THE
DESIGNATED
SURVIVOR

NEIL POLLACK

STRATTON
—PRESS—
Publishing Life

THE DESIGNATED SURVIVOR
Copyright © 2018 **Neil Pollack**

Stratton Press, LLC
1603 Capitol Ave, Suite 310,
Cheyenne, WY 82001
www.stratton-press.com
1-888-323-7009

ISBN (Paperback): 978-1-947355-57-6
ISBN (Ebook): 978-1-64345-018-6

Printed in the United States of America

In memory of my dear parents,
Louis and Molly Pollack

It is forbidden to kill; therefore all murderers are punished unless they kill in large numbers and to the sound of trumpets.

—Voltaire

CHAPTER 1

NEAR FREDERICKSBURG, VIRGINIA, A battered pickup truck wove its way much too quickly down a deserted dirt road under a canopy of leafless deciduous trees and stands of evergreen pines. The vehicle's tires kicked up a cloud of dust that mixed with the exhaust fumes condensing in the frigid mid-January air. The rusted sides of the faded black truck were spattered with dirty gray salt and sand from the plowed main thoroughfares.

The driver, Red Pierce, twenty-seven years old, was small in stature and sported shoulder-length red hair and a clean-shaven, pockmarked face. As usual, a wad of chewing tobacco was tucked under his lip.

Under orders, Red had picked up some guy named Alan Webster—whom he'd never met before—twenty minutes before at his organization's farmhouse headquarters. The truck's heater was going full blast, and Red had stashed his worn and cracked black leather jacket behind his seat. His Black Sabbath T-shirt exposed his thin tattooed arms. His left hand steered the vehicle while his right hand held a bottle of Coors.

The pickup swerved wildly as Red purposely aimed the vehicle's front wheels at roadkill, and he guffawed each time the tires thumped onto a frozen carcass. A dusting of snow still blanketed the shaded forest floor, prompting Red to keep an eye out for deer foraging in the thick woods that might suddenly bound across the narrow road. He didn't relish the thought of having to clean deer blood and guts from his vehicle.

Sitting shotgun, Alan Webster—forty-one years old, tall and strong with a square jaw and military-style crew cut, wearing jeans, combat boots, and a military bomber jacket—asked, "You do this shit often?"

Red cackled. "I like it better when I squash live ones, 'specially squirrels."

Webster shook his head. "How much farther?"

"We've gone 'bout eleven miles. It's a sixteen-mile ride, so that leaves…four more?"

Webster frowned. "If you say so."

Webster's gaze settled on the large black swastika tattoo on Red's forearm, a stare that caught Red's attention.

Red looked at Webster, extended his arm toward him, and said, "Nice, huh?" Red took a final swig from his beer bottle, wiped his mouth on his shoulder sleeve, and then tossed the bottle onto the floor near Webster's feet, where it landed on other bottles, cans, and fast-food wrappers strewn about the sand-laden floor.

Webster shook his head with a disdainful expression. Red's brief comments during the twenty-minute ride told him that Red's engine was at least a quart low. He hoped that he would be dealing with people a lot smarter than the moron sitting beside him.

Red noticed Webster's contemptuous look and said, "Everybody likes it." Red cranked his window halfway down and spat a wad of chewing tobacco toward the dirt road. A blast of cold air rushed in, interfering with Red's aim, and tobacco and saliva hit the inside of the window and began to slide down it, leaving a dark brown streak.

Webster made no attempt to soften the sarcasm as he asked, "This Vance Galvin…is he as smart as you?"

Red's face turned sour. He knew that Webster was disrespecting him, and if it hadn't been for the major wanting to see Webster, he might have put a bullet in Webster's head. "The major ain't no one to mess with."

Webster said, "I'll see what the major is like, and if I don't like what I see, I'm out of there."

The pickup turned onto a paved road and, minutes later, passed the Spotsylvania Confederate Cemetery, where thousands of

Confederate soldiers were laid to rest, many of whom had died in the Battle of Fredericksburg, fought in December of 1862 between General Robert E. Lee's Confederate Army of Northern Virginia and General Ambrose Burnside's Union Army of the Potomac. It was one of the most one-sided battles of the Civil War, with Union casualties more than twice as heavy as those suffered by the Confederates.

Webster solemnly stared at the neat rows of white marble headstones and said reverently, "A great victory for the South happened near here. Too bad there weren't enough of them."

Red pointed at the vast sea of headstones and remarked, "The Feds think the Civil War is over. Well, it ain't."

Webster nodded. It was the only thing Red had said during the ride that he agreed with.

CHAPTER 2

VANCE GALVIN WAITED patiently for Red to arrive with Alan Webster. Galvin believed patience was the greatest of virtues; he'd waited almost forty years for his moment to arrive. He sat behind a dilapidated wooden desk in a ramshackle one-room cabin lit only by sunlight that filtered in through filthy windows. His battery-operated cassette player was blaring Aaron Copland's "Fanfare for the Common Man," which always inspired Galvin. He believed he was the common man for whom there would one day be much fanfare. Copland was his second favorite after Richard Wagner—an anti-Semite known to be Adolf Hitler's preferred composer—whose music Galvin believed would one day replace America's ridiculous national anthem. In fact, he'd recently read a poll that said 22 percent of Americans would have been happy to have Bruce Springsteen, of "Born in the USA" fame, write a new national anthem. Galvin was certain Wagner's music would be far more appropriate.

He'd heard that Webster was ex-military and a natural leader who'd been trained in heavy artillery. Galvin knew that although his men were loyal to the cause, most were poorly educated and unskilled. He needed someone who could help lead his men into battle, and he would soon know if this Alan Webster fit the bill.

Galvin heard a vehicle approaching. He turned off the cassette, got up, walked over to a brownish stained window, peered outside, and saw Red's truck skidding to a halt.

The truck's abrupt stop sent the empty beer bottles rattling around the floor of the truck at Webster's feet. Webster turned toward

Red. "You knew you were picking me up, and you couldn't find the time to clean this shit up?"

As Webster began to open his door, Red grabbed his arm to stop him. "Maybe you and me will have it out some day."

Webster snorted dismissively, jerked his arm from Red's grasp, and opened his door.

The two men exited the truck, casting long dark shadows in the brilliant early-morning sunlight. It was eighteen degrees Fahrenheit, and Webster marveled at how the coldest days of winter always seemed the sunniest.

Next to the cabin lay a large grass field in which Webster spotted a dozen ragged-looking men firing weapons at bottles and tin cans. Most of the shots missed their targets. Webster shook his head and thought, *What am I getting myself into?*

Red led Webster toward the cabin, passing a scruffy-bearded Jim Suggs, who was barking instructions at the dozen men. Some of the men, including Suggs, were dressed in hunters' camouflage jackets.

Watching the pitiful display, Suggs shouted, "Hit the fucking targets!"

Again Webster shook his head and thought, *I picked the wrong militia to try to join.* He knew militias were active in all fifty states, with membership estimated as high as sixty thousand. Webster was in full agreement with these groups that believed the federal government posed a threat to their freedom, especially through its attempts to limit the Second Amendment right to bear arms.

Although there were dozens of militia groups Webster could have attempted to join, this particular one held a special interest for him. He hoped he wouldn't be further disappointed as he shot another glance at the ragtag group of men.

They reached the cabin door. Red opened it, and the two men entered.

Seated again behind his desk, Vance Galvin motioned for the two men to approach. Galvin was in his early sixties, tall and ruggedly handsome, and despite his age, he sported a full head of dark brown wavy hair with only a few gray streaks. His deep-set black eyes attempted to convey a subtle message to Webster: *Don't mess with me.* Galvin scrutinized Webster, and he spoke with a commanding voice. "Come closer, please."

Webster and Red approached Galvin's desk. The two men stopped in front of the desk, behind which hung a huge red-and-black Nazi flag.

Galvin said, "So you're Alan Webster."

"I am."

Galvin stared at Webster for a moment and said, "I understand you served in the first Iraqi war."

Webster, standing ramrod straight in parade rest position, answered, "Correct." He pointed at the Nazi flag behind Galvin. "I hope you men are planning to do better than they did."

Galvin made a perfunctory turn and said, "They made some good attempts at creating a new world order. I believe we *will* do better."

Webster nodded toward Red and then toward the flag. "I heard you're not a neo-Nazi group, so why all the swastikas?"

Galvin appeared bemused as he contemplated his answer. "We respect what the Germans tried to do to keep our race pure, but no, we're not neo-Nazis. Those skinhead types get involved in petty stuff…beating up old Jewish women and homos. They even deny the existence of the Holocaust. Why would they deny the grand attempt to exterminate the Christ-killers who will burn in hell for eternity? Our project has a loftier purpose."

Webster stared at Galvin and didn't reply. He had seen and heard nothing thus far that would allow him to trust in Galvin or his men's abilities. He knew Galvin had checked him out and expected Webster to be joining them. Webster was uncertain how Galvin would react if he refused admission to the group.

Galvin stared back, attempting to size up Webster. "So now you wanna become a Patriot?" he finally said.

Webster folded his arms across his chest and replied, "Assuming you're Major Vance Galvin, let's just say I *did.*"

"I'm sorry," he said. "I thought you knew who I was."

"An introduction would have been nice."

Galvin squinted. "Okay, let's cut the bullshit. Have you changed your mind?"

"Was told y'all have a vision." Webster looked out the window at the yahoos shooting at and missing the bottles and cans, turned, glanced wryly at Red, and then looked back at Galvin. "But I don't see much."

Red suddenly whipped out his Colt .45 and snapped it up against Webster's temple. Red glanced at Galvin, hoping to put a bullet through this smart-ass Webster's skull.

Webster, cool as a cucumber and with his eyes riveted on Galvin, said, "Pimple-face better use it before I break his fucking wrist."

Galvin calmly answered, "Our vision *and* strength lie in a willingness to kill and be killed."

Galvin eyed Red as Red angrily cocked the hammer of his gun, yet Webster still didn't lose his cool.

Galvin slowly shook his head and said with a tight voice, "If you're not interested, maybe it's *auf Wiedersehen*."

Webster dropped to the floor, ducking the barrel of Red's .45, and kicked Red under the chin with the heel of his boot. Red's head snapped back. Lightning-fast, Webster swept Red's legs from under him, grabbed his wrist, wrenched the gun from his grasp, and bounded back to his feet. Webster extended the gun's grip toward Galvin while Red wailed like a baby on the floor, appearing confused and stunned, like a duck hit in the head.

Galvin was impressed with Webster. He smiled as he accepted the gun and holstered it in the back of his pants.

"Stop your crying," Galvin admonished. "And get up off the floor. You'll live."

Red groaned and then fell silent as he sat up, still wondering what had hit him.

Red typified the kind of follower Galvin sought out. Mostly uneducated, Red, whose given name was Marlon (named for Marlon Brando), had been a social outcast for most of his life, never truly fitting in and never participating in any team sports. He had been born to a fourteen-year-old single mother. His nineteen-year-old father had run off with another teenager before he was born, and Red never met him. When he was four, his mother placed Red in the care of his maternal grandmother, who did the best she could to raise him, but her alcoholism and the parade of "uncles" who visited regularly had negative effects on Red.

Although he couldn't have verbalized his feelings, Red tried to feel superior by putting others down, and minorities were always the easiest targets. Red also instinctively knew that there were far worse things that could happen to a person than physical pain. The old saying that sticks and stones could break his bones but names could never harm him, he knew, was terribly wrong. The beatings he had received as a child from his grandmother and schoolmates never lasted as long or hurt as much as the name-calling. As an adult, he had seen again and again in altercations at bars and strip clubs that a put-down could be more troublesome than merely getting into a fistfight, especially for men. Without having learned it formally, Red understood that humans needed to be accepted by a group—any group—in order to survive, an instinct handed down from his cave-man ancestors who, without the natural defenses of other animals, needed to act as a unit in order to hunt and to protect their offspring from predators. Being expelled from the group was essentially a death sentence. Therefore, being dissed was potentially a harbinger of far worse consequences than a beating.

With Galvin, Red finally had found his place in life, and he would do anything to protect it.

Galvin addressed Webster. "Grapevine says you might've helped make the big bang in Oklahoma City. Are you clean?"

Webster took a pack of cigarettes from his shirt pocket, extracted one, and lit it with his Zippo lighter. He inhaled deeply, blew a smoke ring toward the ceiling, and watched it shimmer and disappear before replying. "I met Tim McVeigh at a gun show. He was passing out literature that exposed the government for the oppressor it is. He was a lot smarter than the press made him out to be. But no, I had nothing to do with Oklahoma City, and yes, I'm squeaky clean. Oklahoma City was revenge for Waco, but accomplished squat. Liberal assholes are still runnin' the show. Time to give America back to real Americans."

Galvin's expression showed he was sold on Webster, and he very much wanted to convince Webster he had made the right choice.

A chagrined and wobbly Red staggered to his feet. His head throbbed as he rubbed his sore wrist, and he shot an indignant glance in Webster's direction.

Galvin became solemn as he remarked, "I'm glad you mentioned Waco." He swallowed hard before continuing. "Had a wife and two children burned up at the Branch Davidians compound by the Feds while I was out procuring weapons. For fifty-one days while they held out, I could do nothing but watch on TV and wait." He pounded his fist on the desktop. "Revenge will be sweet."

Webster was clearly affected by Galvin's loss. "Jesus. Sorry, man."

Galvin was glad that Webster hadn't asked him why someone like him would have been involved with the Branch Davidians religious sect. If he had asked him, Galvin would have skirted the question and then changed the subject. He didn't need for anyone to know what had caused him to seek refuge with the Branch Davidians, a sect under the leadership of the charismatic David Koresh.

Galvin had been arrested in Texas in the late seventies for attempting to smuggle three dozen AK-47s into the United States through a Mexican contact, and he had served eighteen months in Federal prison in Beaumont, Texas. But his relative youth and good looks didn't go unnoticed by many of the other hardcore criminals, some of whom were serving life sentences. Ironically, he had been sexually violated on several occasions by members of a white supremacist group. But his hatred turned toward anyone not white since he believed he'd been betrayed by his Mexican contact, and he had been incarcerated because of that half-breed mongrel. He had vowed never to do business with anyone who wasn't one of God's purebred white Christians.

After prison, he had floundered, wondering why Jesus had forsaken him. But a chance meeting with Lucinda Graham while shopping at a Winn-Dixie had changed his life. He instantly fell in love with the beautiful dark-haired woman, to whom he was attracted, even though she claimed to be one-eighth Native American. She was a high-school dropout who'd been sexually abused as an adolescent by an uncle, and she had found refuge in the Branch Davidians, whose leader, David Koresh, believed himself to be the messiah who would lead his flock to the gates of heaven. Even though Galvin didn't relish being a follower rather than a leader, Lucinda convinced him to give the Branch Davidians a try. David Koresh, upon learning of Galvin's history, gave him the task of procuring guns for the compound, and Galvin was on just such a mission when the Bureau of Alcohol, Tobacco, and Firearms attempted to arrest Koresh at the compound on charges of stockpiling illegal weapons. Galvin had no way of getting back into the surrounded compound, and he could only watch and wait. After a fifty-one-day standoff, the FBI fired tear gas into the compound. Fires broke out and quickly decimated the entire structure, killing David Koresh and fifty-four other adults, including Galvin's wife, Lucinda, and twenty-eight children, two of whom were Galvin's two- and four-year-old girls, Mary and Rachel. Galvin's worst nightmare had been realized.

A contemplative Galvin said to Webster, "David Koresh had the right idea but not the right plan." Galvin leaned across the desk. "Can you help to lead my men into battle?"

"Got the firepower?"

Galvin leaned back and crossed his arms as though pondering how much to reveal. He then leaned forward again and, with clenched fist, spoke from his soul. "Nietzsche dreamed of reaching a higher state of being, of becoming *Übermenschen*...supermen. Supermen destroy their enemies." He unclenched his fist, intertwined the fingers of his hands, and laid them on his desk as he asked, "So what's your story?"

Through gritted teeth, Webster answered, "I hate the sons of bitches, maybe as much as you."

"I meant what's your *story*."

Webster inhaled deeply before responding. "My father's plane was shot down in the Vietnam War when I was only six weeks old. My mother committed suicide when I was seven years old, and I was bounced from foster home to foster home. My life turned to shit after that. He died in a war we could never win."

Galvin nodded. "Don't I know it." In a somber tone, he added, "We all died over there, but some of us came back."

Webster understood Galvin's meaning. He knew how much more traumatic the Vietnam War had been to soldiers compared to the Gulf War of 1991, in which only 146 US service people had died. Operation Desert Storm's ground campaign to liberate Kuwait from Iraqi forces—in which Webster had played a part—had lasted only one hundred hours.

Webster said, "That grapevine you mentioned led me to you. I could've chosen any one of several other militias."

"Okay, so why me?"

"My father wrote about you."

Galvin's eyebrows lowered. "Wrote?"

"He kept a log of sorts of stuff he felt was important. It was stashed away with the few things my mother kept after he died. After she passed, a small box was given to me, which I always kept. It was my only connection to him, along with some photos. A couple of years ago I reread his log. Seems he actually met you some forty years ago."

Galvin leaned back in his chair with a puzzled expression. "Where? And what was his name?"

"Oscar Webster met you in Hawaii when he was on R & R for two weeks. You were also on R & R."

Galvin put his hand to his chin in deep thought. "Oscar...I remember him well. Good-looking guy who looked even better in his flyboy uniform. Really impressed the gals."

"Impressed my mother enough to marry him. She was on vacation in Hawaii when she met him."

"So what did this log tell you about me?" Galvin again folded his arms across his chest.

"My father befriended you, a guy named Frank Valone, and a guy named Stan Urbanski."

Galvin took a deep breath and sighed. "Frank was one of my best friends until we had a huge falling-out. Stan wasn't in the service...was some kind of lawyer. What else did the log tell you?"

Webster glanced at Red and back at Galvin.

Galvin understood. "It's okay. I've hidden nothing from my men."

Webster nodded. "That one drunken and drug-filled night you guys created a plan to overthrow the government."

Galvin slowly nodded back. "All except Stan. Wanted no part of it and thought it was all idle bullshit. We went back to 'Nam. Sorry to hear about Oscar. Never saw or heard from Stan again, but Frank Valone and I concocted a plan that went nowhere. Today, with our network of underground militias, it will work."

Webster pointed at Galvin. "That's why I came to you. But something's bothering me. My father was obviously bright, being a pilot and all. Why did he, and you, want to overthrow the government back then?"

Galvin paused for a moment in thought. "Like hundreds of thousands of other guys, I was drafted into a war we all knew we were losing. Half my company was black guys who only wanted to smoke weed. I was born and raised in Martinsville, Indiana, so I learned long ago not to mix with niggers."

"Indiana?" Webster was puzzled. "That's in the north. And I thought you were from Alabama."

Galvin leaned forward. "History lesson. Martinsville was the birthplace of the Ku Klux Klan in Indiana. Once boasted two hundred fifty thousand members. Half the state legislature in the 1920s was members of the KKK. If America had listened to them, we wouldn't be in the mess we're in today, with immigrants flooding the US. If we don't do something about it, it'll be worse tomorrow. My family moved to 'Bama when I was twelve. My older brother was rejected by the University of Alabama in 1963, yet that same year they started accepting niggers even though Governor George Wallace stood in the doorway to block the entrance. Fucking Kennedy sent in the National Guard. My whole family celebrated when Kennedy's head got blown off. If Wallace hadn't been paralyzed by some crazed gunman, he might have been the next president. The country would have been a better place."

Living in one of the whitest states in the Union until he was twelve, Galvin had almost no interaction with black people. His perceptions of African Americans were forged largely from white people's idle chitchat. So by the time he moved to Alabama in the early sixties, he believed that blacks smelled bad, were certainly not as smart as whites, were very often drunk, did drugs, and were lazy. Upon moving to Alabama he was glad that blacks couldn't swim in the same swimming pools as whites, and he was especially happy that they couldn't use the same bathroom facilities or drink from the same water fountains. Who knew the types of exotic diseases he might get from them? His family was thrilled with the segregationist attitudes of the people of Alabama, including those in state government. Jim Crow laws mandated racial segregation in all public facilities in Southern states, and Galvin believed that these laws protected the God-fearing and law-abiding whites from the decadence and low morals of blacks. The only thing that Galvin could give them credit for was their ability to dance.

Of course, he thought, *just look at where they came from. Jungle bunnies had nothing better to do than to run from predators and dance to the music of drums. Who could argue that keeping niggers separated from whites wasn't a good thing—a God-given thing?*

Galvin had been an excellent student, graduating one year early from high school and attending the same college his brother had been rejected from: the University of Alabama, a school that didn't have a single black player on its football team until 1970. Immediately after graduating in 1970 at age 20, Galvin's unlucky draft number caused him to receive his 1A draft status. Instead of waiting to be inducted into the army, Galvin decided to enlist in the Marines, knowing that they were considered the elite among fighting forces.

Galvin turned toward a large poster of America's minority president that was pinned to the wall behind Webster. He removed Red's gun from his belt, aimed it at the poster, and shot the president between the eyes.

Webster and Red flinched from the unexpected blast.

Smoke poured out of the gun barrel as Galvin calmly asked, "Again, can you help lead my men?"

Jim Suggs barged through the doorway, out of breath, with a pistol in his hand, and he shouted, "Everything okay?"

Galvin waved him off. "Just some target practice at our soon-to-be ex-president." He pointed at the poster.

Suggs glanced at the poster, smiled, and walked back to the firing range.

Galvin asked again, impatiently this time, "Can you help lead my men?"

Webster glanced at Red, who was still rubbing his wrist and glaring at Webster. Webster turned back to Galvin and asked, "What am I leading them to, and why do you think it will work?"

Galvin pondered the question. "I'll tell you only this much. I've got men inside the government in high places that will make my plan work. We're not waiting around for the next election."

"How do you know you can trust them? Maybe they're a plant ready to infiltrate your organization."

"One of them's an old Marine buddy of mine. Let's leave it at that. And my plan will work. God is on our side." His gaze drifted toward a filthy window and up toward the heavens.

Galvin's deep conviction sold Webster. "I can lead 'em to hell and back."

Galvin stood up and extended his hand across the desk toward Webster. "Alan Webster, welcome to the Patriots."

Webster felt that he'd found the home he'd been searching for since his mother's death. He had fantasized about how brave his father must have been, and Webster thought he had found a real home when he joined the service, where he had been shipped out to fight in the first Iraq war. But living in close proximity to many African Americans didn't sit well with him. He'd served admirably in Iraq, earning a corporal's stripe, but after returning home with his unit, he had gotten into many altercations with various black soldiers. His vehement disdain for them finally had earned him a dishonorable discharge, something he blamed on the blacks in his unit.

Webster grasped Galvin's hand with both of his, and he knew he was finally home.

Galvin turned to Red. "Introduce Mr. Webster to Jim Suggs." Then to Webster, he said, "Suggs will give you a brief orientation and get you set up. I'll see you later."

Webster nodded, gave Galvin a snappy salute, turned, and marched out, followed begrudgingly by Red.

As he sat alone in the cabin, Galvin recalled a memory that often pervaded his thoughts when he was left alone—the memory of having to go through a makeshift morgue at a warehouse in order to find and identify his wife and little girls. Even though they had handed him a mask, the stench had been almost too much to bear as he walked the aisles of sheet-covered corpses until he finally spotted what remained of his burned-up wife and innocent little girls. The memory of those moments would remain in his psyche forever, almost never leaving his daily thoughts or his nightly dreams. *No, not dreams*, he thought. *Demons.*

If the federal government had been his enemy before this event, it was now his God-given mission to bring it to its knees and begin a new-world order for America and its true Americans. This would stand as a monument to Lucinda, Mary, and Rachel.

CHAPTER 3

THAT SAME MORNING, US Secretary of Agriculture John Simpson, tall and distinguished with graying temples, limped slightly as he walked into his spacious office in the heart of Washington, DC. He sank into his high-backed leather chair. His thick dark eyebrows complemented an expression that almost always appeared serious. His limp was the result of a college football injury, but he never corrected anyone who assumed he'd gotten it in the Vietnam War.

He ignored the landline telephone on his desk and instead picked up his cell phone.

He drew a shallow breath as he marveled at how it had come to be that in just four more days, on January 20, he could potentially be the next president of the United States. Born and raised on a farm fifty miles outside of Manhattan, Kansas, he'd been a good student in school, earning high enough grades to receive a scholarship at Kansas State University, where he majored in agricultural economics. Although it was highly unpopular during the end of the Vietnam War era, he joined the university's ROTC, taking enough elective leadership and military courses to earn him a commission as a second lieutenant when he enlisted in the army. Most of his friends were doing anything in 1972 to stay out of the war, but Simpson had grown up hearing his father's stories of the Second World War, stories his father reluctantly told at John's insistence.

His father, like many other young farm boys, had enlisted in the army directly after the Japanese attack on Pearl Harbor. Immediately after basic training, his father was shipped out to the Philippines, where, after the notorious three-month Battle of Bataan, he was one of fifteen thousand Americans taken prisoner by the Imperial Japanese Army. The soldiers were forced to march eighty miles from Bataan to their prison camp in what infamously came to be known as the Bataan Death March.

Although it was like pulling teeth, over the years young John learned from his father that the Japanese had been unprepared for the number of prisoners they were responsible for, with no organized plan for how to handle them. The prisoners were given no food for the first three days and were only allowed to drink water from filthy water-buffalo wallows on the side of the road. Japanese troops frequently beat and bayonetted prisoners who fell behind. Prisoners were made to bury their comrades alive, and any refusal to do so was met with execution and punishment to fellow soldiers. Many soldiers who fell behind were beheaded by Japanese officers practicing with their samurai swords. His father even saw the charred remains of a soldier who had been set on fire with gasoline while still alive.

Hundreds of American soldiers died during the march, and thousands more died after reaching the prison camp. They died from starvation and disease at a rate of thirty to fifty per day, and were buried in mass graves. The only time John Simpson ever saw his father cry was while he recounted his experiences in the war.

The impressionable young John Simpson learned that the Japanese culture at that time embraced the view that any warrior who surrendered had no honor and was therefore not to be treated as a human being. American prisoners were thus considered no more than animals. Thus, in late 1972, when the opportunity arrived for John Simpson to join the military and fight against East Asian people, he did so with the hope of killing as many as he could, but he was disappointed when the US pulled its combat troops out of Vietnam only one month after his basic training. He never saw any action but was still considered a Vietnam veteran.

Upon finishing his two-year enlistment, he remained a Wildcat, attending law school at Kansas State. Upon graduation, he landed a job with a prestigious law firm in Topeka. His background and good looks soon attracted the attention of the Republican Party, who encouraged him to run for the local congressional seat, which he won easily in his mostly Republican district. During his tenure, he earned high marks from Republicans for pushing for farmers' rights and for championing loose gun-control laws. After winning nine consecutive terms, aided by his farming background, he was appointed secretary of agriculture even though he was a Republican, since the president wanted to demonstrate bipartisanship in his cabinet.

Simpson had been raised to be highly religious, and his family never missed Sunday church. He was proud to be an American and to stand for the rights of individuals. As secretary of agriculture, he kept his personal views on nonfarming issues to himself. He secretly despised anyone who talked of gun control, hated mandated universal health care, and thought that socialism was insidiously creeping into every aspect of American society. In Simpson's mind, this expansion of socialism was taking the country one step closer to communism, something that millions of Americans had fought to defeat in Vietnam, where tens of thousands had made the ultimate sacrifice.

He dialed his cell phone.

Sixty-three-year-old Congressman Brett J. Mannings, with a bulldog face and body to match, sat at his desk and answered his ringing cell phone.

John Simpson said, "Brett, same place. Ten minutes." Simpson hung up without Mannings uttering a word. Mannings had grown up being called BJ but hadn't used the nickname since the early seventies, and for good reason.

Mannings knew what the clandestine meeting was for. He would soon find out if it was going to be possible for the United States to have a bright new beginning. He had waited a long time for this possibility, having made friends with Vance Galvin in Vietnam, and he'd learned much from him. Mannings felt that time was of the essence, not only for the United States but also for himself. Always a smoker, he had high blood pressure and hardening of the arteries, and he knew that no male in his family had ever lived to seventy. He felt that if he had to die, it might as well be for something righteous, something that he believed was God's will, and not because of some unfortunate genetic twist of fate.

Ten minutes after the phone call, Mannings walked up to a waiting Simpson in the basement of the Jamie L. Whitten Building that housed the Department of Agriculture Administration. Simpson scanned the dimly lit basement corridor, making certain they were alone.

Simpson began to speak in a hushed but forceful tone. His contempt was palpable. "The president's policies will destroy us. At this rate, whites will be in the minority. It'll be hell on earth."

Manning's thick neck bulged as he said, "The answer, damn it!"

Simpson again scanned the corridor and then turned to Mannings. "This year's State of the Union rotation came down to me and the secretaries of energy and labor. Labor is Mexican-born, so that left me and energy. I told the president I needed to be with my sick mother in Kansas. I'm the one. I'm the designated survivor."

Mannings smiled and nodded. "The designated survivor. The doomsday survivor. The only one left after we wipe out the president and line of succession." His shoulders relaxed. He looked up, raised his thick hands as though praying to the heavens, and grinned crookedly. "So it begins."

Lowering his arms, Mannings saluted Simpson military style and addressed him with extreme respect. "The king is dead. Long live the king."

Simpson smiled wryly and replied, "Brett, it'll be 'hail to the chief.'" He again glanced up and down the corridor as he continued, "This Vance Galvin is the only one who knows about you. Do you still trust him?"

Mannings nodded. "Semper fi still holds true. My 'Nam buddy and I will both need your executive pardons, Mr. Future President."

The two men stared at each other for a moment and then parted in opposite directions.

Mannings didn't fault Simpson for being skeptical of Vance Galvin since Simpson only knew what Mannings had told him about Galvin. But unbeknownst to Simpson and everyone but Galvin and a few former cohorts, Mannings had participated with Galvin in several violent antigovernment activities after Vietnam. Fortunately, he was not one of the ringleaders and was known only as BJ to everyone involved except Galvin, so he was never indicted or even suspected of any wrongdoing. Thus he was able to continue his life as normal, law-abiding citizen Brett J. Mannings, whose personality and strength of mind and body enabled him eventually to win a congressional seat.

As far as Mannings was concerned, Vance Galvin was the salt of the earth, someone he knew could be depended on in any given situation.

Simpson, on the other hand, walked away with mixed emotions. He was well aware of the risks involved, including the worst-case scenario of being branded a traitor to the United States. If everything went wrong, the result for him would be either life imprisonment or the death penalty.

On the positive side, if everything went as planned, he would become the next president of the United States. He often dreamed of how much good he could accomplish in that role. His strict, religious upbringing had helped to shape his character. As president, he would work to overturn *Roe V. Wade* since he believed life began at conception. He knew that in order to do so, he would have to appoint Supreme Court justices who would do exactly that. He would also attempt to have the Supreme Court rule unconstitutional the laws of states that allowed civil unions and marriages between gays and lesbians. What was next, laws allowing people to marry their own pets? He laughed to himself at the thought, but he believed there might actually be liberals who would vote for such a ridiculous thing.

He also thought that public school systems were failing since the United States ranked well below many other nations in math and science. The answer, he believed, was to allow children to enroll in any school of their choice; if parents chose a religious school for their children, that education should be paid for by the same tax dollars that paid for public schools. And as far as health care was concerned, he would fight to overturn anything that smacked of universal health care. He was certain the only way to solve the health-care dilemma was to make health care available only to those who could afford it. He knew that this position seemed harsh, but he thought that health care would act as an effective incentive for people to work hard so that they could earn enough money to afford such things. *Isn't that how our capitalistic society is supposed to work—with individuals taking responsibility for themselves?*

And above all else, he would see to it that this nation remained the white Christian nation he believed the founding fathers intended it to be.

Simpson drew a deep, calming breath. He knew that the stakes were incalculable, but he believed with all his heart that God was on his side.

CHAPTER 4

LATER THAT SAME COLD January morning, Tim Connor—thirty-four, average height, wiry physique, and boyishly handsome, with brown hair cut athletically short—banged incessantly on the apartment door of a run-down apartment building in a seedy section of Baltimore, Maryland. The building was within eyesight of the steel trusses and arched brick façade of Oriole Park at Camden Yards, home of the Baltimore Orioles baseball team. Finally, Dan Connor's big, burly frame appeared in the doorway. He was clearly drunk, holding a can of beer, and dressed only in a torn undershirt and boxer shorts.

Dan, slurring his words, said, "Tim, my long-lost son...been weeks."

Tim smirked. "Been calling you for days, Daniel."

"So you do love your ol' man. Still goin' out with what's her name, who I never even met?"

Tim answered, "Look at you. Are you ever sober?"

"Raised you good myself, did'n' I?" He stumbled back two steps.

Tim entered the room and closed the door behind him. Dan followed Tim and then flopped down onto a threadbare sofa. It was a tiny studio apartment. A small bathroom was situated near the kitchenette. Much of Dan's clothing was strewn about the room, draped over chairs and scattered on the hardwood floors. Condensation from Dan's cooking formed frosted decorations on the window above the sink.

Tim shook his head and then softened his tone as he said, "Allie's been talking about quitting her computer job and becoming a Hollywood actress. Unbelievable."

Dan waved his hand across the ceiling and said as though reciting poetry, "Set her free like a bird. It comes back, she's yours." He shrugged his shoulders. "Somethin' like that."

Dan slowly closed his eyes and fell asleep on the sofa, still holding the can of beer.

Tim gently removed the can from Dan's grasp and placed it on a small table next to the couch. He then turned to walk out, passing various old photos on the wall, mostly of him and Dan and a cherished German shepherd that had died ten years earlier. He smiled sadly and shook his head as he opened the door and walked out.

Tim's relationship with his father had never been a close one. Tim's mother had died giving birth to him, and so it had been left to Dan Connor to raise their only child, Tim. But as far back as Tim could recall, his father had always had a severe drinking problem. Every year or two they had to move from one city or state to another, and Tim blamed it on Dan's drinking, which he believed caused Dan to lose one menial job after another. Tim had no idea how many landlords Dan owed rent to.

If there was a soft side to Dan, Tim had never witnessed it. His father had never been the hugging and kissing type, and Tim eventually had come to feel that his father believed demonstrating affection would somehow influence Tim to become gay, something Dan and his generation had been raised to dread. A homosexual son was something to be ashamed of and would certainly reflect poorly on that son's upbringing.

But Tim had long ago become accustomed to Dan's ways, and over the years he'd come to understand that many men had similar relationships with their fathers, men who believed they had to be both physically and emotionally strong. Crying was certainly never an option, at least not in front of anyone.

The one true bright spot in Tim's relationship with his father was learning martial arts from him. His father had served in the Vietnam War and had been a martial arts instructor in the service. The only times Tim and his father touched each other in close proximity were when Dan demonstrated certain techniques for vanquishing or even killing an opponent. To Dan's credit, Tim couldn't recall Dan ever laying a hand on him in anger.

Tim was bright and loved to read, but he had been only an average student; his formal education had been stunted by constant moves from school to school. He always had to scramble to catch up to the new school's curriculum and sometimes found a new class heavily into material he'd never studied before. But Tim managed to graduate from high school, and with some advice (but never funding) from his father, he opened a small storefront martial arts school near downtown Baltimore where he taught youngsters the thing he truly knew best.

After his beloved German shepherd Patton died, Tim had immediately gone to the local pound, where one particular golden retriever puppy caught his eye. He named the dog Bruce after his favorite martial arts devotee, Bruce Lee. Bruce, now ten years old, had become lethargic and seemed to be in pain, and Tim had dropped him off at the veterinarian for tests. Tim hoped to receive good news later that day regarding his best friend.

The true love of Tim's life was Allie Sommers. They had met almost two years earlier and had been instantly attracted to each other. She had graduated from the University of Maryland with a degree in computer science, but acting had always been her passion, and she had recently discussed with Tim the possibility of quitting her job to become an actress. Tim thought it foolish to give up a good job for something that seemed like pie in the sky to him. He hoped it was merely a passing phase.

At five o'clock that afternoon, Allie Sommers—twenty-seven years old and attractive, with long auburn hair, striking green eyes, and a figure that made men's heads turn—entered Bruce's Martial Arts School, Tim's small storefront business wedged between Thai and Mexican restaurants near downtown Baltimore.

She observed Tim as he instructed ten white-robed eight-year-old students. The school's walls were covered with martial arts posters, many of which prominently depicted Bruce Lee. The center of the school was covered in soft mats. The children's parents stood off to the side, waiting to pick up their kids.

Tim spotted Allie, but he remained focused on his students.

Allie sat down at his desk, nervously fingering the airline ticket in her coat pocket while watching Tim instruct the youngsters in various moves and skills. She was impressed at how he handled them, and she eyed Tim with admiration.

Allie noticed one little boy named Brian, who stood off to the side, crying to his mother. Brian had only one arm.

Tim paused his instructions, turned to Brian, and gently attempted to coax him into joining the others. "C'mon, Brian. You can do it. Just do what you've practiced."

Brian shook his head. Brian's mother looked at Tim and said with a forced smile, "Maybe next time."

The telephone on Tim's desk rang, and Allie answered it. "Bruce's."

Tim resumed his lessons but noticed Allie's worried expression. She hung up as Tim approached. Allie stuffed the plane ticket deeper into her pocket.

A half hour later, Tim and Allie sat in the sanitized white-and-lime-green office of Dr. Susan Fromm, the veterinarian, who was wearing her white lab coat. Her hair was tied back in a severe bun, which accentuated her narrow face. Tim held his golden retriever in his lap as they faced Dr. Fromm across her desk.

A concerned Fromm said, "Bruce's cancer is terminal. I think you should consider putting him to sleep."

Tim answered caustically, "There a shortage of laboratory dogs?"

The doctor was taken aback by the remark.

Allie shot Tim a look tinged with disappointment.

Seeing Allie's expression, Tim softened and accepted the inevitable. "Best friend and watchdog forever." He affectionately rubbed Bruce's neck.

Dr. Fromm understood. "You can save your old friend weeks of suffering."

Tim held on tightly to Bruce as Bruce whimpered, licking Tim's hand. Tim's shoulders sagged. He looked directly into Bruce's sad eyes and said tenderly, "Don't worry, boy. I'll be safe."

Allie began to cry as Tim's eyes welled up.

"I wanna hold him when…" Tim choked up.

The doctor sympathetically replied, "Sure."

A while later, Tim and Allie somberly exited the back door, which led to the parking lot. Tim carried a large sealed plastic bag. In spite of the doctor's recommendation that Bruce be cremated, Tim insisted on finding a burial plot for Bruce. Tim's mother had been cremated and her ashes scattered somewhere in Virginia, and Tim felt a deep-seated need to have something more tangible than a spirit to be able to visit.

Later that day, Jimmy—proud that his flattened nose and the scars above both eyes made him appear every bit the thug he was— nervously hesitated in front of the door to Tim's one-bedroom apartment in a middle-class section of Baltimore.

Jimmy's heavy fist pounded on the door. He waited and then pounded again. He was about to turn to leave when the door swung open to an apartment decorated in Ikea's light-colored do-it-yourself wooden furniture.

Jimmy instinctively put his arms up for protection and backed away, but nothing happened. Tim stood alone in the doorway as Jimmy anxiously peered through the open door behind Tim.

"Bruce isn't home," Tim said flatly.

Jimmy was relieved. He hated that dog and knew the feeling was mutual. "Richie wants his fifteen Cs."

Allie appeared behind Tim. She'd heard the brief conversation, which prompted her to contemplate the kind of man Tim was dealing with. She wasn't impressed and thought, *If Tim owes fifteen hundred dollars to a man like this lowlife, how much more gambling money might he owe to others?*

Jimmy glanced at the attractive young woman standing behind Tim, and he winked at her.

Tim noticed the wink and unceremoniously slammed the door on Jimmy.

Tim turned around and saw Allie taking her checkbook from her purse. His expression said, "Don't even suggest it."

She sighed as she shoved her checkbook back into her purse. "You promised to give it up."

"I said I'd try, and I am." He knew he sounded unconvincing.

Allie grabbed her coat from the back of a kitchen chair.

Tim said, "Don't go."

With a weary voice, she said, "I just don't feel like arguing right now."

Allie opened the door and left, more disappointed than angry, knowing that Tim's promises to stop gambling apparently meant nothing. Maybe his actions would make it easier for her when she confronted him with her plane ticket to California.

Tim picked up a feeding bowl with "Bruce" written on its side, and he gazed at it sadly as he dropped it into a garbage pail. He paused, retrieved the bowl, and placed it tenderly on a shelf as tears streaked down his cheeks.

Allie was almost glad that she didn't have to deal right then with the fact that she had plans to live in the Hollywood, California, area for at least enough time for her to find out if there might be a career in acting waiting for her.

Her family was musically inclined; her father played the guitar and her mother the piano, although neither was very talented. But her parents made certain that Allie received professional piano lessons from age five, and Allie had indeed become quite talented. But her true passion was always acting. She also took dance lessons, and when the opportunity arose in school to participate in school plays, her attractiveness and talents landed her many leading roles from seventh grade through her senior year in high school.

In college she continued to pursue her passion for acting, but she knew that earning a living from acting was a long shot, so she majored in computer science, knowing that computers would always serve as a fallback position if a career in acting wasn't in the cards.

In the five years since her college graduation, she'd sent out résumés and attended many cattle-call auditions with no real results, only occasionally landing minor parts in local theater productions.

She was now earning a fair salary with a local Baltimore computer company, but was mostly bored to tears. She had read that if someone was truly interested in a career in acting, the best places were New York City and Los Angeles. She had never loved the winters in Baltimore, and she figured they would be even worse in New York, so she chose Los Angeles. Maybe some Hollywood movie producer would spot her and make her a star. She thought, *Isn't that how Lana Turner was discovered?* She'd read that the shapely Lana Turner had been discovered at age sixteen by a movie director when she decided to ditch high school one day and grab a Coke at Schwab's Pharmacy on Sunset Strip. The rest, as they say, was history.

She thought she would give it at least two months in LA. If it didn't work out, computer jobs were always in demand back home.

Her biggest concern was how Tim would react to her leaving him, even if it was only for a couple of months. She knew he would wonder what would happen if she got discovered and landed some high-paying jobs in Hollywood. She didn't know how she would respond to that question. Maybe she'd come back to Baltimore and find some paying jobs there, or maybe Tim could relocate his school to California. She had no idea what the future would bring, but she felt compelled to follow this path.

She loved Tim and hoped he'd understand and allow her this chance. She didn't have a clue what his reaction would be, but she knew she needed to tell him about her decision as soon as possible.

CHAPTER 5

AT TEN THAT EVENING, Dan Connor was the lone patron in a time-worn Irish Pub located three blocks from his apartment. The small and cozy pub always smelled like a combination of beer and polished wood. Dan sat half asleep on a stool at the bar. A burning cigarette with a long cylinder of unflicked ash hung from between his nicotine-stained fingers.

The old bartender, Scotty, stood behind the bar and reached out gently to touch Dan's arm. Dan stirred, and in his rich brogue, Scotty said, "Dan, time to go home."

With bloodshot eyes, Dan responded as well as he could, "I am home, Scotty."

Scotty nodded. "Yeah. You okay?"

"Be a cold day in January Dan Connor can't walk home three blocks."

"Danny, it *is* a cold day in January."

Dan barely slid off his stool as he said, "See ya tomorrow, Scotty m'boy." Dan put on his coat, walked unsteadily out of the pub into the chilly night. It was a familiar routine—pump gas for customers at the local BP station by day and then drink himself into a stupor by night. The drink helped him to forget many things, especially how he'd lost his one true love so many years ago at the hands of Vance Galvin. Dan had managed to avoid being killed by Galvin or one of his men for so long by constantly moving from city to city and state to state. He'd often dreamed of how he would destroy Galvin if he ever got the chance. Alcohol allowed him to repress his many terrible memories. Alcohol was his safe haven, sending him each night to a dreamless abyss.

He had girlfriends from time to time, but none seemed to be able to fill the void. He had served in the Marines during the Vietnam War and had seen things that he chose never to discuss with anyone, not even his son, Tim.

The general public had heard about the My Lai Massacre in which American soldiers—a few bad apples, the government claimed—slaughtered hundreds of Vietnamese civilians. But Dan and many other soldiers like him knew from experience that My Lai was far from an isolated incident; rather it was the result of a standard order to kill anything that moved. The attitude of a military brass, obsessed with body counts, had predictable and barbaric consequences. Torture, rape, and wanton murder of South Vietnamese civilians were far more commonplace than the military leadership admitted. Flashbacks to Vietnam weighed heavily on Dan's soul— memories that occasionally surfaced like a monster from the deep.

He stepped out into the cold night, turned his collar up to defend against the chilly breeze, and thought, *Oh well, at least I didn't die or come home crippled. At least I got to see Tim become a strong and decent man.*

Dan walked unsteadily down the sidewalk toward his apartment building. He turned up a side street and flipped his lit cigarette butt into the street just as three black men in their early twenties blocked his path. Dan stopped and stared at the three men. He instantaneously knew this could not be good.

The tallest of the three demanded, "Give it up, man."

Dan noticed the gun in the man's hand. A sardonic smile crossed Dan's face as he said, "Didn't expect black guys."

Clearly confused, the tall man moved in closer, as though ready to shoot.

Dan backed away, reached under his jacket, and whipped out a gun, but before Dan could get a shot off, the tall man fired and hit Dan in the chest. Dan was knocked backward off his feet. His gun flew out of his hand and slid under a parked car.

The three men hovered over Dan and took his money and watch. One of the men tried to retrieve Dan's gun from under the car, but a nearby woman's screams prompted them to flee into darkness, leaving the gun behind.

Dan lay flat on his back and watched the moon change from silver to yellow to black as crimson blood painted the sidewalk. His last thoughts before blacking out were that this was not the way it was supposed to end.

At eleven that same evening, Tim and four other men played Texas hold 'em at a table in a smoke-filled room strewn with evidence of fast food and beer. The flop showed a king, a jack, a nine, a three, and a two.

Tim had almost no money left in front of him. The player to his left, Arnie, continuously blew cigar smoke in Tim's direction. Tim glanced at his hole cards—two kings—and he turned toward Arnie.

"Been blowin' shit my way all night, pal."

Arnie, whose face resembled that of a boxer who'd had one too many fights, swept his hand across the room and fired back, "Don't see no No Smokin' sign. Play the damn hand."

More smoke drifted its way into Tim's face. Highly annoyed, Tim waited for the smoke to clear. Arnie purposely blew more smoke in Tim's direction.

Tim shot an angry glance at Arnie just as they heard a knock at the door. One of the other players got up and opened it.

Thirty-four-year-old Sam Breen, short and thin, a close friend of Tim's, rushed into the room through a curtain of smoke and exclaimed, "Tim, your father's been shot!"

Tim was momentarily stunned, but he continued to gaze at his cards.

Sam approached the table. "Hear me? Muggers outside Scotty's."

Tim slowly shook his head and said with a dreary sigh, "Scotty's...figures. How bad?"

"In the hospital is all I know." Sam thought that the ominous news would make Tim want to rush out.

Instead, Tim turned away from Sam, leered at Arnie, and threw fifty dollars into the pot. Tim had chosen to believe that his strong-as-an-ox father was merely wounded and would be okay.

Arnie reached down, threw money in, and said, "Make it a C-note."

Tim called the bet by dropping in his last fifty.

Arnie showed his hole cards: a queen and a ten. His straight beat Tim's three kings.

A smug Arnie said, "Lucky night, right, pal?"

Tim pulled back in his chair, stood up, wheeled toward Arnie, and angrily said, "Go fuck yourself."

Arnie sprang to his feet, whipped out a gun and aimed it at Tim's chest, only a foot away. "How 'bout a father-and-son twofer?"

Tim was only slightly surprised at the sight of the gun; he knew what sort of men frequented the card game. He knew this was probably just a show of bravado from Arnie, but he couldn't be certain, and he nervously backed up a step.

Arnie stepped closer to Tim, pressed the gun against Tim's chest, and pushed Tim backward with it.

Sam glared at Arnie and said, "You're a fuckin' hero with that gun." Although short and slight in stature, Sam had learned that talking tough could often make up for his lack of size. Having been bullied while growing up, he believed he could wiggle out of any jam if given an inch.

Tim's fear was evident on his face. "Sam, shut up!"

Arnie's face bore a sinister smile as he thrust the gun back in his jacket pocket and stood nose to nose with Tim, egging him on. "Come on, Mary." He waved his hands toward himself as if to say, "Take your best shot."

Sam smiled in anticipation, knowing Tim's expertise, as Arnie poked Tim's chest with his finger, pushing him backward again, but Tim merely stepped back. A disappointed expression crossed Sam's face.

Arnie laughed and said, "Ain't worth wasting a bullet. Get the fuck out, and take pipsqueak with you."

Sam's eyes screamed for Tim to do something, but Tim simply brushed past Arnie and walked out. Sam followed with Arnie's laughter ringing in his ears.

Sam had been belittled by that jerk, and he dearly wanted Tim to knock his teeth out. *Another bully going unpunished,* he thought. He knew life wasn't always fair.

They made their way to Sam's car, and Sam drove in uncomfortable silence until Tim remarked, "He'll live. He's tough."

Sam turned toward Tim. "Thought tough ran in your family. Your old man would've decked him."

Tim shouted back, "It's a fucking card game!"

"Lost more than a card game," he said casually as he tended to his driving.

"I teach self-defense to kids…and my hands won't stop a bullet, remember?" Tim lifted his shirt to reveal a terrible scar on his side.

Sam looked down, ashamed. He definitely remembered how Tim had gotten the scar.

Tim spoke calmly. "Guy's connected. Maybe I win a battle but lose the war."

Sam realized Tim was correct. Tim didn't need to fear the kind of revenge wiseguys like Arnie were capable of.

Changing the subject, Tim remarked, "Even more important, don't tell Allie where you found me."

"Of course." Sam knew that Tim had a gambling problem—no, an addiction—and he had tried to convince Tim to give it up, but Sam knew that this was apparently easier said than done as his car approached the hospital.

CHAPTER 6

DAN CONNOR LAY on a hospital bed in the emergency room of Johns Hopkins University Hospital with tubes and monitors all around. From a large crucifix over the bed, Jesus sadly stared down at them.

Detective Jim Sykes, a thirty-year veteran with the Baltimore Police Force, was attempting to question Dan despite the obvious disapproval of the nurse standing beside the bed. Sykes was wearing the typical uniform of a detective—a dark suit and a tie to match. He was in his late fifties and was generally considered thin for his age, although he sported a bit of a belly. He constantly vowed to himself to begin working out, but it never seemed to happen. His hair was turning gray and thinning at the top, which made his narrow face appear even longer.

Detective Sykes leaned toward Dan and asked, "Who shot you?"

Dan's breathing was labored, and his eyes were shut.

The nurse said, "He needs rest."

Sykes ignored her as he asked again, "Can you describe who shot you?"

Dan struggled to open his eyes. He turned toward Sykes and said, "Three…white guys." Dan's eyes closed.

Sykes frowned at Dan. The nurse frowned at Sykes.

Jim Sykes had been on the police force since he was twenty-six. He had served two years in the Marines shortly after high school, one of those years in Vietnam, where he saw limited action. After the service, he enrolled at Towson University in Baltimore County, where he majored in criminal justice. It was practically ordained that

42

he would become a police officer, since both his father and grandfather had served on the Baltimore Police Force. He had heard all the stories about payoffs and graft, and he had made it his sworn duty to do anything in his power to prove that not all cops were crooked and always on the take.

To Sykes, this crime was merely another senseless shooting that would probably go unsolved—so many of these types of cases did. As frustrating as this fact was, Sykes took solace in the knowledge that felonies like this were almost never the only offenses these perpetrators carried out. They lived in a world of crime, and many of them were killed by other thugs, or they eventually were caught and incarcerated for some other offense. Many would die from drug overdoses. Sykes believed in the old adage that crime doesn't pay. His reputation as an honest, hardworking cop had earned him his detective's shield, which he wore proudly.

Tim rushed in, out of breath.

The nurse stepped in front of Tim and asked, "Are you related?"

Tim anxiously peered around the nurse. "His son. How's he doin'?"

The nurse looked concerned as she said, "I'll get the doctor." She left the room.

Sykes approached Tim, hand outstretched. "Detective Sykes."

Tim shook hands with Sykes. "What's the story?" Tim stared at his father's ashen face. He hadn't expected his broad-shouldered father to look this bad.

Sykes turned toward Dan. "He was shot in the chest during an apparent mugging. He said three white males were involved. We found a gun. Did he own one?"

Tim shrugged. "Maybe it was theirs."

"Found it under a car. Wasn't fired. We're checking it out." He glanced back at Dan and saw that his eyes were still closed.

Dr. Stevens walked in. He was forty and wore a white lab coat and a stethoscope around his neck. He had met Detective Sykes a few minutes earlier. He looked at Tim and said, "I'm Dr. Stevens. And you are?"

"Tim Connor, his son. How is he?"

Dr. Stevens pursed his lips and said, "He's lost a lot of blood."

The expression on the doctor's face conveyed the seriousness of the situation to Tim. "Can he hear me?"

Dr. Stevens glanced at Dan, whose breathing was becoming increasingly labored. "Make it brief."

Tim knelt next to his father and gently touched his shoulder. "Daniel, it's Tim."

Dan's eyelids fluttered and then opened. He turned toward Tim. His eyes revealed recognition as he struggled to speak.

Tim leaned his head close to his father's lips.

Dan whispered into Tim's ear.

Tim suddenly pulled back, surprised.

Dan appeared to summon every ounce of strength to speak again, but then his eyes opened wide, his body tensed, and the monitors began wailing. Dr. Stevens abruptly pushed Tim aside.

Tim called out, "What's happening?" His eyes darted from person to person as he felt his heart pound in his chest.

Several nurses rushed into the room. One nurse drew the curtain around the bed. Tim paced back and forth outside. Although he had never felt very close to his father, the man who was possibly dying on the other side of that curtain was still the only parent he'd ever known. With no siblings and no relatives that he knew of, the death of his father would not only make him an orphan but would also render him as a man without a country—Dan Connor was still his home base. Suddenly, the fact that Dan was a drunk who lost many jobs and had made them move numerous times while Tim was growing up didn't seem to matter. He prayed that his father would be going home sometime soon. Behind the curtain, someone shouted, "Clear!" He heard the sound of paddles sending electric shock waves through his father's heart.

A half hour later, Sam was standing in the hospital lobby, smoking directly under a No Smoking sign when he saw Tim approaching. He still felt guilty for having accused Tim of being a coward, especially knowing how Tim had gotten that scar.

Tim turned a corner and walked over to Sam. "He's gone," he sadly said.

Sam dropped the cigarette onto the tiled floor and stepped on it. "Shit. Sorry. You okay?"

Tim shrugged his shoulders and walked toward the exit. He was having trouble understanding his own emotions. His father had been heavily into drinking as far back as Tim could remember. Even though Dan had been trained in hand-to-hand combat, he had never beaten Tim. Tim had always felt a coldness between them, but Dan was his father, the only parent Tim had ever known. Yet here he was, only minutes after his father's passing, feeling less sad than when Bruce died. *Is there something wrong with me?* he asked himself. Maybe man's best friend, an innocent creature who gave constant, unconditional love, could actually have more of an emotional effect on a person than a parent. Still, he felt guilty for not feeling worse about his father's death.

A minute later, they solemnly reached Sam's car.

Before getting into the car, Tim asked, "You know how in movies the father dies and says somethin' meaningful?"

Sam opened his door and said, "Make-believe bullshit."

Tim leaned against the car next to Sam's door and lit a cigarette. "His last words to me were, 'Find section 2, block 5, lot 9.' Great, huh?"

Sam cocked his head to the side, thinking.

"Probably drunk," Tim concluded as he exhaled smoke through his nostrils.

Sam scratched his head and said, "Maybe he left you a piece of property. Sounds kinda like it. Look into it."

"How?"

"You go to City Hall and look up some records."

"I can't think about stuff like that right now."

Sam thought for a moment. "Tell you what. I'll go see if it means anything. Maybe you're a millionaire."

They both chuckled at the ridiculous thought.

Tim tossed his cigarette onto the blacktop and stepped on it. "Yeah, and my mother was the Queen of England."

They got into the car and drove off.

Sam had first met Tim when Tim transferred to Sam's high school at the start of eleventh grade. Tim had always been a good athlete, and he had made both the basketball and baseball teams. Unfortunately for Sam, he was quite short and quite thin and didn't have a father around to play ball with, so he'd always lacked the size and skills required to be a decent athlete.

Even though Tim was accustomed to being bounced around from town to town and constantly having to make new friends, it was never easy. But Sam was drawn to him from the start. Since Tim was new to Sam's school, he was appreciative that Sam made such an effort to befriend him. For Sam, being able to say that he was good friends with Tim elevated his status with the other kids, who had always found Sam an easy target for bullying—something Sam had lived with since grade school. The larger, more athletic boys found Sam to be easy pickings and often shoved him around or simply made fun of him. Occasionally, Sam fought back, only to end up with a bloody nose or lip. But it was the name-calling that stung the most. Sam had read that bullying in schools was becoming a national epidemic, but the knowledge that he wasn't alone didn't heal his bruised ego at all.

When Tim and Sam were nineteen years old, they attended a local bar late one evening and ordered their usual beers. Although officially desegregated, many of the local Baltimore bars were frequented by all-white or all-black patrons. One of Tim's former baseball teammates from high school walked in with two friends; all three of them were black. Tim had never had any close black friends, but he had come to know and respect Spencer Givens. Tim had played left field while Spencer had played second base. They hadn't seen each other since graduation one year earlier.

Tim waved to Spencer, who walked over and shook hands with him. Spencer and Sam only knew each other by sight, and they nodded at each other. After a few minutes of reminiscing about old times, one of the other patrons, a man in his early twenties who appeared to be inebriated, told Spencer and his two friends to find a bar with their own kind.

Spencer understood the unwritten rule, and he was willing to leave with his two friends, but Sam, who saw another bully trying to exert his power, told the man to shut the hell up. The man stepped forward as though seeking a fight, but Tim stepped between them. Knowing he had friends to protect him emboldened Sam. The man told Sam to meet him outside, but Sam told him to go fuck himself. The three black youths waved to Tim and prudently left the bar.

A few minutes later, the drunken man stormed out in a huff.

Sam and Tim finished their beers and walked out. In the parking lot, they were confronted by the furious man, who was now holding a gun in his hand and cursing at them. Unable to let go of years of being bullied, Sam stood defiantly and cursed back at the man.

The man raised the gun.

Tim pushed Sam out of the way just as the gun went off. The bullet grazed Tim's side, eventually creating a nasty scar.

The man ran off, and they never saw him again.

Sam had vowed then that he'd do anything for his friend Tim.

CHAPTER 7

THE NEXT MORNING, a pickup truck drove down a long straight paved road lined with telephone poles like crosses along the Appian Way. The truck turned onto a winding dirt road surrounded by a dense forest of trees and shrubs. The lone driver, Alan Webster, saw the lookout and waved. The lookout acknowledged Webster and waved him through. The truck finally screeched to a halt, kicking up a cloud of dust in front of an old farmhouse. Smoke billowed out of the stone chimney. No other houses were visible.

Webster jumped out of the truck, carrying a newspaper.

He entered the farmhouse through an unlocked door and rushed across the ancient wooden floor into the living room.

Vance Galvin sat there alone, eating a breakfast of cereal and milk at a small table situated in front of a blazing fireplace. He looked up.

Webster threw the newspaper onto the table without saying a word, and he waited for Galvin to read it.

Galvin saw the concern on Webster's face. He picked up the paper, which was open to the headline, "Mugging Victim Was Wanted by FBI." Included was a photo of Dan Connor.

Galvin proceeded to read the article: "Daniel Connor, recently shot and killed by muggers, was living a lie. Formerly Frank Valone, he was wanted by the FBI for questioning regarding bombings and killings during the Vietnam War era by a group called the Patriots headed by Vance Galvin. Galvin served three months in prison for violent acts as a Ku Klux Klan member in the early '70s, and eighteen months in Federal prison for gun smuggling. Connor is survived by a son, Timothy."

Galvin pulled a hunting knife from a sheath strapped to his ankle and violently stabbed the photo of Dan Connor between the eyes. He gripped the knife until his knuckles went white as his mind churned through myriad memories. He released his grasp, but the knife remained stuck in the table, standing perpendicular to Dan Connor's photo.

"He was my brother," he said softly. Galvin looked up and saw Webster looking confused with his head cocked to the side. "One of my band of brothers in 'Nam. I loved him…then." Galvin choked up with emotion.

Webster nodded. "I know how you feel, but you're named. You compromised?"

Galvin's shoulders sagged, and he exhaled heavily.

Webster knew that Galvin was shouldering many responsibilities. He sat down on a chair at the table across from Galvin, his back to the dancing flames of the fireplace. In an understanding tone, he said, "Machiavelli said leaders are measured by their reaction to adversity." He waited for Galvin to respond.

Galvin's dark eyes met Webster's, and he sat up straight again. "Concocted a plan we had no organization for. Thanks to the Internet, now we do. Frank stole information, and we better locate it before the feds. We tried but never found the bastard. Obviously changed his name to Daniel Connor and vanished. We need to find where Frank…this Daniel Connor…lived and find where this Timmy Connor lives."

Webster glanced at the article and said, "Timothy. Says Timothy."

Galvin hesitated for a moment. "Yeah…Timothy Connor."

"But why bother? Any information he might've had is decades old. And why find the son?"

Galvin appeared to think for a moment and then answered, "Frank stole stuff that includes names and photos of some of us Patriots, maybe of places we own, and a detailed plan of how to overthrow the government."

Webster leaned back in his chair, thought for a moment, and then said in a subdued voice, "Maybe you should scrap the plan."

Galvin contemplated the suggestion, but only for a moment. He ate a spoonful of cereal and then responded, "Our properties were unoccupied for over three decades. If the feds knew about 'em, they'd have been seized long ago. We're safe for now, so long as we have Connor's info." He took another spoonful.

Webster shook his head. "Look, you haven't told me or any of your local redneck yahoos what the plan is, but if this Frank Valone, or Daniel Connor, hasn't done anything with the information after all these years, why would the son do anything, especially since he probably knows nothing about you or your plans?"

"You'll have to trust me on this. We need to find the information."

Webster stared at Galvin. He wasn't satisfied with Galvin's answer, but he was willing to accept it for now. "And your men. These aren't the best and brightest."

"I know that, but they're loyal and willing to die for the cause. Once you're informed of the plan, you'll see I know what I'm doing." Galvin stared at the glowing embers of the fireplace. "I wanted Frank dead for almost forty years. The timing of his death couldn't have been worse."

Galvin stood up, walked over to the window, and stared at the sky. He spoke as though he'd just seen Moses's burning bush. "I've been ordained to carry out God's will, and now he's testing me. I will not fail."

Galvin turned back to a highly impressed Webster.

Webster nodded and reverently said, "Knew there was a calling for me."

Galvin continued, "The Branch Davidians leader, David Koresh, thought he was the next messiah. He died in their Waco compound when he was thirty-three years old. See the connection?" Galvin hoped he would.

Webster thought for a moment, and he replied as though a light bulb had just switched on in his head. "Like Jesus."

Galvin grinned with satisfaction. "Exactly. I believe Koresh's death was preordained, leaving the work to me." Galvin then added, "Gotta use the phone."

Webster obediently took his cue to leave and walk outside.

Galvin picked up the phone and dialed. Hearing Brett Mannings pick up, Galvin said, "BJ, we got a problem."

The congressman's bulldog face turned red as he spoke on his cell phone while seated in his Congressional office. "I told you not to call me that! I saw the article. Find a solution, understood? Meet at the spot tomorrow, 8:00 a.m."

Galvin began to tremble. "They put me in prison with those homos, not you, remember?"

Mannings hung up.

Galvin slammed the cell phone onto the table, and then he slowly calmed himself. "Your fantasy...my destiny. You'll legislate. I'll exterminate."

Galvin knew BJ would be a good soldier and would go down fighting if he had to. Despite BJ's past, he'd somehow never attracted the government's attention. Maybe BJ's good luck would hold out.

BJ was one of the strongest men Galvin had ever known. Yet in spite of his imposing size, BJ had managed to remain invisible to the authorities even though he'd participated with Galvin in crimes that could have put both of them away for life.

BJ had served in Galvin's unit in Vietnam, where Galvin had learned of BJ's philosophical compatibility with Galvin regarding race, religion, and patriotic fervor. Galvin had always been the more vocal of the two and had natural leadership qualities, and he was therefore more up-front and open about his emotions. Like the soldiers of Christ during the Crusades, Galvin was always on a mission, one that induced him to join a Ku Klux Klan group in the early seventies. A few years later he was convicted of hate crimes and, along with a few other white supremacists, was given three months in a minimum-security prison for using a baseball bat to attack and nearly kill several African American teenagers. Luckily for BJ, he was home with the flu that night.

BJ was with Galvin during several murders, crimes for which Galvin, the known ringleader, and a few others were wanted.

Like Galvin, BJ was involved in gun smuggling. Galvin thought that BJ's four-leaf clover must have been in full bloom when Galvin's truck was randomly stopped and searched as it crossed the Mexican border, but BJ's truck was waved through.

While growing up, Galvin had always thought he'd be lucky, since he believed in St. Patrick's three-leaf clover, which represented the Holy Trinity. But events in Galvin's life demonstrated that the Holy Trinity hadn't been very lucky for him to this point.

Galvin believed that BJ Mannings would be his four-leaf clover.

CHAPTER 8

THAT SAME MORNING, TIM was reading his newspaper over a cup of coffee. He usually enjoyed reading the sports section first, and then he would quickly peruse the headlines of the news section, stopping to read only those articles whose headlines caught his attention. He slowly turned the pages until a headline on page 8 practically choked him. He read the article, leaped to his feet, grabbed the phone, and dialed.

Allie was sitting at her upright piano playing a melodic classical tune. She had read that Billy Joel had been classically trained on the piano, and she thought maybe she'd write something like "Piano Woman" as a response to the pop artist's famous song. She smiled to herself.

Fletcher, Allie's sand-colored cairn terrier, sat at Allie's feet, licking her bare toes while she continued to play.

Although she was highly organized in her work and in most aspects of her life, the one failing she had always had since she was a little girl was an inexplicable inability to keep a clean house. As a child, her bedroom was forever covered in clothing and other odds and ends, completely obscuring the wall-to-wall carpeting. As an adult, not much had changed, and her apartment was in total disarray. Clothes, makeup, brushes, dishes, and other items were strewn everywhere.

The telephone rang, and she picked up after several rings, having had trouble finding it under a pile of clothing. "Hello."

It was Tim, and he sounded upset. "Some jerk must have told the press some bogus shit about my father."

"What are you talking about?"

"It's in today's paper, page 8."

"What's it say?"

"That my father was some kind of terrorist whose real name was Frank Valone."

"What?" She sounded incredulous. "How can that be? It's got to be some kind of mistake."

"Maybe I'll sue the bastard that printed this shit."

"Stay there. I'm coming over." She knew that the last thing Tim needed was to have to worry about defending the only thing Dan Connor had left on this earth—his good name. And certainly Tim didn't want to be known as the son of a terrorist.

Ten minutes later, Tim made sandwiches while Allie sat at his kitchen table reading the article. Tim placed two plates with the sandwiches on the table and sat down. He began eating voraciously while Allie finished the article. Her eyes tracked upward toward Tim as she asked, "Can any of this be true?" She picked up her sandwich and took a small bite.

Tim swallowed and answered, "How could it be? That drunk—a terrorist named Frank Valone? Gotta be bullshit. Sam called, and I told him the same thing."

"How long have you known Sam?"

"Since high school. Saved his life," he said matter-of-factly.

She put down her sandwich without taking another bite, and her green eyes stared wide-eyed at Tim.

Tim noticed her expression, took a bite out of his sandwich, and explained, "Some asshole pulls a gun on him. I shove Sam out of the way. Bullet grazes me. Left me with that scar you asked me about, but at that time, I didn't feel like telling you about it. He'd do it for me."

Allie shook her head. "I see why you didn't want to tell me." She loved Tim but hated the types of men he associated with, especially gamblers. Maybe she could eventually convince him to change.

Tim decided to change the subject. "By the way, Karen next door got married yesterday." Tim bit into his sandwich and stared at her.

Allie didn't answer.

He waited and then asked, "You listening?"

She brushed her hair from her face and said, "In your usual roundabout way, you mean to ask why *we* don't get married."

Tim smirked. "Get your ears cleaned."

Allie remained silent. They'd had this conversation several times before.

Tim placed his hand gently on top of hers. "What if you moved in?"

"We'd be at each other's throats." She removed her hand.

"We're different. So what?"

Allie's face bore the trace of a smile. "The Venus and Mars thing?"

Tim said cynically, "The stuck-up bitch and Neanderthal thing."

Allie sighed. "I'm going nowhere, glued to a desk, punching keys all day."

Tim finished his sandwich. "Make a lot more than I do." He picked up her remaining half sandwich and bit into it.

"You're smarter than you think."

"I barely finished high school."

"Street smart. Common sense. And you're a businessman."

"One little martial arts school."

"Which could become two, then three...who knows? And you're so good with kids. How's that little Brian with one arm doing?"

"Still afraid to mix it up with the other kids."

Allie nervously fingered the plane ticket in her pocket. The doorbell rang. Tim strode to the door, opened it, and saw Detective Sykes standing there with another man who was much bigger and younger than Sykes. Both men were dressed in dark pin-striped suits and ties.

Sykes asked, "Mind if Detective Landers and I come in?"

Tim waved them in, and they entered the apartment.

Tim turned to Allie and introduced the men to her. "Allie, Detectives Sykes and Landers," he said, pointing them out.

Allie and Sykes nodded toward each other. Landers, with a crew cut and a shirt collar that seemed too tight for his thick neck, stood stone-faced.

Sykes got right to the point. "The gun that we found under the car was unregistered, but we ran the prints. It was your father's gun."

Landers interjected, "You know him by any other name?"

Tim's back straightened. "Of course not."

Landers, not looking very pleased, tossed an old black-and-white mug shot of Tim's father onto the kitchen table. "Your father's name was Frank Valone. Hope *you're* not like that creep."

The unexpected insult jarred Tim, but he ignored it and pressed on. "Was he Mafia or something?" he asked as he glanced down at the photograph. It was clearly a picture of his father as a young man, and the name underneath was Frank Valone.

Sykes answered, "Worse. He was on the FBI's most wanted list. He was part of a group calling themselves the Patriots who waged war against the government."

Tim frowned. "Him? When? And why?" He again examined the photograph and wondered how it was possible for his father to have kept this from him for so long. He looked up. "And why was this mug shot taken?"

Sykes explained, "Times were different. People protested the Vietnam War, and others said stuff like 'America—love it or leave it.' Kids eighteen and nineteen years old were sent off ten thousand miles to fight a war no one seemed to want to fight."

"Where's my father fit into this?"

Landers sarcastically remarked, "Your father won the Bronze Star."

"What? Never told me about it." Tim was having trouble processing all these new revelations.

Sykes said, "Like many who served, he came back convinced it was wrong. Got hooked up with this radical group. FBI was hot on their tail when the group vanished, except for a Walter 'Mick' Yeager. Your father was arrested some time earlier for disturbing the peace during a march protesting the war, but like so many others who were arrested at that time, he was never arraigned."

Landers disdainfully said, "Don't try to con us and say you know nothin' about this."

Tim shrugged. "I don't."

"You're really that dumb, huh?" Landers acridly said.

Tim shot Landers a menacing look. "Lose the gun and you'll see how dumb I can be."

Allie was taken aback by all this and sternly said, "I think that's enough, boys."

The much-larger Landers was surprised by Tim's reaction, and he stood erect in response to the threat.

Sykes quickly intervened. "Okay, enough shit."

Tim glared at Landers and then turned back toward Sykes. "So you're the *good* cop. What happened to this Mick Yeager?"

Sykes looked puzzled.

"Might've been my father's friend. Do you know where he is?" With all these crazy revelations, Tim thought maybe this Yeager guy would be able to help him make sense of his father's newly revealed past.

Sykes thumbed through some notes on his pad. He read a portion and looked up. "Deemed unfit for trial. Institutionalized in '74. He now resides at the Morton Psychiatric Hospital in Northern Virginia. By the way, your father described his assailants as three white men. A woman eyewitness saw three black men."

"Prejudice can do that," Allie remarked with a knowing expression.

Sykes turned to her. "The woman is black."

Silence filled the room, as no one had an answer to this little mystery.

Sykes handed Tim his card. "Call if you think of something. My cell phone's listed, so don't hesitate to call me anytime, day or night."

"Sure."

Landers collected the old photo from the table, and he and Sykes walked out.

Allie exhaled. "Glad that's over with. You know, you've got to get over to your father's place and clean it out."

"Like I care. I didn't even know his real name." Tim's head was swimming. He'd often wondered why they had had to move so many times. Dan had always said it had to do with some job or some cheaper apartment to rent. As a child, he'd never questioned these moves. Now if what he had just heard was correct, it made sense.

Allie touched his arm. "It's no good not to grieve."

His shoulders slumped. "Felt worse when Bruce died."

Allie said sternly, "The man raised you by himself."

"Drunk."

"Maybe he had big problems," she said, empathizing with what she believed Tim's father must have been dealing with all those years.

Tim responded sarcastically, "Like what?"

Tim grabbed the last of Allie's sandwich and polished it off as Allie answered, "You're the one who should know. And he was obviously hiding from the law. Pretty big problems, if you ask me."

"Never spoke to me about any problems—and never mentioned anything about some Patriot group or anything else."

"Maybe you never listened," she said.

"Look." He raised his voice. "He was a shitty father. He blamed me for my mother dying at childbirth. And if I don't feel like grieving, that's my business."

"Did he ever say he blamed you for her death?"

He took a moment to contemplate her question and softly reflected, "I always felt the guilt. Some kids didn't have fathers, but everyone had a mother. He was a piece of steel—strong and cold."

"So you stopped calling him Dad?"

He sighed. "An ocean of booze came between us."

Allie's face softened. She understood his resentment. "I'll pick out a nice suit for your father to wear."

Tim didn't think his father even owned a suit, let alone a nice one. He would check to see, but if he was correct, he would have to call the funeral home and see what they could provide for his father.

A half hour later, Tim and Allie entered Dan Connor's apartment with Tim's spare key. To their shock and dismay, the small apartment had been ransacked. Drawers were wide open, clothes were tossed everywhere, and the closet had been taken apart.

Allie gasped. "What happened?"

Tim wasn't as surprised as Allie. He picked up a cushion from the floor, replaced it on the couch, and flopped down on it. "I'm certain it was the cops or the FBI looking for who knows what." He surveyed the mess. "Goddamn it! Now I gotta clean this shit up."

Tim and Allie proceeded to rearrange things and straighten up the apartment. Photos were scattered about on the floor. Allie collected them. "Weird," she said. "The first time I get to see this place is after he's dead."

While Tim placed items into trash bags and boxes, Allie noticed a framed photograph of Dan Connor in uniform on one wall. She turned toward Tim. "Your father was in the army?"

Tim turned to see her staring at the photograph. "Marines. He was a hand-to-hand combat instructor. It was the one thing we had in common—love of martial arts."

"It's in your DNA." She picked up some clothing from the floor. Underneath was an old photo album. She picked up the album and began to thumb through its pages. She could clearly see that some of the photos were missing from the difference between the faded background and the unfaded squares where the photos had been. She looked up at Tim. "I found an old photo album, but some photos are missing. Did he give some of these old photos to you?"

Tim glanced at the album. "I never even knew he had it. Must have had it stashed someplace. Toss it with the rest of the junk. I'll look at it later." They continued to clean and straighten up the apartment.

An hour later, Tim, Allie, and Sam were seated around Tim's kitchen table. Tim and Sam smoked cigarettes while Allie rummaged through some of the things that they had thrown into bags and boxes and taken from Dan's apartment.

Sam began to explain what he'd discovered at city hall. "I had somebody help me check out those numbers on their computer. No piece of property matches the numbers your father gave you."

"Maybe it's not in Baltimore," Allie offered.

Tim seemed amused. "He was drunk. He couldn't even see the guys who shot him were black."

"You ever live in another state?" Allie asked.

"Lots. We moved from Baltimore to Virginia and then to Pennsylvania for a while and back to Baltimore. He could never hold on to a job."

"What'd he do in Vietnam?" Sam asked.

"Never talked about it. I asked him a few times, but he'd say something like, 'It doesn't matter.'"

Allie nodded. "Probably too traumatic."

"We never talked much about anything. He said I was wasting my life gambling, but who the hell was he to talk about waste?"

"Who's coming to the funeral?" Sam asked.

"A few friends, maybe."

"No cousins or other relatives?"

"Never had any."

Sam rubbed his chin. "Can't veterans be buried in national cemeteries?"

"His will said under no circumstances was he to be buried in a national cemetery."

Allie asked, "Isn't that strange, especially when you now have to go pay for a cemetery plot?"

Tim had no answer. Apparently, there had been a lot of strange things going on in his father's life that he knew nothing about. He certainly could understand his father's need to hide the truth about the crimes he had helped to commit. But what about his father's last words to him—"Section 2, block 5, lot 9"? And if he was drunk or delirious, it would have been difficult for him to state those numbers with such clarity and conviction. He recalled that Dan had attempted to speak again just before the monitors started wailing and Tim was abruptly shoved aside. What else had Dan wanted to say to him? Sam was correct. They were the last words of a dying man to his son. They had to mean something, but with Dan gone, the little riddle would probably remain forever unsolved.

CHAPTER 9

Stan Urbanski was not happy with his life. During his lifetime he'd seen many others who were less fortunate than he, and yet they often seemed far happier with their place on this earth than he was. Yes, he was short, balding, and had a pudgy, cherubic face, but there were certainly millions of people fatter, uglier, shorter, and with afflictions he wouldn't have wished on his worst enemy, but then why did they always seem more content with their lives?

He had attended some fine schools, earning his law degree, but he knew he wasn't cut out for this type of work, constantly seeking new clients and often needing to exaggerate the truth—many would have called it lying. It was work he was uncomfortable with, never having been a good salesman. He often wished he would have become a teacher. He loved kids and felt that at least he wouldn't have had to lie to his students. College professor—yes, that was what he should have become.

But now he felt life had totally betrayed him. He sat at his modern glass-topped kitchen table, shirtless and perspiring, and swigged from a bottle of expensive Pinot Noir until it was polished off. He wiped his mouth with his hand and then tenderly leaned a handwritten note against the table's beautiful fake floral centerpiece.

He'd seen many movies and documentaries about the horrors of prison life, and on occasion he had visited clients who'd broken the law. Serving any amount of time in prison terrified him, and he might soon have to face his worst nightmare.

He had a lovely four-thousand-square-foot contemporary home just outside Philadelphia, with fine trimmed hedges, a lush and green lawn, and a beautiful swimming pool and spa with a slate waterfall in his spacious backyard. The driveway always boasted two late-model expensive foreign cars. Life seemed to be good.

Unfortunately, keeping up appearances took a constant flow of income—income that eventually couldn't match his expenses. He had a church-group client who had been required to place five hundred thousand dollars into Stan's escrow account to be used to settle a lawsuit at a later date. Like many lawsuits, this one took years to settle, but finally it had, and Stan couldn't write the five-hundred-thousand-dollar check. The money was practically all gone.

These past few years had taken its toll of both his bank account and his marriage. His divorce had become final two months before. His wife had taken up with a neighbor with whom she had been cheating for more than a year, and she had recently married and moved in with him. It was the talk of the neighborhood, and Stan found it difficult to shop in the area for fear of running into his former wife or her new husband, and he believed that even people he didn't recognize were whispering about him.

Although he had known he was breaking the law, he had dipped into the escrow account three years earlier with the thought that he'd quickly repay it, and no one would be the wiser. But as each month passed, the mortgage and car payments had come due, along with the credit card bills, the country club bill, and so on, and he dipped into the account a little more each month. He'd lost most of his life savings in the market crash of 2008, and he had taken out a second mortgage on his home. His income had dropped to a fraction of what it once had been, and now he was about to lose his house to the bank. Disbarment and prison. Life was not worth living any more.

He staggered into his closed three-car garage and climbed into his Lexus sedan. Tears, sweat, and mucus from a runny nose mingled in droplets that fell from his chin. He turned the key and closed his eyes as exhaust fumes filled the air. He began to breathe deeply, gulping the toxic air in an ocean of gloom. The carbon monoxide would make the pain vanish forever.

He always kept a cell phone in the cup holder of his car, and its sudden ring startled him. He glanced at the number and name of the caller, and he sighed. He reached for the phone, hesitated, and then answered.

"Kim?"

His daughter, Kim, lived in an apartment in Philadelphia with her husband and four-year-old son, David, who was playing at Kim's feet. "Hi, Dad. How you feeling?"

Tears rolled down his face as he answered, "My disbarment... and everything."

"You're still coming to David's birthday party next week, right?"

Stan inhaled deeply. There were only two things he loved more than life itself—his daughter and his grandson—and now he was reminded of them. His quaking hand shut off the engine, and his forehead dropped to the steering wheel in surrender as he said, "Wouldn't miss it, sweetheart." He mopped his brow with his hand.

He ended the call and forlornly stumbled back into the house. He sat down at his kitchen table, picked up the note he'd left, and put it in his pants pocket. For some strange reason, he suddenly felt empowered by the realization that his life was now in his own hands, not those of some judge or jury. He could kill himself today, tomorrow, or any damn time he chose. It was weird. He hadn't felt this good in a long time. He was now in full control of the situation—something he hadn't felt in quite some time. He hoped his high spirits would last.

Later that night, Stan slouched on his living-room couch alone, looking at, but not really watching, the news on his big-screen hi-definition television. The newscaster briefly described the mugging and death of a man wanted by the FBI for almost forty years named Frank Valone. The mention of that name made Stan's eyes open wide. "So they finally got to Frank," he said out loud.

He had met Frank Valone while on an extended vacation in Hawaii. Frank was exactly the opposite of Stan in many ways, from size and looks to personality, and Stan was immediately attracted to him. Frank had been in the Marines when they met, and he would soon be headed back to Vietnam. Frank had introduced him to two other servicemen, Vance Galvin and Oscar Webster, who were also in Hawaii for R & R and who would also be returning to Vietnam. Galvin was the most serious of the four and was always railing about how corrupt and horrible the government was. Oscar Webster was a pilot who, like Frank and Galvin, was disenchanted with the war. Oscar had flown many missions, and he knew he had killed not only enemy combatants but also many innocent civilians, including women and children, some of whom had been killed in horrible fashion by napalm. Oscar had seen the famous photo of a twelve-year-old Vietnamese girl running naked on a road, screaming in pain after napalm had burned every stitch of clothing from her body. The brass summarily dismissed incidents like this as collateral damage. Oscar believed his own psyche was also collateral damage; he could never reconcile the deaths of so many innocent Vietnamese with the expressed goals of the United States. It weighed heavily on his soul.

Before the three servicemen arrived in Hawaii, Stan had met what he thought was the most beautiful woman he'd ever seen. Beverly Lundquist was tall and blonde but took a liking to Stan. It was the age of casual sex, and Stan had sex with her several times over the course of the week. Unfortunately for Stan, when the handsome fighter pilot Oscar Webster came on the scene, Bev dropped him like a hot potato and took up with Oscar. Stan later learned that Bev married Oscar between Oscar's first and second tours of duty.

Every night for two weeks, the four men went drinking, sometimes smoking marijuana as well. During those two weeks, Galvin, Frank, Oscar, and Stan often discussed how to end the war, which included the overthrow of the US government. Stan didn't have the same hatred of the government as the other three, and he knew their hatred was probably the result of witnessing atrocities in Vietnam. Stan eventually went back to Philadelphia, and the three of them returned to the war, but not before they swore to keep in touch with each other once the war ended.

Stan did keep in touch with both Vance Galvin and Frank Valone for a short time, but eventually he lost contact with them, especially once he read in newspaper accounts that Frank Valone and Vance Galvin were wanted by the FBI. Unfortunately for Oscar

Webster, his plane was shot down, and he was listed for a time as missing in action. His remains were never found, and his MIA status was not changed to KIA until six years later.

After the newscaster's report on the death of Frank Valone, something stirred in Stan. He got up from his couch and began to traverse various parts of the house, searching for something he hadn't worn in more years than he could remember. He tossed things out of drawers and haphazardly pushed things aside. He was on a mission.

He eventually attacked a desk drawer. He paused, reached into the drawer, and reverently picked up a solid metal bracelet. The bracelet was a simple piece of shiny steel curved into a bracelet. On the surface, etched in black block lettering, was the name Major Oscar Webster. Underneath the name was the date: May 15, 1972. It was the date Oscar first went missing in action. These bracelets had been sold to the public in order to raise money for POW and MIA families. Stan had worn his for several years in honor of Oscar.

Stan slipped the bracelet over his wrist. It felt right.

He sat down at his computer desk and began to type. Minutes later, a Google search revealed a photograph of Major Oscar Webster smiling for the camera in his flight gear next to his Air Force jet. Below the photo was a synopsis, which read, "Major Oscar Webster of Richmond, Virginia, was assigned to a bombing mission in Laos when his aircraft was hit by enemy fire on May 15, 1972. Like most who were lost in Laos, Webster was never classified as a prisoner of war. No remains were ever found, and Webster was declared deceased in 1978. His name is inscribed at the Wall in our nation's capital on panel 05E, line 038. He left behind a wife, Beverly, and a six-year-old son, Alan."

Stan focused on the numbers 1978 and six. "Bev gave birth in '72?"

He had never thrown out an old address book, and he began to rifle through his drawers until he found it. There it was: Oscar Webster's address back in 1972 in Fairfax, Virginia.

He picked up the phone and dialed Kim's number. "Kim, I'll be gone a few days. If I'm not at the party, I'll send something."

"Where you going?"

"To find my first love. You might even have a half brother."

Kim was taken aback at the remark and could only muster a weak response. "What? You're kidding, right?"

"I'm serious. Long before I married your mother, I had an affair with a beautiful woman who gave birth nine months later. It's possible that that child is mine. I need to find out if it is."

Kim's head was filled with all kinds of thoughts. She knew her father was going through a very rough period, and she concluded that perhaps he was fantasizing about some previous affair. Maybe he hoped she would go running to tell her mother, for some malicious reason, although she could understand why he might want to try to hurt his ex-wife. "Okay, Dad, but let me know what you find out."

"Sure, sweetheart, the minute I do." He hung up.

Stan had done the calculations in his head. He knew that Beverly had given birth almost exactly nine months after Hawaii. In the pre-AIDS era, when unprotected sex was rampant, many men—including Stan—relied on women to provide some sort of birth control. Stan knew that Alan Webster could just as easily be Oscar's child. He hoped to be able to find out, and this newborn quest gave him something to think about other than prison or suicide—at least for the time being.

CHAPTER 10

THE NEXT MORNING, Tim, Allie, Sam, and a few close friends of Dan, including Scotty, watched somberly as the plain pine casket was lowered into the grave at the Gardens of Faith Cemetery on Trumps Mill Road at the intersection of Interstates 95 and 695. The branches of the leafless trees were taking a beating from the cold, crisp wind. The breaths of the mourners became puffs of disappearing clouds against the brilliantly clear blue sky.

Allie glanced at Tim and detected no emotion on his face. She wondered if he was very good at masking his feelings or if he truly had little regard for his father. She looked around and noticed that Scotty the bartender was wiping a tear from his eye, seemingly more emotionally involved in Dan Connor's passing than Dan's own son. She thought how interesting it was that Tim had shown such grief over his dog, Bruce, and yet hardly any thus far over his father.

Oh well, she thought. *Life is apparently cruel to some people, enough so that some poor souls are even able to take the life of their own mother or father, but they would run into a burning house to save their cherished dog.*

Tim had chosen to have a simple, inexpensive graveside service. He'd grown up with no religious education, but he knew he was a Christian of sorts. Tim thought that, with their moving around so much, there had been little chance to belong to any particular church. As the cemetery's stand-in chaplain gave a brief boilerplate eulogy for Dan, Tim recalled several instances in the past when he had been asked about his religion. He'd always felt as though he had absolutely no religious affiliation, but he chose to answer that he was a Christian. Saying he was an atheist or agnostic took too much explanation, especially since he wasn't sure if he was actually either one. He believed that if a person chose to accept the premise that God existed, he or she could do so without belonging to any particular religion. He was no historian, but he'd learned over the years that millions had been slaughtered in religion's name over the millennia, and continued to be up to the present time. No, Tim thought, if there was a God, you didn't have to join some group to believe in him.

The service over, the mourners walked somberly past the many well-tended graves toward their vehicles.

Allie took Tim's hand in hers, and she asked as they approached the road, "How are you doing?"

Tim shrugged and continued walking, not knowing how to express his mixed emotions.

Allie suddenly grabbed Sam and Tim's arms to stop them. She pointed at a sign. It read, "Section 1, Block 3, Plots 1-43."

Tim and Sam looked up in the direction she had pointed. Neither man understood what she was pointing at.

Allie turned to Tim and asked, "What were your father's last words again?"

"Why's it matter?"

"Just tell me," she said impatiently.

"Find section 2, block 5, lot 9. Okay?"

"Look at that sign." She pointed at it once again.

They both now saw what she was referring to, but both men were still confused.

"Could he have said *plot* and not *lot*?" she inquired.

"If he did, what for?" Tim replied.

She contemplated his question. "I don't know…maybe he already owned a grave."

Tim continued to walk toward the car, ignoring her remark, but she grabbed his arm to stop him and asked, "You know what you just paid for that two-by-nothing grave?"

"Way too much." He lit a cigarette.

"Maybe you could sell the one he might own and break even."

Tim smiled broadly. "That's what I like about you. You think like a businesswoman."

"Then humor me. I think we should go to the office and get a map of this cemetery." She placed her hands on her hips and waited for a response.

Tim glanced at Sam. Sam shrugged his shoulders, and Tim said, "I'm pretty certain he said *lot*, but I'll try anything at this point."

They turned and strode toward the cemetery office.

Minutes later, the three walked among rows of graves. Sam held a map of the grave sites. He looked up and scanned the area. "This place gives me the willies."

Allie thought for a moment and mused, "You know, maybe Tim's mother is buried here."

Tim shook his head emphatically. "Impossible. He told me she was cremated."

They continued to search for signs that might lead them to plot number 9.

"Maybe some pirate treasure!" Sam chuckled.

Tim pouted. "Jesus. Mr. and Mrs. Sherlock Holmes."

They continued to walk between the graves, counting them until they came to plot 9 of section 2, block 5. The headstone was inscribed, "George Martin Gruber, July 12, 1886–October 16, 1942."

Allie joked, "I don't think that's your mother."

Sam frowned. "Those numbers gotta mean something. I mean, those were the man's last words to his son." He turned and faced Tim. "You got some digging to do."

Tim and Allie looked at Sam with amused expressions.

Sam immediately understood and laughed at his unintended pun.

Back at Tim's apartment, while Tim and Sam rummaged through Dan's things, Allie began turning the pages of the old photo album she had found. One of the photos showed Dan in uniform receiving the Bronze Star. "Hey, Sam, look at this." She handed the photo to Sam, who was quite surprised.

Sam turned to Tim and said, "I didn't know your father was a friggin' hero."

Tim glanced at the photo and sighed. "Didn't know he got a medal until the cops told me and Allie, but I still can't believe he never told me about it. You would think he'd be proud to tell people about it, especially his own son."

Sam handed the photo album over to Tim.

Tim slowly turned the pages until he saw a photo that made him gasp.

Sam and Allie heard the sound, and they turned toward Tim, who looked like he'd just seen a ghost.

Tim looked up at them and declared, "The son of a bitch lied! All these years. He lied."

Allie said, "What are you talking about?"

He handed the photo album to Allie, who shared it with Sam.

Tim pointed at a photo of Tim and a young woman. The photo was labeled, "Timmy, age two, and his mom, Sara."

Allie and Sam exchanged surprised glances; Tim had told them that his mother had died giving birth to him.

Allie put her arm around Tim's shoulder, knowing how he must be feeling. Why would Dan have told Tim his mother had died giving birth to him if it wasn't true?

Tim was visibly shaken by the revelation. After a brief, uncomfortable pause, Tim broke the silence. "If she didn't die giving birth to me and was alive until I was at least two, could my mother still be alive?" He searched Allie and Sam's faces.

They had no answers for him.

"Also," Tim continued, "maybe that's why he told me she was cremated—so I would never ask to visit her grave. Jesus—it all adds up. Maybe she actually is still alive, but if so, why would he never tell me about her?"

No one had a solution. Sam took hold of the album and began to view the rest of the photos. A minute later, he remarked, "Look how many show your father and this Mick Yeager guy." He pointed at several photos of a young Dan Connor and Mick Yeager in uniform.

Tim said, "Let me see them." He looked at the photos. "Maybe he can tell me something about my mother."

"How?" Sam asked.

"We know where he's living," Allie said. "I think we should go there when we get a chance."

Tim sat down at his kitchen table and stared at the photo of him with his mom. He looked up at Allie longingly and said with a lump in his throat, "She was beautiful, don't you think?"

Allie softly responded, "Yes, she was."

He shook his head as a tear rolled down his cheek for the mother he never got to know. His thoughts careened from pillar to post. How old had he been when she vanished? He now knew she had been with him until he was at least two years old. She might have breast-fed him and nurtured him, and yet he could recall absolutely nothing about her. And if she really was still alive, and if he could find her, then he would no longer be parentless. *My God*, he thought, *what a reunion that would be*. Maybe she would inform him of relatives he'd never known about. Maybe he even had some half brothers or half sisters. The possibilities seemed endless as he continued to stare at his mother's photograph. He thought if this Mick Yeager was actually a good friend, perhaps he might reveal the truth about his mother.

CHAPTER 11

IN THE EARLY AFTERNOON, after Sam had gone home, Tim pulled on his work boots and then went over to his closet for his jacket.

"I hope we're not going to be disappointed with this Mick Yeager guy," Allie said. "What if he's crazy or just some vegetable?"

Tim put on his jacket. "I'm a gambler. What can I lose?"

She cynically said, "Yeah, some gambler." She knew he owed someone named Richie fifteen hundred dollars, money he didn't have.

Tim understood what she meant. He knew she hated his gambling and that she thought it a bad habit, but Tim felt he could stop whenever he chose. "You know what gambling is? It's not betting on a sure thing or when there's nothin' to lose."

Tim walked to the door, ready to leave for the Morton Hospital.

Allie stopped him by saying, "Then I think we're a long shot."

Tim turned around and said, "Maybe we're not a sure thing, but it'll be a hell of a ride."

Chin up, she said, "My ride's to Hollywood." Her hand shook as she took the plane ticket from her pocket and held it out for him to view.

After he stared at the ticket for what seemed to her an eternity, Tim snarled, "Were you gonna send me a goddamn picture postcard from Hollywood?"

Allie took a tentative step backward. "Gonna prove you're a Neanderthal?" Tim had never laid a hand on her, but she'd had experiences before with a man who reacted freely with his hands in situations far less troublesome than this.

Tim was visibly stung by her remark. "What will it take to prove that I'm no caveman? How much time before the window stops taking bets?"

Her eyes misted as she said, "It's post time."

In a soft voice, Tim said, "Maybe I can change your mind?"

Allie's shoulders sagged. "It's not you...it's me. Acting in school made me feel alive. I'm dying at my job. If I don't try now, I know it'll be never."

Tim asked gently, "You good enough for Hollywood?"

"I need to find out," she said as tears welled up in her eyes and began to run down her cheeks.

Tim tenderly placed his arm around her shoulder. "Come on. We gotta visit a mental case."

They left for the hospital in Tim's old white Pontiac Tempest.

A half hour later, Tim and Allie entered the Morton Psychiatric Hospital. Built in 1933, it was an imposing structure that had originally housed the criminally insane, a term used far more frequently during the first half of the twentieth century. Although the bars over the windows weren't needed for the vast majority of the current patients, they never had been removed and still gave the solid sandstone building the look and feel of a prison.

They approached the counter and asked the middle-aged female receptionist if they could visit with Walter Yeager. The receptionist asked for photo ID, and both Tim and Allie complied. She entered their names on her computer, printed out a sticky name badge for each of them to wear, and then picked up a phone and called a Dr. Sung. After hanging up she told them to go to Dr. Sung's office in room 117 down the hall. They slapped the badges onto their chests.

Arriving at the open door to room 117, they saw Dr. Sung—a second-generation American whose family hailed from China—sitting behind his large, highly polished oak desk. He waved them in, and they introduced themselves.

Sung came right to the point. "I understand you'd like to visit with Walter Yeager."

Tim answered, "Yes, if that's okay."

"What is your relationship to him and the nature of your visit?"

"My father and Mick—apparently that's what my father called him—were very close friends. Fought in Vietnam together. There are things about my father that I believe Mick might be able to tell me."

"Your father is deceased?"

"Yes. Dan Connor died a few days ago."

"Sorry to hear that, but Walter—that's what I prefer to call him—hasn't had a visitor in thirty years. I'm uncertain as to how he will react to seeing the two of you."

"We'll ask a few questions and then go."

Allie asked, "Is he imprisoned here?"

Sung took a moment to ponder the best way to answer her question. "If a family member took custody, they'd release him. But with nowhere to go, he's serving sort of a life sentence here."

"Is he sane?" Tim asked.

"Harmless, but perfectly sane? Not quite. I doubt he'll agree to see you."

"Please, it's very important to us," Tim implored.

Sung tapped his fingers on the desktop, and then said, "I can try, but no guarantees. Wait here. I'll be right back." He got up and left the room.

Allie turned to Tim. "If this guy isn't sane, how do we know anything he tells us will even be the truth?"

"We'll have to wait and see. Who knows if he'll even see us?"

Sung entered Mick's room. Walter "Mick" Yeager was an anachronism dressed in sixties attire—psychedelic shirt, beads, vest with tassels, bell bottom pants, and sandals. His long graying hair was tied back in a ten-inch ponytail. Mick was sitting in a chair looking out of the window as the Rolling Stones played "Satisfaction" on his cassette player.

Sung gently knocked on the open door. "Excuse me, Walter. There's a young man and woman in my office asking to speak with you."

Mick looked at Dr. Sung as though he hadn't heard him. "What?" Mick lowered the volume on the cassette.

"Tim Connor and Allie Sommers want to ask some questions about Tim's father, a man named Dan Connor. Would it be okay if they visited you?"

Mick was bewildered. He'd had no visitors for so long that these two could not be bringing good news. "Don't know 'em and don't know no Dan Connor. Send them away. Send them away." He waved his arm toward Sung and then turned the volume back up on the cassette.

"You're sure?"

Mick shouted, "Send them away!"

Dr. Sung detected Mick becoming agitated and soothingly said, "All right, Walter. No problem. See you later." Sung walked out to the sound of the Rolling Stones singing, "I can't get no sat-is-fac-tion."

A minute later, Dr. Sung returned to his office with a disappointed expression. He stood in the open doorway and said, "I'm sorry, but he refuses to see you. He's improved markedly over the years, and I can't risk destabilizing him. Again, sorry." He waited for them to get up and leave.

Allie swiveled in her chair toward Tim and said in a loud whisper, "Tell him the other name."

Tim understood and turned back to Dr. Sung. "Please try again, but this time tell him I'm the son of Frank Valone."

"Look, don't take it personally. I really don't think he wants to see anyone." He stood in the doorway, conveying more than a subtle hint that it was time for them to leave.

Allie said, "Please, just mention that name. If it doesn't work, we'll go immediately."

Sung had plenty of paperwork piled on his desk, but he didn't want get into a shouting match in an attempt to throw them out. He took a deep breath, and said, "Okay, I mention...what was that name?"

"Frank Valone," Tim said.

"Frank Valone, and then that's it. Understood?"

"Absolutely," Tim answered.

Sung again left the office and walked into Mick's room. The Rolling Stones were now belting out "Angie" on his cassette.

"Walter, sorry to bother you again."

Mick turned down the volume and stared at Sung.

"This Tim Connor says he's the son of someone named Frank Valone. Does that name mean anything to you?"

Mick's eyes blinked rapidly for several seconds. His head began to move in a circle, and he said nothing, appearing to Sung to have entered some kind of trance.

Sung stepped up to Mick's chair and put his arm around Mick. "Walter, Walter, it's okay. I'll send them away immediately."

Mick didn't respond, so Sung turned to leave, hoping that Mick wouldn't regress from whatever was causing this apparent trauma.

Just as Sung was walking through the door, Mick shouted, "Wait!"

Sung turned back to Mick.

"Tell them…tell them…tell them okay."

"You're certain?"

Mick hesitated and weakly said, "Yeah."

Sung quickly returned to his office and declared, "That name sure did the trick. But understand that he can be brilliant or delusional, and sometimes it's hard to tell which one he's being."

Tim and Allie stood up. They were satisfied that at least they might be able to determine if this psychiatric patient could be of any help regarding Tim's mother and Dan's secretive past.

Tim and Allie followed Dr. Sung down a long corridor to Yeager's room. Dr. Sung stood at the door and announced, "Walter, your guests are here."

Mick sat in a chair looking out the window. This time it was Janis Joplin they heard crooning on his cassette player, "Freedom's just another word for nothin' left to lose…"

Dr. Sung took it in stride when Mick didn't answer, and he motioned for them to enter. "Go ahead. It's okay."

Tim and Allie cautiously entered the room, not knowing what to expect.

Dr. Sung left the room and returned to his office. He used his intercom to alert a nurse to remain within earshot of Mick's room, just in case.

Tim and Allie were taken aback by Mick's attire and appearance. They stood there in silence until Janis stopped singing and Mick turned off the cassette.

He slowly turned toward them and said, "Janis Joplin. Saw her at Woodstock. Best damn time of my life, skinny-dippin' with babes in mud ponds. Sex, drugs, and rock 'n' roll. Were you guys there?"

Allie smiled. "I wasn't born yet."

Mick hit his own forehead with the palm of his hand. "Idiot!"

Mick's eyes slowly focused on Tim. He seemed to study his face before saying, "So you're Frank's kid?"

Tim quickly responded, "I always knew my father as Dan Connor, which is why I'm here. I'm hoping you might be able to tell me something about him. I recently found out that his real name was Frank Valone."

Mick's face turned to stone. He looked into the distance with what fellow soldiers would have described as a thousand-yard stare.

Tim glanced at Allie and then back at Mick. "Mick, I'm sure you remember him, don't you?"

The recollection of Frank once again caused Mick to blink several times before answering, "Sure. I know Frank."

Mick seemed to want to change the subject. He turned to Allie. "Who's the groovy chick?"

"My girlfriend, Allie," Tim answered.

"Bowling alley?" Mick smiled.

Allie replied, "As in Allison."

Mick grinned broadly. "Just funnin' ya. So how's big old Frank?"

"Killed a couple of days ago by muggers," Tim answered.

Mick's face turned serious. "You sure? Killed by muggers?"

Tim was uncertain why Mick would question the manner of Dan's death, but he thought it best not to press him. Maybe the years in psych wards had dulled his mind. "Yeah, three white or black guys," Tim answered.

Mick shook his head. "I don't dig, man."

"A black woman says it was three black guys. My father, on his deathbed, told the cops it was three white guys."

Mick seemed deep in thought, and then suddenly he burst out laughing, almost uncontrollably. Holding his sides, he said, "Be just like your old man, that son of a gun. Far out!" He knew exactly why his old Marine buddy might have said that, but he didn't want to discuss or even think about the horrible events of the past.

Tim and Allie glanced at each other. Tim asked, "Whaddaya mean?"

Mick stopped laughing, leaned toward the two of them, and whispered, "Spring me to a Stones concert, and I'll spill my guts."

Mick unexpectedly got out of his chair, jutted out his lower lip, and began to strut around the floor, mimicking Mick Jagger's wild, lanky style.

Tim and Allie tried hard not to laugh.

"Listen," Tim said as his eyes followed the strutting Mick around the room, "I can try to get you to a Rolling Stones concert, but first I need to know if you can leave with us. I'll talk to Dr. Sung and see what he says."

Mick stopped strutting and smiled at them. "I always wanted to see the Rolling Stones in person."

Tim said, "Okay, let's see what we can do."

Tim and Allie returned to Dr. Sung's office. After informing him of their conversation with Mick, Sung said, "All right. But he's got to be back by six tonight. We've taken him on a few very local excursions over the past few years. But remember—once he leaves his cocoon, he can become disoriented. If he does, I suggest you return him immediately." His tone was quite serious.

Allie nervously twirled her finger through her long auburn hair. She wasn't certain this was a good idea.

The two returned to Mick to give him the good news but, upon entering, they saw Mick curled up in a fetal position in his chair.

Mick saw them enter and said, "Ain't goin'. I'm not safe out there."

"I'm sure you'll be perfectly safe," Allie said.

Still in the fetal position, Mick said, "Sure. Just like poor old Frank was."

Tim softly said, "He was at the wrong place at the wrong time. I'm sure you'll be okay."

"You sure he was killed by muggers?" It sounded more like a statement than a question.

Allie replied, "Absolutely."

Allie and Tim both wondered why Mick was questioning who had killed Dan, but they thought it best not to push Mick on the subject.

Tim walked to Mick and said soothingly, "The shrink says you been out before and was okay. Look, I'll get you that Stones ticket. Scout's honor." Tim put up two fingers in a scout-like salute.

Mick grinned and nervously agreed. "Okay."

They checked Mick out at the front desk and left in Tim's car.

During the half-hour ride to Tim's apartment, Mick continuously expressed his amazement at how much had changed over the forty years that had passed since his incarceration. Many shopping centers and even larger shopping malls had sprung up, as well as many housing projects and a few tall office buildings and multistory apartment complexes. It all seemed to fascinate him, and he hummed several Rolling Stones tunes along the way.

Tim thought they were probably wasting their time but that it was still worth the effort. Maybe Mick would actually have answers for them.

Tim and Allie took Mick to Tim's apartment, where they sat down at Tim's kitchen table.

Mick surveyed the small apartment and said, "Nice pad. Maybe I can crash here sometime?"

Tim raised an eyebrow.

"Got a joint?" Mick asked. "Man, could use a toke...but a beer'll do."

Allie opened the refrigerator, cracked open a can of beer, and handed it to Mick, who took a swig, wiped his mouth with his sleeve, and then released a long sigh.

Allie sat down at the table and said, "Tell us about Tim's father."

Mick put down his beer. Then he abruptly launched into his life story, as if long-closed floodgates had finally burst open: "Met Frank at Parris Island, early '71. We were gonna kill us some gooks and end the war. We were young. What the hell'd we know? It wasn't too bad at first. I had my Stones music—"

Allie interrupted, nodding. "Mick Jagger—Mick Yeager."

Mick nodded as well and continued, "Then it all turned to shit. While kids back home were droppin' out, I had buddies shot and killed just 'cause they sparked up a cigarette at night outside their hooches. Didn't take too many enemy human-wave assaults by hardcore suicidals to get us thinkin' about nothin' red, white, and blue. Us grunts would slosh through mud and heavy rain on search-and-destroy missions. Our second lieutenant, Sadler, had a hard-on for gooks. After a firefight, your father and me got separated from the unit with Sadler. We come across a small village suspected of harboring VC. Sadler rounds up the remaining men, about fifteen old men and young boys. He grills 'em, but no one speaks English. Sadler goes nuts—shoots 'em up one by one. Charlie's frozen in place. I yell 'Stop!' and get in front of one of 'em and take a round in the shoulder. Your father shoots Sadler in the back—*ratta-tat-tat*—and pulls me out."

Tim and Allie were both mesmerized and said nothing.

Tim now realized why his father never had told him that story. Shooting your second lieutenant in the back was nothing to brag about.

Mick wiped his sweaty forehead with his sleeve, lit a cigarette with a lighter, took a deep drag, exhaled a cloud of smoke, and continued his monologue. "Jesus himself could never conceive of such sin. I tell the brass your dad saved me after a terrible firefight with the VC. They fuckin' give him a medal!" Mick laughed scornfully. "I was with him when he threw that piece of shit over the White House fence."

Mick stood up and again mimicked Jagger's strut. He seemed to be somewhere else again.

They heard a knock at the door.

Mick stopped strutting and stood watching as Tim opened the door.

Sam walked in.

Tim said, "Just in time to meet an old corps buddy of my father's—Walter 'Mick' Yeager."

Sam and Mick shook hands. Sam eyed Mick from ponytail to sandals as he asked, "What's with the outfit?"

Everyone ignored the question.

Allie said, "Have a seat, Sam."

Sam sat next to Allie at the table. Mick still stood next to it.

Tim remarked to Sam, "Mick's telling us how my father won that medal—by shooting his lieutenant in the back!"

Mick angrily retorted, "Cut the ol' man some slack, man. Saved ten asses...*my* ass! Back then, they were gooks. Now they're nightmares." Mick began to shake visibly. He felt his legs turning to wax, and he sat down heavily on one of the chairs at the kitchen table.

Tim sat down again at the table opposite Mick, crossed his arms, and showed no emotion as he continued to grill Mick. "The cops mentioned involvement in some kind of paramilitary group."

Mick squirmed in his seat. "Don't know nothin' 'bout that, man"

Silence reigned while Tim eyed Mick suspiciously.

Mick bit his lower lip so hard it began to bleed.

Allie noticed, pointed at his lip, and said, "You...your lip is bleeding."

Mick licked his lip and said wistfully, "Some wounds never heal."

Allie nodded, empathizing with Mick.

Tim appeared unimpressed. He said, "Do you know anything about my mother?"

Mick looked confused. "Do I know her?"

"If you were such good buddies with my father, you must have known her."

"What's her name?"

Tim was uncertain how he should answer the question. "It probably would have been either Sara Connor or Sara Valone."

Mick looked like a deer caught in a car's brilliant headlights. He hesitated and said, "Don't know nothin'. I'd like to go back now." Mick's face contorted.

The other three were confused by Mick's reactions, but then again, he was unstable and couldn't be relied upon to give cogent and lucid answers consistently.

Tim thought Mick might crack up at any moment. "Okay. I guess I got all I'm going to. Time to go back...*man.*"

Allie looked at Tim. "We still have an hour or two."

Mick had composed himself and answered, "It's cool. I really need to get back." He was drained emotionally and couldn't wait to return to the safety of his chrysalis.

They all stood up and walked to the door.

Tim turned to Sam. "Wanna come along?"

"Nah. I'll stay and make myself a sandwich."

As they left, Mick turned to Sam and flashed him the two-fingered peace sign used by the antiwar movement in the sixties and seventies.

CHAPTER 12

TWENTY MINUTES LATER, WHILE Tim and Allie were driving Mick back from Baltimore to the Morton Hospital in Virginia, Galvin, Webster, Red, and Suggs pulled up in two cars down the block from Tim's apartment. Red, sitting in the front seat of Galvin's car, fondled his Smith & Wesson like a lover.

Galvin said, "Remember, if he's not there, we pick the lock and search the place. If we find what we want, we're out of there. If not, we wait for Connor. If he's in there, leave the questioning to me."

The four men exited the cars and walked to Tim's door. Webster rang the bell and waited. They expected little or no resistance.

Moments later, Sam opened the door.

The four men rushed in, pushed Sam deeper into the room, and slammed the door behind them.

Sam exclaimed, "What the fuck?" His eyes darted from one man to the next.

Red jerked Sam's arms behind his back and handcuffed him to a kitchen chair. Red was purposely rough with Sam, and Red was enjoying this.

Sam knew there would be no use resisting all four since he saw the guns they carried, but he hoped they would rob the place and get the hell out of there. He was scared but was still able to act cool. "Take whatever you want, but there's nothin' here to take."

While the others began to tear the apartment apart, searching, Galvin knelt in front of Sam, examined his face, and remarked with a puzzled expression, "You're Dan Connor's kid?"

He nervously answered, "Sam Breen. It's Tim's apartment, and I guarantee he's not rich." Sam wondered about the reference to Dan Connor and Tim, which meant this was no ordinary robbery. They apparently wanted something from Tim. He hoped they'd find what they were searching for and get out.

"You got ID, son?" Galvin asked.

"Back pocket." At least he could prove he wasn't the one they were looking for.

Galvin reached behind Sam and found his wallet. He extracted his license and then angrily hurled everything against the wall.

Now Sam knew for certain that these men wanted to find Tim. Observing how angry this man was, Sam was smart enough to keep quiet as the men continued to tear the place apart—but what they were looking for Sam couldn't begin to guess.

Minutes later, after the small apartment had been turned inside out, the men stood around Sam.

"Nothing here, Major," Suggs said.

Galvin turned to Sam. "Where's Tim Connor?"

Sam said, "I have no idea." He thought if he acted tough they would believe him and leave. He wore the bravest face he could muster.

Red stepped forward and punched Sam's face with his leather-gloved fist. Both of Sam's nostrils exploded with blood as his nose shattered.

Sam now realized he was in big trouble, and he began to shake as his eyes welled up and his head began to throb. His brave face became a mask of fear.

Galvin spoke calmly. "Must be real friendly leaving you alone in his apartment. What's he know about us?"

"Who the hell *are* you?" asked Sam.

Galvin coldly remarked, "You're about to find out."

Red again smashed Sam's face with his fist.

Sam felt the pain radiate throughout his skull, and he screamed, "What do you guys want?"

Galvin stepped in closer. "We need to know where Tim Connor is right now. Tell us and we'll be on our way. No more harm done."

Sam was breathing heavily, and his head felt like it was ready to explode. "Look, all I know is that he went to take an old friend of his father's back home." He knew he sounded like a pleading little boy, but he didn't care.

Galvin perked up. "What friend, and how old?"

Sam spat blood from his mouth and replied, "Some guy he served with in Vietnam."

Now Galvin's interest was piqued. He believed he knew all of Frank's former Vietnam buddies. "What's this friend's name?"

Sam knew he had to tell them, but his nervousness and the blows to his face had wiped the name from his memory. He stuttered, "I c-can't remember."

Galvin was annoyed. "Red, maybe our friend needs a little more persuasion." He gestured toward the stove. "Turn on the gas range and heat up your knife."

"Wait," Sam pleaded, his blood still running across his mouth and chin. "I'm trying to remember—I really am."

Red went to the stove, turned on one of the gas burners, and put the tip of his hunting knife into the flame as Sam struggled to recall the name before they did something horrible to him. Would they pluck out his eyes? Cut off his balls? His dire thoughts made his heart pound in his chest as perspiration soaked his clothes.

Tim, Allie, and Mick got out of Tim's car, and Allie escorted Mick toward the hospital entrance. Mick stopped and turned to Tim. "There's lots more to your old man."

Tim wasn't impressed. He thought that the person Mick had known so long ago was probably not the same man who'd raised him. "Gave me a roof over my head and turned me on to martial arts. Other than that, he was a drunk who dragged me from place to place and showed me about the same warmth he showed your lieutenant."

Mick began to shake. "Watch it, buddy. He was a good friend." Then he shouted, "*Chat dau ho chung!*"

Tim and Allie could clearly see that Mick was in another place and another time. Mick began to cry, his body quaking.

Allie placed her arm around Mick and helped him to the door.

Tim made a face. *Who cares?* he thought. They disappeared into the hospital.

Sam's body was trembling uncontrollably. He'd been bullied many times before, but never anything remotely resembling this.

Galvin spoke to Red. "Let's see if we can persuade our friend to give us some answers."

Red removed his knife from the open flame of the gas range. The tip of the knife was glowing. Suggs held Sam's hand in place as Red approached with the glowing tip. He pressed the tip against the back of Sam's hand.

Red was in ecstasy as Sam screamed in agony as the knife seared his skin. The pungent odor of burnt flesh filled the air.

Sam suddenly recalled a name and shouted, "Mick! They went to see a guy named Mick!" Sam felt a fierce knot forming in his stomach, but he hoped the name would satisfy them. He stared at Galvin through blurry eyes for some sign that his ordeal was over.

The name jarred Galvin for a second before he remembered that Mick was probably a vegetable stashed away in some nuthouse. It didn't surprise him that Frank might have told Tim about Mick. *But still,* he thought, *what if Mick has somewhat recovered after all these years, and what if Mick knows what Frank knew?*

Red put the knife back into the flame, hoping to be able to use it again. He was enjoying watching Sam squirm.

Galvin leaned over toward Sam. "See, I knew you weren't that dumb. Now where is this Mick now? Where did Connor go, and when will he be back?"

This time Sam knew he was in even bigger trouble since he had no idea where they were taking Mick. At the time, it hadn't mattered to Sam where they were going, and he'd paid no attention to it. "I swear I don't know. Please. I beg you to believe me. I don't know where they went. Don't you think I would tell you if I knew?" He glanced at the glowing knife amid spasms of terror.

Galvin wasn't impressed. "Just like you couldn't remember his name until we decided to use Red's knife."

The lingering pain from the knife caused Sam's mind to shift into overdrive. "Okay, let me think a minute," he pleaded as he choked back a sob. He knew he might have to lie and was trying to buy some time. Maybe somebody had heard his screams and called the cops. Or maybe they would believe what he told them and leave. He prayed something good would happen as he tried to concoct some believable story.

Tim and Allie were now on the way back to Tim's apartment after dropping Mick off at the hospital.

They drove in total silence until Allie said, "I know how you feel, but Mick was only trying to explain—"

"Now I'm hearing more shit. My father's buried. Time to let him rot." Tim instantly regretted saying it out loud, but he felt that Dan deserved his scorn.

For Allie, having grown up with two loving parents, it was difficult to empathize with Tim's lack of sympathy for his father, but she knew Tim's experiences were his own, and he would have to reconcile himself with his past on his own terms.

Red brought the red-hot knife toward Sam's face. Sam yelled, "Okay, I remember!"

A disappointed Red moved the knife away.

Galvin said, "Okay, where'd he go?"

Sam gave them an address. He stared at them, praying they would believe him and leave.

Galvin knew he was lying, but he had to be certain. "Is that where Mick lives?"

"Yeah…yeah, that's it."

Galvin paused, and said, "You're a lying sack of shit." He knew Mick was in some hospital, but not which one.

Galvin looked at Red. "Red, do your thing, and no mercy this time."

Sam's whole body began to quake as he struggled with every ounce of strength to break free of the handcuffs, reacting instinctively like an animal chewing its own leg off to free itself from a trap.

Red was gleeful. He brought the knife toward Sam's left eye. Red was prepared to burn Sam's eyes out if need be, and he was looking forward to seeing his reaction.

Sam, who'd been bullied so much in the past, suddenly thrust his head forward and clamped his teeth onto Red's forearm, biting as hard as he could, drawing blood.

Red screamed, grabbed the knife with his other hand, and plunged it into Sam's neck.

Webster winced as blood and steam shot out of Sam's neck.

Red pried open Sam's jaw and yanked his arm from Sam's mouth.

Sam made gurgling noises, suffered for a full minute, choking on his own blood, and then finally died.

Webster angrily shouted, "Could've used him as bait, you dumb shithead!"

Red yelled back, "Fuckin' bit me! Maybe I got rabies!"

A furious Red kicked over Sam's chair. Sam fell on his side in a puddle of blood.

Galvin took control and spoke calmly to Webster. "Okay, so it's *auf Wiedersehen*. Red's candle may not burn the brightest, but he'd leap into flaming hell for me."

"Damn right!" Red shouted, grasping his bleeding arm. "Now I probably got AIDS!"

Webster stared at Red and Galvin. He knew Red was a sadist who had the brains of a walnut, but it was Galvin's lack of sympathy for this innocent guy named Sam that worried him. A leader had to be strong, yes. But a leader also had to have some humanity. The fact that he didn't detect this trait in Galvin worried Webster to his core.

After an uncomfortable silence, Tim glanced at Allie in the passenger seat and said, "I'm starving."

"I'll tell Sam to meet us at Friday's." She dialed her cell phone, heard it ring four times, and then got Sam's voice mail. "Hi, Sam. We're going to Friday's for lunch. If you want you can meet us there. Bye."

She ended the call. "He didn't pick up. Let's eat and then go to my place. I've got to walk Fletcher."

"Okay."

The four men heard Sam's cell phone ringing from his pocket. Sam still lay on his side, drenched in his own blood. Suggs asked, "Should we answer it?"

Galvin replied, "Let it ring. If we answer it, it'll raise suspicions."

A half hour later, Red sat eating peanuts, throwing the shells at Sam's body.

"Sooner or later," Webster said, "he'll be missed, and they'll definitely check here."

Galvin nodded. "We'll wait a while longer or until the body starts to stink." No one but Galvin knew how important it was to make certain the information Frank had stolen didn't fall into the hands of the authorities, and Galvin was willing to wait as long as it took to find Tim Connor.

CHAPTER 13

THAT SAME DAY, STAN Urbanski left his home in Philadelphia at nine o'clock in the morning in search of something he knew was merely wishful thinking, but at least it was giving him the impetus to do something other than sitting alone in his big house and feeling sorry for himself.

Driving his late-model Lexus on I-95 from Philadelphia, it took only twenty minutes to cross into Delaware, and only another twenty minutes to pass through the Union's second-smallest state and into Maryland, home of Antietam National Battlefield, site of the bloodiest single-day battle of the Civil War, where more than twenty-three thousand Union and Confederate soldiers were killed or wounded. Fifty minutes later, he passed through Baltimore near Fort McHenry, a star-shaped brick fort whose bombardment by the British during the War of 1812 inspired Francis Scott Key to pen "The Star-Spangled Banner." Key had been detained aboard a truce ship, from which he watched the battle rage through the day and night. Upon seeing the star-spangled banner still aloft "by the dawn's early light," he knew that the beleaguered defenders had held firm.

Another forty minutes passed before Stan found himself in the nation's capital. After spotting signs for the National Mall, Stan felt drawn like iron filings to a magnet toward a place he'd never been before.

Just northeast of the Lincoln Memorial and adjacent to the National Mall in Constitution Gardens is the Vietnam Veterans Memorial, which consists of three separate parts: *The Three Soldiers,* the Vietnam Women's Memorial, and the Vietnam Veterans Memorial Wall. Stan parked his car and reverently approached his destination.

Completed in 1982, the Wall consists of two slabs of gabbro, an igneous rock, and is two hundred fifty feet long. The polished gabbro was chosen for its reflective quality, and Stan Urbanski was able to see his stout reflection clearly as he searched among the 58,318 names of Vietnam War era dead and missing servicemen and women engraved in the panels. He passed other people, most of them walking slowly or standing reverently in front of a name. Some made impressions of the names by rubbing pencils or chalk onto pieces of paper. Some softly cried.

Stan found the panel he was looking for. He stepped forward and solemnly touched the name of Oscar Webster. Tears began to run down his cheek. His hand held a time-worn photograph of his father, who had been killed in the Korean War during the harsh winter of 1953, when Stan was just six years old.

The Korean War was the first major armed involvement between free-world and Communist forces as the cold war became inflamed. The Korean War was also known as the forgotten war, since it was sandwiched between the sheer size of World War II and the controversial Vietnam War.

His father, Captain Nicholas Urbanski—a first-generation child of Polish immigrants—enlisted in the Air Force at the end of the Second World War. By the beginning of the Korean conflict in 1950, he was piloting aging B-29 bombers with the Fifth Air Force. In February of 1953, on a bombing raid forty miles north of Pyongyang, his B-29 was on a mission to destroy railroads and bridges when the plane encountered heavy antiaircraft fire and went down. The bodies were returned to the US in an exchange program for North Korean dead in 1955.

Stan spoke softly to the photograph. "All heroes…just like you, Dad."

Stan looked up at the sun, which was shining brightly on that crisp January morning, and he then looked back at Oscar Webster's name and said, "See you soon, buddy." He left for his car, believing his time on this earth was nearing its end. He wasn't a religious man, but at that moment he felt he'd soon be seeing his father once again.

Stan returned to his Lexus and crossed the Potomac River into Northern Virginia, where he was drawn to Arlington National Cemetery, feeling compelled to visit the grave of President John F. Kennedy. Although it was the most visited grave site in the country, the frosty January temperature kept away all but a hearty few.

Stan stood somberly in front of the eternal flame under which his most cherished president was buried. Next to JFK lay two of his children who had died in infancy, and also his wife, Jacqueline Kennedy Onassis. Stan had been in his high-school biology class when the public address system announced the almost inconceivable news. Stan believed that JFK's assassination was the beginning of the end of America's last age of innocence. The ten years between the end of the Korean War and JFK's death had seen the emergence of rock 'n' roll, television shows such as *I Love Lucy* and *The Brady Bunch*, and an America that emerged as a world power and beacon of freedom for the world to admire. Housing developments and shopping centers were springing up all over the country, and American manufacturing was second to none, acting as the world's car dealer, food grower, and clothier.

After JFK's assassination in 1963 came the Vietnam War, the incredible rise of the drug culture, the age of free sex, the assassination of Martin Luther King Jr., race riots in many major cities, the assassination of Robert Kennedy, the advent of rampant inflation, and gasoline shortages that engendered huge lines at the pump. New York City was just one of many other great cities on the brink of declaring bankruptcy. The final blow to America's confidence was dealt during the Iranian hostage crisis of 1979. Fifty-two American diplomats were held hostage for 444 days by the government of Iran. Rather than flex its vast military might, the US attempted a failed rescue mission that resulted in the deaths of eight servicemen. During this time, the Soviet Union invaded Afghanistan, and America's tepid response was to pull out of the 1980 Moscow Olympics. The United States appeared to be an emasculated shadow of its former self. These events contributed heavily to Jimmy Carter's defeat by Ronald

Reagan. There was a general feeling that the America Stan had grown up in was no longer a shining beacon of light for the world to follow.

With a heavy heart, Stan left the cemetery for Fairfax, Virginia, a small city of approximately twenty-two thousand located a few miles from the Maryland border. He arrived at the address listed in his old address book, but as he expected, numerous tenants had come and gone since Oscar died. Stan proceeded to knock on several apartment doors, asking if anyone remembered the Webster family. Finally, one elderly female tenant recalled that Beverly Webster had a sister, Carla Spangler, who lived in a garden apartment complex called Biltmore Park, and she believed Carla still lived there.

A short while later, after speaking with the superintendent at Biltmore Park, Stan knocked on a door in the apartment complex. An old woman, appearing about eighty years old, opened the door slightly, with the chain still attached. She silently scrutinized Stan and waited.

Her blank stare prompted Stan to speak first. "Oscar and Beverly Webster used to live nearby. I found a neighbor who told me his sister-in-law…you, I'm guessing…lived here."

Without opening the door any wider, she said coldly, "Oscar's dead over thirty years." With a puzzled expression, she continued, "And how do you know where he lived so long ago? In fact, he was there only once for a short visit just after getting married. Had to go back to the war."

"We met in Hawaii and exchanged addresses. Never threw out my old address book. Oscar had a son. I wore this bracelet during the Vietnam War and would like to give it to him." Stan held out his wrist for the old woman to see the bracelet.

She nodded as though showing approval. "You serve with Oscar?"

"I was never in the service." He thought, *Thank God for that.*

The old woman unlatched the chain and opened the door, but looked at him skeptically. "Then what's it to you?" She stood there in an old flowered house dress and worn-out pink cotton slippers.

"I looked on the Internet and saw that Bev had a son. I just feel like he should be the one to have it."

"Where'd you get the bracelet?"

"They were sold to support the families of MIAs and POWs."

Her eyes narrowed. "A war protester."

Stan remarked, "If they'd listened, Oscar and thousands like him would still be alive. My father was killed in Korea, but at least we got his body and tags back."

Following an uncomfortable silence, the old woman mellowed. "Alan was practically a newborn when his father was lost. His mother, my younger sister, couldn't cope after that. She eventually killed herself."

The old woman detected a surprised look on Stan's face. "Guess you didn't know. Anyhow, Alan joined the Marines. Maybe because of his father, but maybe because he had nowhere to go. Haven't seen Alan in maybe fifteen years."

"Where's he stationed?"

"Last I knew, Quantico."

Stan thanked the woman for her time and left.

Before traveling to Quantico, he took a fifteen-minute detour to Manassas. Manassas National Battle Field Park, also known as Bull Run, was the site of two Confederate victories. It was here that General Jackson earned the nickname Stonewall. When the second battle ended, the Confederacy was at the height of its power. Stan viewed the blood-soaked battlegrounds with the thought that the brave, defeated Union soldiers who laid down their lives here were at least fighting for noble causes: the end of slavery and to keep the union whole. He was never certain what cause his father died for in Korea. He solemnly stared at the huge battlefield and left for his car.

An hour later, Stan arrived at Marine Corps Base Quantico, one of the largest US Marine Corps bases in the world. The base was the site of the Marine Corps Combat Development Command and the presidential helicopter squadron. Also located on 570 acres of the base was the FBI Academy training site for new special agents, who had to pass a twenty-week training course.

The town of Quantico had a population of less than six hundred and was bordered by the Marine Corps base on three sides, the Potomac River on the fourth. The base was a miniature city that housed more than twelve thousand military and civilian personnel and their families.

Stan arrived at the front gate, where he couldn't help but notice the imposing statue of four Marines raising the American flag atop Mt. Suribachi on Iwo Jima, fashioned after the iconic Pulitzer Prize–winning photograph taken in 1945 by Joe Rosenthal. The Battle of Iwo Jima was a major battle on that Pacific Island that boasted three valuable airfields. Seventy thousand US troops fought twenty-two thousand Japanese soldiers; almost seven thousand US troops were killed, and almost twenty-one thousand were wounded. Of the twenty-two thousand Japanese soldiers, only two hundred sixteen were taken prisoner. Some of these were captured only because they had been knocked unconscious or otherwise disabled. The rest were killed or missing and presumed dead. The incredible number of dead Japanese soldiers stood as glaring testimony to the Imperial Japanese Army's willingness to fight to the bitter end, a fact that weighed heavily on President Harry Truman's decision to drop atomic bombs on Hiroshima and Nagasaki rather than invade the Japanese mainland. It was estimated that the invasion might require a force of one million troops, with a high cost of a hundred thousand American soldiers killed and wounded. It was also estimated that many more Japanese would be killed in an invasion than those killed in the two unlucky cities due, in part, to conventional carpet-bombing of its cities and an invasion force that would be compelled to fight in the streets of Tokyo and many other major Japanese cities.

Stan had to pass through an armed gate, where he had to provide ID and state his business at the base. He was issued a one-day pass, given directions to his destination, and allowed onto base property.

Ten minutes later, Stan stood at a counter in the Marine Records Office and spoke with a serious-looking young Marine sergeant, who read from his computer. "Alan Webster was discharged after nine years with loss of pension. Records show his father was KIA in 'Nam. You serve with his father?"

"Too busy protesting," Stan said proudly.

With disdain, the sergeant replied, "Oh, a real hero."

Stan didn't shrink from the sergeant's admonishment. "You're not old enough to remember. You had to be there." Stan recalled the intense arguments concerning the war. It wasn't easy, especially in the early years of the war, to speak out against a war when many said, "My country, right or wrong." When he ran for president in 2004, Senator John Kerry, a decorated Vietnam War hero, was still paying a high price among many veterans for speaking out against the war back in 1971. Kerry testified before the Senate and told of atrocities being committed by US troops. He called for the immediate withdrawal of US troops and asked, "How do you ask a man to be the last man to die in Vietnam? How do you ask a man to be the last man to die for a mistake?" Stan had always thought that if your country was wrong, you were obligated to do something to try to fix it. And Kerry had tried to do exactly that.

With impatience, the sergeant said, "Sir, state your business with him."

"I'd like to give this bracelet to his son." He held it out for the sergeant.

The sergeant stared at the bracelet for a moment, and he asked with an accusatory tone, "Guilt?"

Stan had now become annoyed with the sergeant's lack of understanding. Stan knew that time had proven the protestors right and the warmongers wrong. He asked, chafing, "Do you know where he is now?"

The sergeant glanced at the screen. "Only his last known address in Stafford. But that's as of five years ago."

"How far is that by car?"

"Fifteen, twenty minutes."

Stan wrote the address and then left with the sergeant's accusatory expression fresh on his mind, practically calling him a coward. Was he a coward? No—not even when he did everything he could to avoid being drafted into the Vietnam War. He always thought that if America had been under attack, like at Pearl Harbor, he wouldn't have thought twice about defending the nation, himself, and his family. But being an inquisitive student in both high school and college, he'd read as much as he could about the US's reasons for waging a war ten thousand miles away against a people who had not attacked the US and were no threat to its national security.

He read that although many nations had invaded Vietnam—the Chinese, the Japanese, the French, and now the Americans—no one had been able to conquer a people determined to defend their own country. In 1954, Ho Chi Minh's Viet Minh forces decisively defeated the French at Dien Bien Phu. The Geneva conference that followed divided the country into North and South Vietnam, and the North became Communist and the South did not. But Ho Chi Minh, the North Vietnamese leader, wanted to unite his country, and it was this fact that gave rise to the Viet Cong—South Vietnamese who fought on the side of the North against the tall invaders from ten thousand miles away.

By 1967, Stan and much of America knew that the war was a mistake. It seemed to divide the US along lines of education: college students and graduates knew the war was wrong while most others simply said, "America—love it or leave it." The war would drag on for almost six more years and would become the first war America could clearly claim as a loss, with almost sixty thousand Americans dead. Saigon became Ho Chi Minh City, and Vietnam became one country under Communist rule, which was exactly what the United States was trying to prevent in the first place.

Stan traveled from Philadelphia to New York City in 1967 to attend two peace rallies. At one, three hundred thousand people marched down Fifth Avenue behind a huge sign that read, "Hell No, We Won't Go." Stan took a turn carrying the sign and saw many men in suits and ties snapping photographs, and he thought they might be FBI agents taking photos for their files.

He remembered high-school kids, maybe thirty of them, throwing light bulbs and balloons filled with paint at the marchers while running across Central Park's igneous outcrops carrying an American flag. Stan saw this as blind patriotic obedience, and he wondered if there would have been a Second World War had the German people not followed Hitler so blindly.

Another march that he attended ended in front of the United Nations building, where folk singers like Pete Seeger railed against the war. Stan fondly recalled the feeling of camaraderie that permeated the immense crowd as they sang "We Shall Overcome." The marchers hoped to end the war quickly and bring the troops home. They couldn't have imagined that the war would churn on for almost six more years at considerable cost.

While still in college, Stan attempted to avoid the draft by enlisting in the Air Force Reserves. He was required to pass a physical at the local army base, and he and a friend, also attempting to enlist in the reserves, were able to drive their own car to the base, where they were treated differently from the rest, who were mostly draftees. Stan and his friend were ushered to the front of every line, and he passed the physical with flying colors. Stan went to the bathroom just before they needed a urine sample, so as the two friends stood next to each other with cups in their hands in front of a communal urinal, Stan turned to his friend and said, "Give me some," to which his friend obliged. Unfortunately, one of the sergeants in charge saw this act and shouted, "They're pissing for each other." To which another soldier shouted, "If they want to get in that badly, who gives a shit?"

Unfortunately for Stan, he was never called up by the Air Force Reserves and instead received his 1A notice immediately after graduation. He read that the Tet Offensive had recently killed two thousand American soldiers in just one month—good and obedient soldiers whom he believed had died for no good reason. Stan vowed to do anything to avoid becoming some politician's cannon fodder, even if it meant leaving America for Canada.

Now that he was certain to be drafted and would probably end up in Vietnam, he was obligated to take a second physical examination—one he hoped he would fail—but this time he was required to take a bus from his local draft board to the army base. The dour faces of the young men on that bus mirrored his own feelings about potentially sloshing through muck and mire to kill people he had never met and who never wanted to do him or any other American any harm.

This physical bore no resemblance to the first. Now he was at the end of very long lines, wearing only his undershorts, and being screamed at by officers as though the draftees were already in uniform. Stan attempted to fail every test he could, including the hearing test in which he purposely raised the wrong hand at the wrong times. He somehow passed the test.

When it was Stan's turn to stand in line for his blood pressure and heart rate to be taken, a young man directly in front of him kept itching and scratching his beet-red skin. When they took this man's heart rate it was 180, and his blood pressure was 170 over 120. He failed. It wasn't until later that Stan learned many men failed their physicals by taking high doses of amphetamines just before the exam.

Stan saw one young man faint immediately after having his blood taken, falling straight back like a felled tree, landing on his head on the hard floor with the sound of a watermelon being smashed. Stan never found out what happened to the guy but figured he had failed too.

Many friends and acquaintances had gotten out in a variety of ways. After initially passing his physical, one friend had gone on the Stillman water diet, eating only meat and water for six weeks until his six-foot frame carried only 117 pounds. He looked worse than Mahatma Gandhi after his most serious hunger strike. The young man's eye sockets resembled those of some unworldly zombie. Immediately before being sworn in, he told the officer he believed he was underweight and that they must have made a mistake. They weighed him again, making certain all his weight was on the scale, and he was declared unfit for duty. He ate seven Twinkies on the way home from the army base.

Others avoided serving by being overweight, voraciously eating as many fats and starches as possible until they crossed the overweight threshold. Some young men called Suicide Anonymous every week for long periods of time in order to establish their mental disability. Of course, the counselors at the other end were always gratified at how they were able to prevent the young men from killing themselves. One young man saw a psychiatrist for more than a year in an attempt to gain deferment, but unfortunately for him, he passed. He was so incensed at not failing the exam that he leaped onto one of the desks, threw his stack of medical records into the air, and screamed at the top of his lungs, "I'm crazy! You can't take me! I'm crazy!" The medical personnel helped him off the desk and failed him.

Many others had connections, either politically or through some payoff. Some parents, who knew a judge or connected politician, managed to get the local draft board to vacate their sons' names from the list of potential draftees. And certainly, for the right price, some draft board members could be bought.

As a result, the Vietnam War was fought disproportionately by minorities and poor whites.

After passing his second physical exam, Stan thought that he might actually have to flee to Canada as he'd read so many others had done. Finally, a friend of his brother told him to find something wrong with himself. Stan could only recall a knee injury that he'd gotten while skiing. While it only bothered him sporadically and hurt only slightly, he decided he had nothing to lose by seeing an orthopedic surgeon. This particular surgeon claimed to have gotten five out of the seven young men he had examined out of the draft, but the caveat was that there was something wrong with all five. Stan was told that if there was nothing truly wrong with him, he could leave with no charge. Stan complained of constant pain in his knee, which kept him from walking any long distance. The doctor took X-rays, saw a little something there, wrote a diagnosis, and thought it might be enough to give Stan a desk job in the army. Stan requested a third physical in which he would only have to see an orthopedic specialist at the army base. He did so and, to his utter amazement, was given the designation 1Y—permanent deferment. He would only be drafted if there was a nuclear war or if America was invaded. In Stan's mind, he was probably out for good.

As soon as Stan received his deferment, he was so thrilled at the news that he began to run to his car on the base parking lot; he could hardly wait to get home and tell everyone of the good news. Suddenly, he remembered why the army had refused him. He murmured under his breath, "You idiot!" He grabbed his knee, fell on the ground, and limped the rest of the way to his car. He irrationally expected some officer to shout in the distance, "You, you're lying. You can run, so get on the plane and get to Vietnam right now!" Stan never served and would never again suffer the degree of paranoia he felt at that moment.

After arriving in Stafford twenty minutes later, Stan rang a doorbell in a dumpy, run-down garden apartment complex. A teen-aged boy opened the door.

Stan asked, "Does Alan Webster live here?"

The boy shook his head. "Wrong apartment."

The door closed. Stan looked at the mailbox, which said Albertson. Stan scratched his head and then gazed up and down the block. He spotted two men talking to each other who appeared to be about the same age as Alan Webster—about forty or so. One man was wearing a Baltimore Orioles baseball cap.

Stan approached them and asked, "Excuse me, do you know an Alan Webster?"

The man with the cap said, "I knew Al. Bill collector?"

Stan chuckled. "No, I'm not a bill collector. I knew Alan's father. I'd like to give this to his son."

Stan held out the bracelet for the two of them to view.

The two men saw the bracelet with Oscar Webster's name and the date he was first listed as missing in action.

The capped man looked up and asked, "Were you there?"

Stan hesitated. After his experiences with the old woman and the sergeant, he thought it easier to simply lie. "Don't like to talk about it. Do you know where he is now?"

The capped man thought for a moment. "Harry at Harry's Bar might know. But if you find Al, be careful."

"Why is that?"

"You a WASP?"

Stan was puzzled.

"You know—white Anglo-Saxon Protestant?"

"Polish Catholic. So what?"

The capped man pointed in the direction of a black woman walking farther down the block. "Al moved out because blacks were moving in. I'd watch out if I were you."

Stan shrugged. "What could happen?"

His eyes opened wide. "How 'bout getting killed?"

Stan smiled serenely. "No big deal."

The two men stared oddly at Stan as he sauntered away.

Minutes later, Stan was seated on a stool at Harry's Bar, a sleazy little corner establishment patronized by locals who drank too much, cheated on their spouses too much, and complained about life too much. Stan waved and caught the attention of the grossly overweight bartender, who happened to be Harry. As usual, Harry, whose nose was swollen from years of heavy drinking, was tending bar in the half-empty place, which reeked of stale tobacco and body odor.

Harry approached Stan and casually asked, "What's your poison?"

"Thanks, but nothing right now. I was told you know a guy named Alan Webster."

"Yeah, I know Al," Harry said.

"Do you know where can I find him?"

Harry squinted. "You a cop?"

Stan lied again. "Served with his father, Oscar. I'd like to give his son this." He showed Harry the bracelet.

Harry nodded. "His father died when Al was a kid. Why're you looking for him after all this time?"

Again, Stan thought it best to lie. "I was watching an old Vietnam War movie. It reminded me of Oscar."

"Some kind of flashback or somethin'?" he said with empathy.

"Went through a lot together." Stan attempted to appear as though he'd seen things he'd rather not talk about.

Harry was genuinely affected by Stan's reticence. "Jesus, must've been rough."

"You have no idea," he said, involuntarily choking up. His eyes suddenly welled up as his mind drifted, recalling in that instant just how rough his life recently had been and how much harder it would be if he had to do time in prison, a fallen and disgraced man. He looked at Harry through glazed eyes. "I lost my law practice, lost my wife to a neighbor, losing my house, and might even do prison time—used escrow money. Got nowhere to go except this."

Harry felt for Stan. "Jesus…Listen, Al isn't the nicest guy. Called me his friend, but barkeeps are everybody's friend. He had maybe one guy who really was his friend. Comes in here three, four nights a week, usually around nine. Might know somethin'."

Stan composed himself, swatted a tear from his eye, nodded at Harry, and said, "Thanks. I'll be back around nine."

Stan left the bar knowing that this could be a dead end. If Alan Webster had moved, now he could be anywhere. If so, Stan's quest to find a long-lost son might result in failure, and all Stan could think about was how and when to end it all.

The pain of living was deepening once more.

CHAPTER 14

AT FOUR THAT AFTERNOON, Tim and Allie were lying naked on Allie's bed after showering together. They both sipped bottles of Bud Light, which was usually a prelude to lovemaking, as each of them admired the other's body.

Tim playfully began to sing a hit song from the seventies, and he more or less managed to find the melody: "Gonna find my baby, gonna hold her tight, gonna grab some afternoon delight."

Allie giggled at his rendition and said, tongue-in-cheek, "Gee, maybe we could form a duet—me as the pianist and you the vocalist."

Tim laughed heartily at the thought.

The place was its usual mess. Fletcher eyed the two of them from his vantage point at the foot of the bed.

Allie gently touched the scar on Tim's side. "Stay a while, after," she softly asked.

"What's for dinner?"

She smiled demurely, and Tim rolled over and kissed her.

"Ow!" he exclaimed.

He reached behind him and threw a brush onto the floor. "If you got robbed, how would you know?"

She laughed. "Stuff would be out of place."

Tim and Fletcher looked at each other.

Tim surveyed her lithe, dancer-like body, staring at it as always as if for the first time, from the feminine curve of her hips to the full roundness of her breasts. He ran his fingers across her stomach, and Allie responded by pressing the length of her body against his.

He tenderly kissed her already hardened nipples. She moaned softly, and he kissed her beckoning mouth. They then embraced each other, making love that was familiar but never felt routine.

After they were both spent, Tim was reluctant to bring up the subject, but he asked anyway, "Can I change your mind about an acting career?" Tim reached over her, grabbed his pack of cigarettes and lighter from the end table, and lit one.

Sounding annoyed, she said, "Do you have to? You'll stink up the place."

Tim took one deep drag, extinguished the glowing tip on the side of the metal lighter, and balanced the cigarette on the edge of the ashtray.

Allie continued, "And as far as my nonexistent acting career, I don't know if it will even pan out, but I feel I have to try. Maybe I'll get a job backing up some group with my piano playing. Maybe it'll be right here in Baltimore. But I'd like to at least see what's out there, and my choices were New York or Hollywood."

"New York's a lot closer."

She said lightly, "Hollywood is warmer."

Tim merely nodded and wondered what Allie might cook for dinner.

The four men were now tired, dirty, and disgruntled. Many peanut shells dotted Sam's body.

A testy Webster said, "I'm starving, and this guy's startin' to smell. Unless that's Red's stink."

Red glared harshly at Webster. "Real funny, asshole."

Webster ignored Red and looked at Galvin. "Maybe Connor suspects something."

Galvin thought for a moment. "Getting itchy myself. Cops could show up." He thought for another moment and then decided. "You'll take turns watching from the car. I have an important meeting."

Webster couldn't stand the thought of being cooped up in the same car as Red, and he offered, "Let me get some dinner. I'll kill time for a couple of hours and then bring them back some food."

Galvin nodded his approval. "All right. Suggs and Red, you'll take the first watch."

Red knew why Webster had made the suggestion, and he silently seethed.

Tim pressed his phone to his ear and glanced at Allie's closed bathroom door. He spoke quickly and quietly just as the door opened. "Two hundred. Lakers plus three."

He hung up as Allie emerged from the bathroom. "You're just like your father." Unfortunately for Tim, she'd heard him.

"What's that supposed to mean?"

"You're an addict, and I—"

He raised his hand and said, "Save the speech. I already know you're an actress."

Allie sighed. "We're so…different."

"But that's *good*. Take two people exactly alike, and they add up to two. We could add up to three."

Allie sat down on a chair, looking dejected. "I need something more."

He knew she meant leaving him for California, and realizing that he wasn't going to change her mind, Tim angrily responded, "The ball's always been in your court. I'm done at seven. Be there and I'll know I have a shot. If not, I'll know I don't." His ego had finally caught up to him, and he now believed she thought he wasn't good enough for her.

Tim grabbed his jacket and stormed out of the apartment.

Allie was miserable. She loved Tim, maybe even enough to marry him one day, but she knew she was being drawn toward Hollywood like a tiny boat caught in a maelstrom's powerful current.

CHAPTER 15

AT FIVE TO seven that evening, Allie stood outside Bruce's Martial Arts Studio, unseen in the dark, at the storefront window. She watched as Tim instructed his students.

Tim glanced at the clock on the wall—almost seven, and no Allie. He hoped she would come and maybe with a change of heart, although he doubted it. He knew he loved her. Maybe he was being unreasonable. Maybe she would find out that an acting career wasn't in her future, and they would live happily ever after. Or maybe she wouldn't show up at all, and that would be the end of their relationship.

Ten kids in white robes sat cross-legged as Tim, standing in the center of the mats, coaxed the one-armed Brian to defend himself against another eight-year-old. Brian's mother was on the side, nervously looking on. Several other parents ringed the mats, waiting to pick up their children.

As the two boys stood on the mat in the center of the room, Tim said, "Okay, Brian. Larry's gonna strike at you. You can do it."

Brian looked over at his mother. She nodded approvingly in his direction.

Tim said, "Ready? Begin!"

Eight-year-old Larry stepped forward and took a swing at Brian. Brian stepped back, knocked Larry's arm to the side with his only arm, and swept his leg across Larry's legs. Larry fell.

The other kids began to cheer as Tim exclaimed, pumping his arm twice like Tiger Woods after sinking a forty-foot putt, "Yes! Yes!"

Tim grabbed Brian and hugged him for several seconds as Brian's mother grinned from ear to ear, wiping tears from her eyes.

Tim affectionately patted a proud Brian on his rear end as Brian ran to his mother's arms. "Okay, guys, that's it for today," he announced.

Outside, Allie also brushed tears from her eyes, and she walked past the doorway, leaving.

Tim spotted her at the last moment and ran outside to catch her.

He saw her half a block away, and he shouted, "Allie, stop!" He was confused.

She stopped and turned around.

He strode up to her and noticed her damp eyes. "What's wrong?"

She smiled sadly. "Allergies."

"Where were you going?"

She dabbed her eyes with a tissue. "To find the kind of connection I saw through that window."

Tim shrugged. "I don't get you."

"You just reinforced what I'm missing." It was a difficult decision, but she didn't want to eventually drown in a sea of regret.

He shook his head. "What are you saying?"

She answered with authority, "You made more of an impact on people in the last two minutes than I've made in the past two years."

Tim slowly nodded his head. He was beginning to understand. Then speaking uncharacteristically from his heart, he said, "I don't remember my mother, so I can honestly say this. You're the only woman I've ever truly loved. Does that count for anything?"

She again wiped tears from her eyes as she averted his gaze. "Maybe our differences make us *less* than the sum of our parts."

After gathering up and donning their coats and shoes, the kids and parents began to exit the school, waving good night.

Tim waved back and said to Allie, "This isn't the place to discuss this. Let me lock up and then go back to my apartment."

She reluctantly agreed. She believed he would once again try to dissuade her, but her mind was made up. She had to try or forever lament it.

At eight that evening, Galvin and B. J. Mannings spoke through the open windows of their cars, parked driver's side to driver's side in a deserted parking lot.

Galvin said, "We'll find him. What about the feds?"

The bulldog-faced Mannings said, "If they get their hands on Valone's info, they might have enough to put me away with a bunch of degenerate animals. I'll die carrying out the plan before they get me. Part of why I'm seeking the presidential nomination. Got nothing to lose if your plan never gets off the ground, but let's hope your men can hit the Capitol first." Mannings knew that Frank had pilfered enough information on him to send him away for life or worse. He had told Galvin that he'd die first before being caught. He had no way of knowing whether Galvin believed him, but Mannings knew it was probably the only sure thing in this whole affair.

Galvin smirked. "Don't worry. Got 'em all fooled." Galvin pondered Mannings's statement about dying before serving time, and he thought to himself that he would definitely do the same. The memory of being repeatedly raped by those perverted animals made the decision easy for him. They would never be able to put him in a cage again. He swore it on all that was sacred to him, including the memory of his wife, Lucinda, and his beautiful, innocent little girls.

CHAPTER 16

SUGGS AND RED sat drinking beer in the car they had parked across the street from Tim's apartment. They were waiting either for Tim to show up or for Webster to return with their food—food being more on their minds than Tim Connor.

Red chewed on a wad of chewing tobacco as he asked, "What do you think about the new guy?"

Suggs yawned. "You mean Webster?"

"Yeah, him."

"I guess he's okay. I mean, Galvin likes him, so…"

"Yeah, but he thinks he's hot shit. If he disses me one more time, I just might put a bullet in his skull."

Suggs understood Red's feelings, but he knew Red's mental magazine was often one bullet short. "Listen, you better not talk that way around Galvin, or he or Webster might put one in *your* head."

Red folded his arms across his chest and didn't reply. He smiled to himself as he imagined the satisfaction he'd have in killing Webster.

Several minutes passed. An old white Pontiac pulled up and parked across the street, a bit farther down the block.

Red remarked, "You know what *Pontiac* stands for?"

"No, what?" He watched the doors to the Pontiac open and a man and a woman get out.

Red guffawed before answering. "Poor old nigger thinks it's a Cadillac." He slapped his hand on his thigh and said, "Get it? Poor old—"

"I get it. I get it," Suggs answered, expressionless, now looking at the couple walking up the street toward Tim's apartment. Suggs yawned again. "See if that's him."

Red took a photo out of his pocket that they had taken from Tim's apartment. He checked it out and exclaimed, "Hey, that *is* him."

"Okay, let's move, but the honey could be a complication," Suggs said.

"Not the way I'm feelin'." Red grabbed his crotch and shook it.

The two men exited the car. Red spat out his chewing tobacco, and then he and Suggs ran up to Tim's apartment door just as Tim and Allie were entering.

Tim and Allie had only taken two steps into the apartment when they both screamed at the sight of Sam's body lying in a pool of coagulated blood.

Tim yelled, "Sam!" He thrust his hand into his pocket for his cell phone, and he was about to step toward Sam when the door flew open. Red and Suggs barged into the room, guns drawn.

Tim and Allie turned toward the door, and their bodies went rigid upon seeing the weapons.

Red slammed the door shut and shouted, "Hands up!" He pointed menacingly with his gun and grabbed the phone from Tim's raised hand. Red tossed the phone to Suggs, who dropped it on the floor and crushed it with his boot.

Red looked at a terrified Allie and demanded, "Where's your cell?"

"In my pocket," her quaking voice answered.

"Take it out and toss it to him," he said, pointing at Suggs with his thumb.

Allie's shaking hand reached into her pocket for her cell phone, and then she bent down and slid it along the floor toward Suggs. Suggs stopped it with his foot and then stomped on it, shattering the glass display.

Red ordered, "Now back up against the wall."

Tim stared at Sam's lifeless body, thinking this had to be a dream. "What is it you want? We don't have much money, but whatever we have is yours." Hoping against hope, he added, "Is he still alive?"

Red hollered, "Shut the fuck up and do what I said." He stretched his gun hand toward Tim. "And if you two don't move your asses, you'll be as dead as he is."

Stunned, Tim and Allie fearfully backed up and stood facing the two men. The fact that Sam was lying in a pool of blood made the two of them fear that they would be next. As much as possible, they tried not to look at poor Sam's body. Tim and Allie's eyes darted from Red to Suggs and back to Red.

The memory of the searing pain of being shot darted across Tim's mind, but it didn't hurt as much as the sight of his oldest and best friend lying dead, murdered by these two animals. Tim wanted to crush these two maggots and watch their guts ooze out, but he knew he could do nothing at the moment.

Red looked at Tim. "You're Timothy Connor, right?"

Tim stared fearfully at the gun, but he didn't respond. The memory of the pain from the wound to his side made him wonder how much more painful a shot to the chest might be.

Red said caustically, "Let's see if you remember when I blow your girl's tits off." Red pressed the barrel of the gun against Allie's left breast.

Her eyes, wide with terror, locked with Tim's.

The violation and threat against Allie made Tim's blood run hot. Without thinking, he was ready to defend his intended mate to the death. "Yeah, that's me." Visions of tearing the man's throat out danced across Tim's mind, but unarmed, he knew he still could do nothing.

"Call the Major," Suggs said to Red.

Red took his cell phone and called Galvin's number. After ten seconds he said, "Got him, but he's with some bitch…Okay."

He ended the call and said to Suggs, "He'll be here in ten minutes."

Suggs nodded and then told Tim and Allie, "Turn around and put your hands behind your back."

They begrudgingly turned around and faced the wall. They heard Suggs place his gun on the table and take a pair of handcuffs from his jacket. Red held his gun at Allie's back as Suggs stepped behind Tim.

Feeling frisky, Red playfully poked the muzzle of his gun between Allie's legs, pressing it up against her vulva.

Allie gasped at the invasive touch.

Tim turned his head and saw what Red was doing. Tim's nostrils flared. He snapped his leg up behind him, kicking Suggs in the groin. Suggs grimaced and fell to the floor. Tim pushed Allie to his left as he jumped to his right. Red, taken by surprise, was frozen in place long enough for Tim to pick up a chair and throw it at him. The gun went off, splintering the chair. Suggs got up and reached for his gun, which still was on the table.

Tim leaped at Red. He grabbed Red's gun hand and repeatedly bashed it against the wall until the gun came loose.

Before Suggs could grab his gun, Allie jumped on his back. Suggs attempted to spin and throw her off, but he slipped on Sam's blood, and the two of them crashed to the floor with Allie still holding on for dear life.

Tim's martial arts abilities kicked in. He threw a vicious roundhouse kick that landed against the side of Red's head. Red grimaced and began to fall backward as Tim threw multiple punches at his head and body, and Red was quickly pummeled into submission. He lay on the floor, semiconscious.

Allie was still clinging to Suggs's back, scratching at his eyes with her sharp nails. Suggs managed to shove her off, and as he rose, Tim threw a perfect kick at his midsection. Suggs groaned and dropped to his knees.

Tim shouted, "Run!"

Allie scrambled to her feet, and as they ran toward the door, Allie crouched and scooped up her cell phone. They dashed out of the apartment and ran to Tim's car like two fawns being chased by a lioness. They jumped inside. Tim slammed the pedal to the floor and peeled out.

Allie cried out, "All that blood! And they want you?"

Tim pounded the steering wheel with his fist while Allie nervously looked behind to see if they were being followed. She saw nothing there. They both lit cigarettes and took deep drags.

Tim noticed his hand trembling, and he glanced at Allie, whose whole body was shaking as if caught in an icy blast of wind. He flung his lit cigarette out the window and gripped the wheel tightly, constantly checking his rearview mirror.

Tim told Allie, "If your cell still works, call the cops. Tell 'em what happened."

Allie tried to open her cell. "No good. It's dead. We need to find a pay phone somewhere. Maybe some gas station."

Tim was lost in his own thoughts. "They killed Sam but wanted me alive. Why?" The terrible image of Sam lying dead in his own blood caused Tim to feel as though he was drowning in a sea of sadness.

Allie had no answer for him as she began to seek out a phone booth.

Tim recalled Mick's last remark about there being more to his father, and he thought maybe Mick might have some clue as to what was going on. "Listen, we're gonna go see our friend, Mick. I believe he might know stuff that will help us."

Although still quite upset, she leaned over and gave him an appreciative kiss on the cheek as tears rolled down her face.

Tim proudly said, "*That* gamble paid off big time."

For once she agreed as she continued to look for a phone booth. Minutes later they spotted one outside a Shell station. They felt lucky, as many phone booths had been removed since cell phones became common. They stopped and called Sykes, informing him of the horrible events.

At nine that same evening, Stan once again sat in Harry's Bar, this time at a small table in the moderately crowded and noisy tavern.

A huge man walked in, and Harry waved him to the bar. Harry said something to the man and then nodded in Stan's direction.

Stan saw this and stood up as John Herrmann approached. Herrmann took off his jacket, and even though it was winter, he wore only a Van Halen T-shirt underneath. His large exposed arms were covered with tattoos. His huge beefy hands looked like they could have picked up a grand piano.

He towered over Stan as Stan said, "I hear you're Al Webster's friend."

Herrmann replied casually, "Who the fuck're you?"

"A friend of his father's."

Herrmann eyed him suspiciously. "Bullshit. Father's long dead."

"He got hit over Laos. I flew missions to find him," he lied. "Almost bought it myself."

Herrmann was impressed. He motioned for the two of them to sit at the bar, and after being seated, Herrmann thawed. "So whadd-aya want?"

"To give Alan this." He held out his wrist.

Now Herrmann was really impressed. "Fuck, man. Where'd you get that?"

"Been wearing it all these years. Oscar would've wanted me to give it to his son."

Normally, Herrmann would never divulge anything to some-one he'd never met before. But this innocuous-looking little man appeared truly to mean no harm and like he merely wanted to give Webster his father's bracelet. "Look. Last week he comes and tells me he's goin' into the hills. Gives me an address and says if I don't hear from him in twenty-four hours, to call the cops and tell 'em where to go."

Stan leaned closer to Herrmann. "And?"

"And nothin'. Calls the next day and says forget our conversa-tion. I don't know if he even went."

"I'd like to go there, just in case."

Herrmann turned toward the bar and shouted over the noisy crowd, "Harry, throw me a pen."

CHAPTER 17

AT 9:15 P.M., TIM and Allie entered the Morton Hospital with myriad thoughts and trepidations bouncing around their skulls like Ping-Pong balls. The drive to the hospital gave them time to recover from their initial shock at seeing poor Sam lying dead in his own blood and barely escaping from Suggs and Red. But now they needed to know why they were after Tim—and the identity of the major their attackers had mentioned. There were too many confusing revelations concerning Dan Connor's—or Frank Valone's—past, and they hoped Mick Yeager might be able to reveal some answers.

Tim vowed to himself that, somehow, those cretin assholes would pay dearly for Sam's death.

Minutes later, they entered Mick's hospital room. Mick was seated in his chair, apparently oblivious to Tim and Allie's agitation. "Back so soon?" he said. "Groovy."

Tim shouted, "Couple of scumbags just killed Sam in my apartment and were waiting for me. Why?"

Mick stared at Tim with a blank expression.

Tim continued, "They trashed my apartment looking for something, and wanted someone they called the major to come over because they had captured me, but for what reason I can't even begin to guess. But I believe you might have some ideas."

Mick bit his lip, and it started to bleed again, but this time they ignored the blood.

Allie asked, "And why'd his father identify three black guys as white?"

Mick curled up tighter in his chair. He knew exactly why Frank might have said that, but he wasn't willing to reveal it to them right now since he loathed discussing sordid events from the past. He turned away from them and stared out the window as he evaded answering truthfully by softly saying, "Frank seen so much injustice done to Negroes. I'm pretty sure he was making amends, saying it was three white dudes."

Allie was baffled. "That's it? Must be more."

Tim raised his voice as he said, "And I never knew my father to be a bleeding-heart liberal."

Mick wore a sad expression as he turned back to them. "Seems you know nothin' about him. Frank was a cool cat."

As soothingly as she could, Allie said, "What you tell us might save Tim's life. Please help us."

Mick pondered Allie's plea. He coughed, lit a cigarette, and then slowly nodded his head as he exhaled. Watching the smoke disappear, he said, "Against the rules, but fuck 'em." He took another deep drag, again watched the smoke vanish, and continued, "Your father and me were sick about the war and shit we did. We returned home and joined a group, the Patriots, that turned out to be more than just antiwar. It was headed by a guy named Vance Galvin. Galvin served in Vietnam in a different unit. He blamed being kicked out of OCS on a black colonel. Black or white, Galvin deserved being canned—fuckin' bigot. We didn't know at first that he did time for some triple K shit."

Mick closed his eyes and remembered the early seventies as he told his tale.

Frank Valone and Mick Yeager sat around a table in a cabin nestled deep in the Virginia countryside. Seated with them was handsome, charismatic Vance Galvin. Nearby, Sara Galvin, very pretty with waist-long blonde hair, listened to music. Next to her was a portable crib that held a crying toddler. She attempted to soothe the young boy with her music.

They all wore tie-dyed clothes except for Galvin, who was in army fatigues.

Galvin addressed Frank and Mick with deep conviction. "With enough explosives and people who believe like we do, we can disrupt the fed's ability to operate—bring down Uncle Sam."

Frank took a sip of his beer. "I know we've got to take drastic measures to end the goddamn war, but we've seen too many innocent people die."

Galvin snorted. "The commies, Jews, and blacks are taking over the fucking government. So what if we kill a few sorry-ass niggers or government workers? If it'll help save the United States for people like us, *real* Americans, who cares? You been with us for three months. You in or out?"

"In. But we're out to destroy property, not people, remember?" Frank answered.

Galvin looked at Mick. "How about you?"

"Count me in, but I agree with Frank."

"Don't worry. If we can avoid killing, we will." Galvin turned toward the crying toddler. "Sara, can't you shut that fucking kid up?"

Tim remarked to Mick, "So you did know my mother. How old was I?"

Mick appeared confused. "Your mother? What gives?"

"Sara was my mother's name."

Allie's eyes opened wide as she said to Tim, "Two Saras?"

Tim and Allie allowed the improbability to sink in.

Mick looked directly at Tim, studying his face. "Sara was Galvin's wife." Mick's jaw dropped. "Holy shit. You do look like Galvin—a lot."

A strained silence filled the air as Tim and Allie tried to assess Mick's statement.

But Tim had heard enough. "Listen—Dan Connor's my father." His head was swimming. Too much was happening all at once. The implication was frighteningly clear. If Sara was his mother, and if Sara was married to Vance Galvin, then Vance Galvin was his real father. Tim shook his head vigorously as though attempting to erase the thought from his mind.

Mick squirmed in his seat. He tensed up and took a drag of his cigarette.

Allie felt that Tim was in denial. Everything that Mick had said made sense to her. Vance Galvin was more than likely Tim's biological father, but she didn't want to press Tim on the issue. Instead, she put her arm around Tim's waist as Tim asked, "So what happened to this Galvin guy? What happened to Sara?"

"The bad stuff started with me, Frank, Galvin, a guy named BJ, and two other guys whose names I don't even remember." Mick closed his eyes again as he continued his tale.

At 2:00 a.m., Galvin, Frank, Mick, BJ, and two other men backed a truck up to the darkened rear of a gun shop. The men noiselessly got out of the truck. BJ climbed a ladder and cut some wires that ran under an eave of the building. He climbed back down and whispered, "All clear."

They had staked the place out earlier and knew where the alarm bells were. Once BJ had cut the wires, the others pried open the rear door with a crowbar and drew deep breaths before they rushed inside.

Once inside, Galvin said in a hushed voice, "BJ, grab ammo."

Galvin and Mick grabbed as many firearms as they could carry and brought them outside. As Mick and Galvin were outside loading guns and ammunition onto the truck, an elderly man and woman entered the room wearing night clothes.

The man held a gun in his hand and shouted, "Put your hands up!"

BJ, Frank, and the other two men inside stopped dead in their tracks.

Galvin and Mick, still outside, heard the man shout. Crouching, Galvin sneaked into the darkened shop, gun drawn, and saw the man holding his gun on the other four. Galvin fired three rapid shots into his chest, killing the man instantly. He fell back, hit a counter, and slithered to the floor. Then as the unarmed woman screamed and backed off, he riddled her with bullets as well. She attempted to scream again, but the bullets had pierced both lungs, and only crimson blood escaped from her mouth as she fell backward, dead before she hit the cold tiled floor.

Bedlam reigned. Frank yelled, "You said no killing."

"And the store would be empty," Mick shouted.

Galvin disdainfully answered, "How could I know they fucking lived in the place? Load the damn truck."

Mick began to sweat as he told the story. "That's when I knew Frank felt like I did, but we were in too far. Still, we didn't know the kind of animal we were dealing with until one day…" Memories that had been bottled up for a long time now came pouring out.

The six men sat in an isolated tiny cabin in the woods, drinking and killing time while Sara breast-fed the toddler.

Galvin addressed the men. "We hole up a couple of days. The weapons will be distributed to militia groups in the area. Meanwhile, we plan the bombing of strategic federal offices."

From outside, BJ rushed through the cabin door. "Some kids are comin' up the road," he exclaimed.

Galvin and the rest of the men looked out the windows and saw three black kids, ranging in age from eleven to fourteen, walking toward the cabin.

The kids stopped in their tracks when they saw a truck and a pickup parked in front of the cabin.

The youngest boy asked the other two, "Somebody moved in?"

The other two had no answer.

Their curiosity prompted them to walk toward the front door.

Inside the cabin, no one knew what to do except Galvin, who grabbed his gun, opened the door, and began firing at the three kids. One bullet smashed though the oldest boy's skull. He dropped like a rag doll as the other two boys stood like statues, frozen in disbelief.

Galvin shot the second boy through the neck. The boy clutched his throat and fell onto his back, writhing in pain and bleeding profusely. The youngest boy screamed, turned around, and began to run for his life.

Galvin took careful aim and hit the boy square in the middle of his back. The powerful bullet propelled the boy forward, and he skidded to a halt face-down on the dirt road.

Galvin muttered, "Fucking niggers." The boy who had been shot in the neck was still moving spastically on the ground. Galvin administered the *coup de grâce* with a bullet that shattered the boy's head.

The other men rushed out the door. All except BJ were horrified at the carnage.

Tension and anger filled the air. Dazed, Mick began singing a Rolling Stones song. "I can't get no sat-is-fac-tion."

Frank screamed at Galvin, "You're a fucking maniac!"

Galvin said, "Would've ratted on us."

"We could've found another cabin or—"

BJ interrupted. "Don't get your balls in an uproar. That's three less niggers left to rape your mother."

Mick stopped singing and, with tears in his eyes, addressed BJ, "Lot of Corps buddies were black. Killing kids…again."

BJ merely waved him off. He knew that probably thousands of Vietnamese children had been killed by American soldiers, mostly as collateral damage from Air Force bombing raids—most horribly from napalm, which could burn the skin right down to the bone but also from mortar and cannon fire and raids on villages. Often, if there was return fire from the Viet Cong, an American unit would dub a village Pinkville and destroy it completely, leading to the slaughter of women and children. But, BJ had always rationalized, this was war, and if a few thousand gooks had to pay the ultimate price, so be it.

BJ had heard Mick tell Galvin of how Mick and Frank's company had come across a village suspected of harboring Viet Cong. They had been in the bush for several weeks and were tired and disgruntled and had heard that the war might soon be coming to an end. They dearly wanted to go home as soon as possible, and if killing a few more of the enemy would hasten their return, that was what they intended to do. But information gleaned from various sources was often wrong or misleading. They thought this particular village was a VC stronghold and raided it with mortar fire, followed by an attack on the village, directing gunfire, grenades, and flamethrowers at the huts. They heard screams and fired indiscriminately without thinking at anything that emerged from the huts. It was all over in a matter of minutes.

When they examined the carnage, they realized that this was no VC stronghold. Mick came upon several huts in which mostly women, children, and elderly people lay dead. Many were dismembered and charred, and the images of infants dying in their mothers' arms had a life-altering effect on Mick. For whatever reason, the events of that day had much more of a debilitating effect on Mick than on Frank.

BJ had seen graphic photos of atrocities in Vietnam, including the infamous photos of the victims of My Lai, where four to five hundred women, children, and elderly people were killed. Many of them were dismembered, and some of the women were raped before being killed by American soldiers in March of 1968. Although the photographs were gruesome, BJ knew from experience that no photo could approach the intensity and raw emotion of seeing the real thing firsthand. Yet BJ wasn't affected very much by the atrocities he'd seen. He rationalized that if they weren't stopped, the commies would eventually make their way to America, maybe with nuclear weapons, and kill millions of American kids. *Better their kids than ours*, BJ had always thought.

Mick began singing again. Frank grabbed Mick in a bear hug as an effort to soothe him. He continued to hold Mick until Mick calmed down, but Mick didn't look emotionally well.

"Bury 'em where no one will find 'em," Galvin said.

Still quite upset, Frank said, "The cops will look here."

Galvin said, "We'll be long gone."

Mick still wasn't doing well. He was doubled over, continuing to sing.

Frank knew that Mick was in deep trouble. Galvin stared suspiciously at Mick and strode toward him with his gun drawn.

Frank shouted, "I'll take care of him." He pushed Galvin away from Mick. Galvin grabbed Frank by the collar and said through gritted teeth, "He can't jeopardize the operation."

Frank grabbed Galvin's collar and, also through gritted teeth, yelled, "I said I'd take care of him!"

They both shoved each other away.

Frank looked at Mick and back at Galvin. "He'll be okay."

Galvin glared at Mick and stormed off.

The men buried the three boys in shallow graves deep in the woods and then loaded up the truck and left. Mick was sickened at the sight of the three boys as dirt was piled onto their lifeless forms.

Allie and Tim stared at Mick. They were spellbound by Mick's stories.

Mick was sweating profusely. He had a faraway look. Suddenly, he blurted out, *"Chat dau ho chung."*

Allie calmly asked, "Mick, what's that mean? You said it earlier tonight."

Mick seemed confused. "What's what mean?"

"I think it was Vietnamese," Allie answered.

Mick looked away and said, "Some old song."

They both stared at Mick. He was clearly hiding something, but for what reasons they couldn't even begin to guess.

Allie brushed her hair from her face, deep in thought. "Three white guys...now it makes sense."

"I agree," Tim said. He turned to Mick. "Does section 2, block 5, lot 9 mean anything to you?"

Through a crooked smile, Mick asked, "Some kind of riddle?"

"How about section 2, block 5, *plot* 9, like in a cemetery." Tim hoped Mick would have an answer, but he didn't expect him to.

Mick pondered the question for a moment and answered, scratching his head, "What's the scoop?"

"Those were my father's last words. Not sure if he said *lot* or *plot*. Does a lot or cemetery plot mean anything to you?"

Mick thought hard. He leaned back, closed his eyes, and said, "That prick Galvin was gonna hurt...you...real bad, so Frank took you."

Confirmation that Vance Galvin and not Dan Connor was his real father made Tim's head feel as though it were being squeezed in a vise.

Allie turned to look at Tim, knowing what he must be feeling at that moment, but Tim was stone-faced.

Mick continued, "Almost caught us when we blew a tire next to a cemetery and hid there overnight. Think he buried somethin'... Anyway, the graves reminded me of the dead bodies I saw. I cracked up, and Frank left me at a hospital. They arrested me, but I was so flipped out they put me into a psych ward and eventually into this place. It's the only cemetery story I got."

"What about Sara...my mother?" Tim was unsure whether he really wanted to hear the truth at this time, but he felt his heart pounding at the thought that she might still be alive.

Mick squirmed in his seat. "Don't know nothin'." He couldn't bring himself to tell them what really had happened to make him crack up at the cemetery. He turned and stared out the window, hoping they wouldn't press him on the issue of Sara.

Tim and Allie believed he was hiding something, but they refrained from grilling Mick too hard.

"Where's this cemetery?" Tim asked.

Mick thought for a few seconds, happy to change the subject. "Passed it all the time...in Fredericksburg—that's it, the Fredericksburg Cemetery. Maybe fifty miles south of Arlington."

Allie looked at Tim. "Now what?"

"I give Detective Sykes a call and see what they found out."

Allie asked Tim, "Where can we go? I'm sure those men are still looking for you."

"Maybe Sykes will have some suggestions."

Tim and Allie said good-bye to Mick, and they went to the main lobby to make the call to Detective Sykes.

Sykes answered his cell phone, told them not to return to either of their apartments, and suggested they meet with him in his office around 10:00 p.m. He explained that he was at Tim's apartment with several crime-scene specialists.

CHAPTER 18

AT 9:30 P.M., DETECTIVES Sykes and Landers were still with the crime-scene specialists examining the gruesome scene in Tim's apartment when fifty-eight-year-old FBI Special Agent Calvin Barnes, a stout black man, appeared at the door and flashed his badge.

Sam's body still lay in a pool of coagulated brown blood.

"Barnes, FBI," he announced to everyone in the room. He stepped into the room and saw Sam's body.

Landers smirked, turned to Sykes, and said just loudly enough for Sykes to hear, "There goes the neighborhood."

Sykes ignored Landers as Barnes walked toward them.

Barnes took a moment to view the gory crime scene and asked, "What've we got?"

"Victim was tortured and murdered," Sykes answered. "Perps turned the place inside out, apparently looking for something."

"That his son?" Barnes pointed at Sam's body.

"Son's friend," Sykes said. "From what we culled from the contents of his wallet, which was strewn about the room, his name is Sam Breen. Tim Connor and his girlfriend called and informed us about this. They arrived here after the victim was murdered and were accosted by two armed men, but they managed to escape from the guys that did this."

"Where's this Tim Connor now?"

"Don't know, but they were apparently after Tim, not the poor soul on the floor," Sykes answered. "I told them to lay low and not go back to their apartments. They agreed to meet with me in my office tonight at ten. By the way, I'm Detective Jim Sykes, and this is Detective Ray Landers."

Barnes nodded toward each man and replied, "Agent Calvin Barnes."

Landers said, "If the FBI is here, you must know something we don't. Why Daniel Connor's—or should I say, Frank Valone's—son?"

Barnes stared skeptically at Landers and then at Sykes.

His hesitation caused Sykes to say, "We're the good guys, remember?"

Barnes thought a moment longer and reluctantly replied, "They were apparently looking for something Frank Valone held over them. From our case files, a Walter Yeager, a former partner in crime of Valone's, was arrested decades ago. It seems there was a huge split between Valone and their leader, Vance Galvin. They were involved in multiple murders and had planned the bombing of many government offices when the whole crew vanished except for Yeager."

Landers asked, "Where's Yeager now?"

"Yeager was deemed unfit for trial, a real nut job, and they put him into prison psychiatric wards for about thirty years. When they decided he'd be no threat to society, they placed him in a mini-mum-security psychiatric hospital. We better bring Timothy Connor in. We might also want to question this Yeager guy. Crazy or not, he might be able to provide some clue as to what the hell's going on here."

Landers grunted. "Mr. Macho Connor is gonna play dumb. Personally, I think he just *is* dumb. You guys know more than what you faxed Sykes about Daniel Connor, don't you?"

Barnes glanced at the crime-scene specialists and said to Sykes and Landers, "Step outside. Got an old story to tell about some real scumbag bigots who don't exactly like us black folk."

Barnes turned and walked toward the door, trailed by the two men.

Landers whispered to Sykes, "Another black FBI guy who thinks he's hot shit."

Sykes softly answered, "All FBI think that."

Landers smiled. "Thought shit only came in one color." He laughed at his joke, but Sykes merely smirked.

Sykes knew that Landers was a closet bigot who enjoyed telling crude jokes to people he thought might appreciate them. Landers's favorite was, "A sixth-grade black boy told his father that during recess he and three white boys measured their penises to see whose was longest, and he had won. The boy asked his father, 'Is it because I'm black?' The father replied, 'No, son. It's because you're seventeen.'"

Landers's feelings on race relations were no different from those of many Americans who'd had little contact with African Americans while growing up. As a police officer in downtown Baltimore, Landers's contact with blacks usually revolved around some crime that had been committed, very often a murder, a drive-by shooting, a robbery, domestic violence, or something along those lines, and it had jaded him. His job didn't give him opportunities to see the many good things that were happening in the black community.

He knew there were multiple reasons for the high rate of crime and incarceration in black communities, but when confronted almost on a daily basis with lawlessness, the main thing that mattered to Landers was the present. Figuring out the whys and wherefores was for bleeding-heart liberals who didn't see the decay and decadence he'd seen. He hadn't the time nor patience to search for the reasons behind the crime; only the results of the crime and catching the perpetrators mattered to him.

Once outside, Barnes related all that the FBI knew of the Patriot group, which included the fact that they were responsible for the deaths of a gun shop owner, the owner's wife, and three black kids.

At just after ten o'clock, Tim and Allie were seated in front of Detective Sykes's metal desk.

Sykes said, "Did the smart thing, coming here."

Tim, still pumped from his adrenaline rush, his leg bouncing nervously, asked, "Why'd they kill Sam?"

"They were apparently searching for something in your apartment."

Confused, Tim asked, "Something they'd kill for?"

"We believe it was something your father had. They trashed his place first and probably assumed you might have it."

Tim glanced at Allie at the disclosure, and he said to Sykes, "We thought it was the cops who had trashed it."

"We did go there to search it, but we got there after they did."

Tim stood up, walked to the window, and stared out for a few seconds. He turned around with a pissed-off expression. "Enough shit. What's goin' on?"

With an air of resignation, Sykes said, "All right...okay." Sykes pointed at Tim's seat, and Tim sat down. Sykes began, "Your father was part of an antiwar group that was also anti a lot of other things. He was involved in killings, but vanished with you and maybe your mother. Never seen or heard from again until the newspaper article. Apparently, your father must have taken incriminating evidence that could be used against the group—and, most likely, against its leaders."

Tim immediately came to his father's defense. He looked Sykes squarely in the eye and said, "He might have been there during those murders, but I know he didn't shoot any of those people. I know he had his faults, but he was a better man than that." His leg began to bounce nervously once more.

Sykes understood Tim's reaction. "Okay, let's just say he was an accessory to murder."

Tim stared straight ahead, expressionless, thinking about Mick's stories. Tim knew his father had been at the scene of these crimes, but it had been Galvin who shot those innocent black kids and store owners, not his father. He thought of Mick's Vietnam experiences and said, "The Vietnam War did some crazy shit to an awful lot of soldiers."

Sykes clearly understood. "I know what you're saying. I was there too but, fortunately, didn't see the kind of action many other grunts did."

Tim said, "Dan told me my mother died giving birth to me, but she might actually still be alive." His leg stopped bouncing. At this point his mother was nothing more than an apparition to him. First he was told that his mother had died during childbirth. Then he found the photo that proved his mother was alive until he was at least two years old. Now it was even possible, although unlikely, that she was still alive, a thought fueled by Mick's avoidance of questions regarding his mother. If something had happened to her all those years ago, wouldn't Mick know about it? Tim made a mental note to pump Mick harder about his mother. He knew it was a long shot, but too many strange things had happened recently, and perhaps his mother being alive would be one more bizarre revelation.

Sykes said, "Maybe we can look into it when this is done. But whatever your father had years ago, they believe you probably have it. There's no statute of limitations on murder. Did your father have a safety deposit box anywhere?"

Tim shook his head. "Not that I know of, but probably not. He never had anything of real value."

"How about some hiding place where he hid cash or—"

Tim impatiently cut him off. "Look. The main thing is we can ID the two morons who killed Sam."

Sykes nodded. "That's why we'll show you some mug shots, maybe get lucky. Then we'll discuss protection for you."

"I don't need it," he said with conviction.

Allie put a hand on Tim's arm. "Your hands won't stop a bullet."

Tim stared at her. It was almost the exact same line he had used with Sam. "Okay. Let's first see if we can ID those scumbags." He turned toward Sykes. "Maybe you can catch them and we won't need your protection."

"All right," said Sykes. "Let's begin."

CHAPTER 19

GALVIN, RED, SUGGS, and Webster sat at a table in the farmhouse. Red's face was badly bruised from Tim's beating. No one looked happy.

Galvin said, "The cops might protect him, but if we're lucky, Tim Connor might not know what he has on us—at least not yet."

Webster asked, "What if Tim Connor has nothing? We searched Valone and Connor's apartments and didn't find a thing."

Galvin thought for a moment. "Here's the deal. Fact: I know Frank took lots of incriminating evidence as insurance against me finding him. I didn't think he'd be stupid enough to keep it with him or in Tim Connor's apartment, but I had to be sure. I'm also certain he'd tell Tim Connor where the information was hidden, just in case we found him. I tried to find him long ago, but since he changed his name and moved around a lot, I never got to him. But I can't take the chance that Tim Connor will be able to get that info and give it to the FBI. We'll still try to get Connor or at least keep him on the run until this is over. I've got a contact with the police who's helping to monitor Connor's movements. I believe we'll get to him soon enough."

Webster asked, "Was there anyone else involved—someone who might know about this information?"

Galvin exhaled heavily. "A guy who served with Frank, Mick Yeager, stole something valuable of mine and helped Frank escape. I found Mick just a couple of months later in a prison psych ward and tried questioning him, but he was so deranged I got nothing out of him. He just kept mumbling something in Vietnamese that I couldn't understand. Anyway, Mick was always a worthless piece of shit. It's Frank that held the answers, and now it's this Tim Connor." Galvin wore a faraway expression.

After a brief pause, Galvin said, "The others are ready. We can't let this stop us, not when we're this close. An all-out assault on the Capitol in two days during the president's State of the Union speech. I can taste victory already."

Webster wanted to interrupt Galvin's monologue and say not only that the plan seemed sketchy at best, but also that an assault would never truly penetrate such a massive building as the Capitol. But Webster allowed Galvin to continue. He would have to reveal something better than this, or Webster was gone.

With utmost fervor, Galvin continued, "Think of it! Total anarchy. Thousands of brothers are waiting to use their weapons. Millions will follow once we Patriots accomplish our mission. Then we take back what was always meant for us and our children...the United States of America."

Galvin looked at Webster and asked, "Al, you got kids, right?"

"Two boys...with my ex-wife."

Galvin reached into his pocket. "Give 'em this from Uncle Vance." With genuine sincerity, Galvin held out a hundred-dollar bill, but Webster refused it with a wave of his hand. Galvin seemed hurt.

With a melancholy expression, Webster said, "Haven't seen 'em in years."

"I know the feeling. In addition to my poor little girls at Waco, I had a son once. He's gone now." Galvin exhaled with a shudder.

"Sorry," said Webster. He didn't know what else to say.

Galvin swallowed hard, looked down at his clasped hands, and attempted to hold back his emotions. A solemn silence followed.

Galvin's sincere offer of a gift to Webster's children was the first time Webster had seen a softer, more compassionate side of Galvin. But Webster understood that human beings had the capacity to kill even when they seemed loving and nurturing to others, just as Hitler had been able to order the deaths of millions while kissing babies and patting young children on their heads. It was the one truism Webster adhered to: people were natural-born killers, and given the right circumstances, anyone could take a life.

Suggs broke the uncomfortable silence. "How many men we got now?"

Galvin looked up. "With several militias working together, we'll have about eighty men laying siege—about half to fire artillery and the other half to drive the vehicles, including the escape vehicles."

"Good men, I hope," Webster said. He glanced over at Red and back at Galvin.

Red caught Webster's subtle movement, and he knew he was being dissed once again. He swore to get his revenge one day.

"Don't worry. It's under control," Galvin answered. "See you bright and early tomorrow."

Webster didn't like Galvin's evasive answer, but he didn't want to confront Galvin in front of Suggs and Red. He walked outside, lit a cigarette, and waited for Suggs and Red to leave.

He watched their vehicle disappear into darkness, and went back inside.

Galvin had picked up his cell phone, intending to call his mole on the police force regarding Mick's whereabouts, when he looked up and was surprised to see Webster still there.

Webster walked up to the table. "Okay. It's time you leveled with me. If you intend for me to be involved in helping lead the charge, I need to know more of the plan. I'm not one of your local village idiots who will blindly charge into battle like the Light Brigade just to be cannon fodder." He folded his arms and waited for an answer. If he didn't like what he heard, he thought he might vanish in the middle of the night. *Let Galvin lead the charge*, he thought, *if he's so certain it's going to work.*

Galvin pondered the request. He needed good men like Webster; he knew he couldn't rely on men like Red. He acquiesced. "Here's the deal. I've been training an elite few to fire a howitzer cannon, mortars, and other types of ordnance, although most already knew how from their military service. I know you're familiar with these weapons."

Webster's eyes opened wide. "You've got cannons and mortars?"

"And a rocket launcher and bazookas," he proudly stated.

Webster sat on one of the chairs across from Galvin. "How'd you get them, and how many do you have?"

"I procured the materiel in a variety of ways. One day I'll tell you all about it, but suffice to say that I have about fifty of these types of weapons, along with AK-47s and over a hundred other assault weapons."

Webster answered with skepticism. "And the government has millions of weapons and an army. Fifty versus that?"

"The plan is to attack the Capitol during the State of the Union address."

"You've said that." Webster was surprised at the simplistic and unrealistic plan. "You'll never kill them all, and probably not the president." He thought the plan was ridiculous, and once again he seriously considered cutting and running.

"Correct. But that's where plan B comes in. I have a trap ready to spring on them from a man on the inside. Let's leave it at that. If all goes as planned, we'll be in charge. For security purposes, I cannot tell you what plan B is, at least not yet, and only a select few know about the attack on the Capitol. Plan B will be revealed just prior to the attack. The object of the attack is to fire an average of ten bombs each as quickly as possible and then escape. The surprise attack will catch them all off guard. Each vehicle will have a backup man who will fire on any cops or Secret Service that may show up. That man will also drive the vehicle toward the outskirts of the city, where they will ditch the vehicles and escape in other vehicles that are parked in various predesignated locations."

Webster pictured the plan but was still skeptical. But maybe once he heard what this plan B was, he'd be less apprehensive. The one thing he believed about Galvin was that he was no idiot, and plan B was obviously more intricate than plan A. He was satisfied, at least for now.

Webster said, "See you tomorrow," and he walked out toward his pickup truck.

This time, Galvin waited until he heard the truck leave, and he dialed a number on his cell. "Yeah," he said, "it's me. Find out where Walter Yeager lives, and get back to me ASAP."

CHAPTER 20

AT 11:00 P.M. IN a trailer park near Richmond, Virginia, the former capital of the Confederacy, Harold Smalls, standing under the lemon glare of a naked light bulb, banged on the door of a dilapidated trailer home. His son, Bobby Smalls, opened the door and hopped out holding a bottle of beer in his hand. Despite the bitter cold, he wore only a flannel shirt for protection. It was evident to Harold that Bobby had had way too much to drink already.

Harold scowled at his son and said, "Word is...real soon, son."

"Ain't soon enough, Pop. Gotta get me 'n' the wife outta this shithole. Mexicans live better'n this."

"Make sure you're sober when the time comes. Never met the major, but believe he's got some good things in store for us."

Bobby said, "I really hope so, Pop. But when are we gonna be told exactly what we're supposed to do?"

"I understand we get our orders right before the operation takes place. You know—security reasons. But I've been told our mission will come within two days, maybe even tomorrow." Harold pointed at the beer bottle. "And for God's sake, stop drinking."

"Okay, Pop." He took another swig of his beer.

"I'll talk to you later." Harold got into his car and drove away.

Bobby Smalls had been raised by Harold after his mother died in a car accident when Bobby was only three. Bobby never was a good student, dropping out of high school after the eleventh grade, and he worked mostly at odd jobs in department stores and at the local filling stations. Harold and Bobby had always lived in trailer parks, which was the only thing Harold could afford on his store clerk's salary.

Living among mostly poor whites, it was inevitable that Bobby would hear disparaging things about minorities, such as how affirmative action was giving good-paying jobs to unqualified blacks. Bobby had always wondered—given that the Civil War had ended some hundred and fifty years earlier—why they had to do that. He had heard it was liberals in Washington, especially Jews, who were behind this travesty of justice.

A friend of his loaned him a book entitled *The Turner Diaries*. Bobby hadn't read a novel since being forced to write a seventh-grade book report, but once he began to read this one, he couldn't put it down. It was written in 1978 by William Luther Pierce, the former leader of a white nationalist organization. The novel depicted a violent revolution in the United States that led to the overthrow of the federal government, nuclear war, and ultimately a race war that resulted in the extermination of all impure groups, such as Jews, gay people, and nonwhites. The novel concluded with the white Aryans eliminating other races. China and the entire eastern half of Asia were destroyed by weapons of mass destruction; blacks were exterminated in Africa as well as in America; and Puerto Ricans, described as "a repulsive mongrel race" were exterminated and their island resettled by whites.

It wasn't a surprise to the FBI that two pages of the book depicting preparation for the bombing of the J. Edgar Hoover Building were found in the getaway car of Timothy McVeigh, the perpetrator of the Oklahoma City bombing.

Bobby Smalls envisioned himself as a leader in the coming apocalypse, with many gorgeous young women begging him to service them.

He had heard that Major Vance Galvin was a God-fearing, righteous man who knew what people like Bobby were going through. Bobby felt that if he'd had the right chance, he could have been anything—maybe even a doctor. Watching the news, he learned that many people, especially blacks, were given something called *entitlements*. He didn't know precisely what that word meant, but he knew it involved giving certain people a lot of money, and he believed that most of those certain people were black. How come good, hardworking whites like him never got any of those entitlements?

He knew that Vance Galvin was working on a plan to take America back for the white Christian race. He realized that *The Turner Diaries* was made-up stuff, but what if some of what that book said could really come true? His young wife, Abby, was always complaining about not having the same nice things as some of the other girls with whom she had graduated from high school. She had worked as a waitress since high school, but now, in her ninth month of pregnancy, she'd had to stop working, and she didn't know when she'd be able to work full-time again. She knew she was a nag at times to Bobby, but unless he was able to get a better job, their crappy old trailer would be the only thing they would ever be able to afford to live in.

Bobby thought—with a baby due soon, and with Abby ceasing to work, at least for a time—that if the major could accomplish his goal of getting America back and not giving free stuff to people who didn't deserve it, he might be able to buy a big house in a real nice neighborhood, where he would be able to live among white folk who thought and believed as he did.

Bobby took another swig of his beer, threw the bottle into a beat-up metal garbage can, and went back into his trailer, where he expected to be harassed by Abby once again.

Bobby thought to himself that he would do anything the major asked of him. The major would come through for him, Abby, and his firstborn child. He was sure of it. The major was his hero. The major would be his savior.

Bobby entered the trailer and saw his plump wife, Abby, sitting on an armchair watching some innocuous television program. Never a beauty to begin with, she had gained about sixty pounds since becoming pregnant, and Bobby couldn't wait for her to give birth, lose a lot of weight, and have normal sex with him again. He thought he loved Abby, but her nagging about him not earning a solid living was eating away at his self-esteem. He knew that about half of all marriages ended in divorce, and he thought that maybe once he had a better job in the new America, he would add to that statistic. He'd seen so many rich guys—even real old and ugly ones—with gorgeous young babes at their sides. Apparently, all it took was money—lots of it. He recalled the Beatles' song that stated, "Money can't buy me love." He couldn't wait to prove them wrong.

CHAPTER 21

TIM AND ALLIE WERE exhausted after sitting at Sykes's desk for almost an hour and a half viewing mug shots. The several hundred photographs had become a blur of unhappy faces of every race and creed. They closed the last book and looked up at Sykes with disappointment on their faces.

Sykes threw his hands in the air in defeat. "Was worth the try." His tone turned serious. "Good chance they know where Allie lives. I'll get you a motel room till we catch them."

Allie scowled. "We have jobs."

Tim sarcastically added, "And she has a plane to catch."

Allie shot a harsh glance at Tim.

Tim avoided her glare.

Sykes understood their dilemma, but he also knew the risks involved. "You want to spend the next few days or weeks crossing your fingers every time you start your car or step out of your doorway?"

Tim paused, deep in thought. "Tell you what. I'll rent a room and call you."

Sykes pondered the request and then frowned. "What are you insinuating?"

"Not a thing. Just playing the odds." He thought it best to make sure no one, not even the police, knew where they were staying.

"Not every deck is stacked against you."

Tim smiled. "I'm making sure nobody deals from the bottom."

Allie said, "I've got to get Fletcher and some of my things first."

Sykes understood. "At least let us escort you to your apartments. They could be waiting for you."

Sykes's suggestion made sense, and they both agreed.

Two patrol cars followed Tim's car. They went to Tim's apartment first. Unbeknownst to them, Red and Suggs were watching from a car parked down the block. The two men knew they could do nothing more than return to Galvin and give him the news that Tim and Allie were being protected.

At ten after midnight that evening, Tim and Allie were busy unpacking in a room at the Skylight Motel, a decent place half an hour from Baltimore. Fletcher lay on the bed watching them.

"Involved in so much shit, yet his dying breath sends me to a grave?" Tim slowly shook his head as he hung his coat in the closet. He felt he couldn't be certain of anything anymore—who his father was, what his birth name was, why Dan Connor would have said those last words to him, why they were being sought by crazed murderers, or why Dan had told him his mother had been cremated after giving birth to him.

Allie continued unpacking and placing things in drawers. "You're guessing, and this Fredericksburg cemetery could be over an hour away."

He finished unpacking and said, "I got a flashlight and a shovel in my car." He was determined to discover once and for all if Dan's last words meant something important.

She sighed in resignation. "I'll Google it and get directions and make sure Mick isn't sending us to a cemetery that doesn't even exist."

She sat at her computer, printed out directions, and read that six Confederate generals and more than thirty-three hundred Southern soldiers were buried there, more than two thousand of them unknown. The cemetery covered many acres and had roadways running through it for vehicular traffic. She further read that the Battle of Fredericksburg was fought in December of 1862 between General Robert E. Lee's Confederate army of Northern Virginia and the Union Army of the Potomac, commanded by Major General Ambrose E. Burnside, after whom sideburns were named. The battle resulted in a great Confederate victory but at considerable human cost to both sides. Almost twenty thousand men were killed, wounded, or listed as captured or missing.

They left at 12:30 a.m. for the Fredericksburg Cemetery. This trip bore no resemblance to Tim's last visit to Fredericksburg. He had gone with his seventh-grade class and had learned that Fredericksburg was a charming community of twenty-five thousand and known as America's friendliest and most historic city. It was situated halfway between Richmond and Washington—the two capitals of the Civil War—near the falls of the Rappahannock River. The railroad lines that had been so crucial to transporting Civil War supplies now brought workers to and from the nation's capital, one hour away.

It was in his seventh-grade class that Tim had learned that many of the stories he'd heard in grade school were actually legend and myth. George Washington knew Fredericksburg well, having grown up just across the Rappahannock River. The myths about chopping down a cherry tree and throwing a coin across the Rappahannock referred to this period in Washington's life, and had been concocted by Parson Weems, known for his fictionalized biography of Washington.

They drove through historic downtown Fredericksburg past several blocks of nineteenth-century two-story brick buildings. They passed Chatham Manor, whose guests had once included George Washington and Thomas Jefferson. Abraham Lincoln conferred with his generals there, and American Red Cross founder, Clara Barton, tended the wounded. Poet Walt Whitman visited for a few hours searching for his brother, who had been wounded in battle.

At 1:35 a.m., they arrived at the corner of William Street and Washington Avenue, the entrance to the cemetery. It was encircled by a six-foot-high brick wall. Tim and Allie drove to a relatively deserted border of the cemetery, parked the car, and got out. Tim helped Allie climb over the brick wall. Once she was on the other side, he threw the shovel over the wall and proceeded to follow her over it.

The full moon helped light the way for them, which was fortunate since they wanted to use the flashlight as sparingly as possible. What they were hoping to do was quite illegal and definitely immoral, and they feared getting caught.

They searched for signs along the roadways that would guide them to section 2, block 5, plot 9. It took a while, but the overhead street signs were clearly marked, and after finding section 2, they searched for block 5. To their relief there was one. They could now look for plot 9.

They made their way among the frost-covered graves. The individual graves bore no numbers, so they couldn't be certain from which end of the row the numbers began. Many of the graves bore no names and were inscribed with only the date of death and the word *unknown*.

Tim had to use his flashlight to view the inscriptions as he counted headstones, trying to locate plot 9.

Allie tried not to walk on top of the graves. "This is creepy," she said.

"It's the live ones that worry me," Tim answered as he directed the flashlight's beam across several more headstones.

They continued past still more headstones. Allie suddenly wheeled around. To her relief, there was nothing there.

Allie whispered, "Even if we find number 9, how do we know for sure it referred to a cemetery or that is was *this* cemetery, and what do we do if we find it? Are we going to dig up some dead body?" Her nerves had held out thus far, but she'd never been in trouble with the authorities, even in school. It was always the mean girls who seemed to end up in the principal's office. She knew that if she and Tim were caught, their fate would be far worse than a trip to the principal's office.

Tim testily answered, "You're picking a fine time to question our being here."

"I guess it's just this place. I'm almost expecting a hand to pop out of one of these graves and pull me into it." Her body shivered for a second.

Tim smiled. "You've seen one too many horror movies."

"Maybe so, but I still can't wait to get out of here." She continued to follow Tim, trying to step around each grave.

Tim continued to shine his light on the headstones, and then there it was. The name on one of the headstones made Tim feel as though he had a touch of vertigo. "Holy shit," he blurted out. He dropped the shovel onto the ground.

"What is it?" Allie stepped closer to Tim, enabling her to see what the light was shining on. She gasped and repeated, "Holy shit."

They both stood staring with mouths agape.

The light illuminated a headstone that was inscribed, "Daniel John Connor, May 11, 1842–December 15, 1862."

Tim somberly said, "John was my father's middle name, too."

Allie turned to Tim and asked, "Could this be a relative of yours?" She immediately felt silly and was about to retract the question, but Tim beat her to the punch.

"Come on. Remember, his real name was Frank Valone. He must have taken the identity of this guy who died over a century ago. His last breath sent me here. Whatever my father buried, it's got to be here."

"I agree," she said. She sounded nervous. "You're not going to dig up some dead body, are you?"

Tim picked up the shovel. "If something's buried here, I'm pretty sure he wouldn't have buried it too far beneath the surface."

"I hope you're right. Your father and Mick probably had only their bare hands or a stick or something to dig with."

Tim began to dig with the shovel while Allie stood watch. Tim had no idea exactly where to dig or how far down he'd have to go. He started near the headstone and worked his way toward the foot of the grave. The hole grew larger as Tim continued to dig. A half hour passed. In spite of the cold temperature, Tim was now dripping wet. Still no results.

Allie looked up at the full moon. An owl hooted, and she shuddered for a moment.

The hole was almost two feet deep over the entire length and width of the grave when Tim's shovel struck metal. He began to dig furiously, pushing the dirt away with his gloved hands until he uncovered a metal box wrapped in plastic. He was fixated on it as he lifted it out of the hole. "I got it!" Tim climbed out of the hole with the box in his hands.

Allie was thrilled. "Let's get the hell out of here."

They both were pushing the dirt back onto the grave, he using the shovel and she her foot, when they spotted a security car approaching along the road with its spotlight scanning the area nearby.

They realized it would soon shine its light on two grave robbers. The sharply defined beam of light was only ten feet away when Tim grasped Allie's arm and, with a strong tug, pulled her down into the hole with him. As they landed in the grave, the rotting casket collapsed under their combined weight. They fell facedown onto dirt, rotted wood, and the remains of a corpse.

Allie was closest to the decomposed face of the real Daniel Connor. Her eyes practically popped out of their sockets, and she was about to scream when Tim clamped his hand over her mouth and whispered, "Pretend you're home."

Her eyes turned quizzical and then serious as she tore his hand from her mouth and whispered back, "I'm pretending it's you!" It was all she could do to keep from vomiting. She closed her eyes and forced herself to think about lying on a tropical island beach with a piña colada in her hand.

From deep inside the grave, Tim saw the spotlight play across the area overhead.

Similar thoughts crossed both their minds. If found, how would they explain lying in the grave they had just dug up? Besides being a ghoulishly horrible act, grave robbing was against the law. They could both see the headlines: "Grave Robber Lovers Sent to Prison."

Allie kept her eyes closed, but the beach and piña colada weren't working, and she desperately tried not to think about the fact that she was practically face-to-face with a decayed corpse. She could do nothing but pray she'd soon be out of there.

They both held their breath as they heard the car approach and then, ever so slowly, fade into the distance.

Tim climbed out of the grave, helped Allie out, and they brushed themselves off. Allie shivered in disgust, thinking that some of what she was wiping from her clothing was dead body.

The desecrated grave would have to remain as it was.

But they believed they'd solved Dan's riddle, although neither could imagine what was in that box. They desperately wanted to examine its contents, but they knew they had to get out of there immediately, so they climbed back over the wall and felt safe once more only when they had begun the drive back to the motel. As excited as they were to examine the box's contents, they agreed it was best to wait until they were in the safety of their well-lit room.

At 4:00 a.m., Tim and Allie, having showered and changed into night clothes, sat on the bed in their motel room. With apprehension and excitement, Tim pried open the box. It contained several photographs with names scribbled on them, a list, some papers, and a letter addressed to Timmy. They each drew a deep breath before reading the letter. It read:

Dear Timmy,

If you ever read this, it is because you are the only one I can ever trust. By mistake, I hooked up with very bad men. Vance Galvin, the leader, is your father. Galvin is a monster who killed your mom. I'm burying information in case they or the cops find us. This information could be my bargaining chip. Photos identify the guys who intend to attack the Capitol building. I'll raise you the best I can.

With much love,
Your new dad

Allie wiped a tear from her eye and wondered how Tim would be affected by these revelations.

Tim sat in stunned silence. The realization that there would be no loving reunion with his mother and that Vance Galvin was truly his biological father was hitting him hard. While growing up he'd often wondered why there was so little resemblance between him and Dan. Dan was three inches taller than Tim and had a much larger frame, outweighing Tim by some seventy pounds, most of which was pure muscle. Tim had rationalized that he obviously took after his mother, of whom he'd never seen a single photograph. He had asked Dan about that fact, and Dan had replied that he'd lost the only photo album he had that contained her photos, but that Sara was beautiful, and Tim always reminded him of her. Tim now realized he'd been nothing more than a wood-brained marionette all along, and Dan had always been the puppeteer pulling the strings.

Allie put her arm around him. "You okay?"

Tim didn't answer. *Am I okay?* he asked himself. For more than thirty years he had thought his mother was dead. Then the possibility had arisen, although remotely, that she was alive, and now this letter confirmed her death. But still, why had Dan told him she had died during childbirth? And had she actually been cremated? If not, where was her grave? And how and why did Dan—Frank Valone—take it upon himself to kidnap him and raise him as his own for all these years?

But Tim now glanced at the material before him and became enrapt once again. Maybe it would contain answers to his questions. He spread the photos out on the bed and then picked them up one by one, examining the faces and names. One of the photos seemed to ring a bell. It depicted a man of perhaps twenty with a bulldog face and a strong physique. The caption identified him only as BJ.

Tim handed the photo to Allie. "This guy...BJ. He look familiar?"

She studied the photo for a moment and shrugged her shoulders. Tim nodded and took the photo back. "Just seems like I've seen him somewhere."

She leaned over and viewed the photo again. "But the guy would have to be over sixty today. I don't see how you'd know him. I wonder if that's the same BJ as the one in Mick's story?"

"Probably."

He stared at the photo for a few more seconds and picked up the papers and the list. After viewing them for a few minutes, he said, "Shows the crimes they committed, their plans to disrupt the government and...attack the Capitol building? Jesus!"

"At any rate, they're still around and believe you have this information," she said. "But exactly why they're willing to kill for it, I have no idea. Maybe we're missing something."

"Maybe if I give it to the cops, they'll have no reason to come after us." He knew it was a weak answer.

As gently as she knew how, she said, "I know you're trying to suppress something."

"Yeah, what?"

"I know you don't want to hear it, but the letter confirms what Mick suggested—this monster, Vance Galvin, is your biological father, and your mother is dead. Maybe he's after you...for you." She held her breath and waited for his response.

Tim lay back on the bed and shielded his eyes from the naked light bulb overhead with his arm. A cascade of conflicting emotions washed over him. "You're right," he said finally. "The idea that Daniel was never my real father and that Galvin is...It's a bit much to handle. Remember, they called someone. It sounded like he was going to be there in ten minutes. What if they were calling this Galvin, my—I hate even saying it—my father, a man who killed his own wife, my mother?" His emotional longitude and latitude had always been sure. Now he was adrift at sea without sextant or compass.

In an understanding tone, she said, "Look, we don't know who they called. We don't even know if this Galvin is still alive."

"True." He lit a cigarette, hoping to relieve some of the tension he was feeling.

She twirled her fingers through her hair. "But I don't get something. If the information is so old, what could be so important? That your father is this Galvin? Okay, so what? Why would they have to kill Sam, and why are they after you?"

"You're probably right. Maybe there's something from the box that we're missing or just don't understand."

"But if this Galvin isn't involved, maybe these jerks will want revenge, like the mafia. Kill our families...pets too." Allie looked at Fletcher with concern.

"But if he is involved, is he that nuts? Christ! I have his genes. Am I like him?" He flung the papers into the air. They fell feather-like onto the bed.

Allie responded, "Monsters don't give birth to little monsters. Although on second thought, all my friends' kids are little monsters."

"Very funny. So as long as we hold this stuff, we hold the trump card."

"It's our only bargaining chip."

"I thought poker was *my* game."

Exhausted, the two attempted to fall asleep, and when they finally did, it was a fitful sleep, one in which Tim dreamed of Sam lying in a pool of his own blood and the mother he didn't remember.

CHAPTER 22

THE BALTIMORE FIELD OFFICE of the Federal Bureau of Investigation was located at 2600 Lord Baltimore Drive, thirty miles from Washington, DC. The FBI's motto was "Fidelity, Bravery, and Integrity," words that Special Agent Calvin Barnes lived by. Part of the bureau's mission was to protect the United States from terrorist attacks, whether foreign or domestic, a mission Agent Barnes took as seriously as anyone, especially since that mission included terrorist acts against African Americans.

Early the following morning, lean and lanky Special Agent Bronowski stood in front of a television while ten other agents, including Agent Calvin Barnes, sat on folding chairs facing him.

Bronowski addressed the agents. "These discs were confiscated from extremist groups—men who love inflicting pain."

Bronowski turned around, pressed a button on the remote, dimmed the lights, and then stood off to the side. They viewed a montage of men training in rural areas, handing out antigovernment propaganda, and so forth.

Bronowski said, "They hate the federal government and are convinced of an army showdown. The men you see training are getting ready for a guerrilla war."

On the screen, men were training in army fatigues and holding many types of weapons. They were taking target practice and learning hand-to-hand combat.

"They fear gun control and what they call Auschwitz cards—forms of identification."

The TV continued to show men learning to set booby traps and firing weapons at posters depicting unflattering caricatures of African Americans, Mexicans, and Jews.

"Training includes mountain survival techniques and setting booby traps. The enemy is us, Jews, immigrants, people of color, and the government."

The video showed beatings and the terrible results of attacks by white supremacist groups on minorities.

"They advise against using a landline telephone with this racist joke: 'Bojangles Robinson ain't the only one who can tap.'"

Calvin Barnes became visibly upset as the disc continued to display killings and other ghastly deeds, many of them against blacks.

"As for gay tolerance..." Bronowski pointed at the screen.

Skinheads carried signs on a recent march in San Francisco. One slogan read, "Praise God for AIDS."

The broadcast then switched to a room full of men who were busy building computer websites.

"Bomb manuals on the Internet, and *The Anarchist Cookbook*, offer recipes for death. Even worse is the fact that the movement has spread, especially after Oklahoma City, and now with a minority president, militias operate in all fifty states, with membership around fifty thousand."

The Anarchist Cookbook, written by William Powell to protest United States involvement in the Vietnam War, was first published in 1971 and contained instructions for the manufacture of explosives and other deadly devices. At the time of its publication, one FBI memo described the book as "one of the crudest, low-brow, paranoiac writing efforts ever attempted." Years later, Powell attempted to have the book removed from circulation since he no longer advocated what he had written. He wrote on his website, "The book, in many respects, was a misguided product of my adolescent anger at the prospect of being drafted and sent to Vietnam to fight a war that I did not believe in."

Bronowski turned off the TV, turned on the lights, and somberly addressed the men. "Unfortunately, they could have millions of sympathizers."

Barnes nodded his head and said to himself, "Gonna see who their enemy is."

Calvin Barnes had been born and raised outside of Tupelo, Mississippi. His father had worked as a porter for the railroad, one of the few nonfarming jobs open to black men. Barnes was the fifth of seven children. The family lived in a two-bedroom apartment, and he grew up sharing a bed with one of his younger brothers. But his family was stable, and his parents impressed upon young Calvin and his siblings the need for a good education. His mother had always wanted to be a teacher but, with seven kids to raise, was relegated to being a full-time housewife, one who helped her kids with their schoolwork.

Having grown up in the South in the late fifties and sixties, Barnes had firsthand knowledge of ingrained prejudices. He'd seen the Whites Only signs and heard the negative talk aimed at black people—their nappy hair was ugly, their women were not as beautiful as white women, and so forth. He had heard many people telling blacks, "Go back to Africa," a phrase which always puzzled the young Barnes. He'd never been to Africa. In fact, his family's oral history told of his ancestors coming to America in the late 1600s and early 1700s. He also knew that they came unwillingly as slaves, ripped from their families and everything they knew, dragged here on horrible slave ships and sold like farm animals, often being treated worse than those animals.

He was a graduate of Morgan State University in Baltimore. Morgan State was a historically African American university, and almost 90 percent of its student body was black. It was purchased by the state of Maryland in 1939 in response to a state study that determined Maryland needed to provide more opportunities for its black citizens. Barnes had discussed many topics regarding blacks in America with fellow black students and teachers. The ironic thing, he had learned, was that most of the people yelling for them to go back to Africa had ancestors who had come to the United States during the mid-nineteenth and early twentieth centuries. Knowing that his family had been in America longer than most white families, Barnes believed he was as much an American as anyone, perhaps even more so.

During the tumultuous sixties and seventies, slogans like "Black is beautiful" and "I'm black and I'm proud" bolstered his confidence that things in America were changing and that maybe one day there would even be a black president. Who knew?

After college, he was drafted into the war in Vietnam, and he served mostly behind the front lines in supply depots. The war was actually the first time in his life when he was able to have close relationships with anyone who wasn't black, and he'd learned there were many white folks who believed, as he did, that black people had been dealt a poor hand in the form of slavery, Jim Crow laws, and segregation.

Barnes received high grades in college, and he was accepted into the FBI on his own merit, receiving his training at Quantico, although there were always doubting looks and hushed discussions among some white FBI agents. Barnes knew affirmative action would be a burden he'd always have to bear. He had nothing but disdain for those who broadly characterized African Americans as lazy and on welfare or who thought America was on its way to becoming a socialist nation. He'd taken a course in college that categorized the United States as both capitalistic and socialistic almost from the start. The professor asked, "What pays for the military, roads, dams, bridges, public schools, the post office, the salaries of government officials?" His answer was simple: taxes. It seemed to Barnes that many US citizens needed a primer on American history to understand that America made money through capitalism but needed a socialistic society to enhance everyone's lives.

Barnes smiled to himself, knowing that his own position with the FBI was also funded by taxes and that his oath of office required him to protect and defend even those who disparaged him and his race.

CHAPTER 23

GALVIN, WEBSTER, AND THREE local militia leaders—Luke Tyler, Smitty Brown, and Bob Stern—sat around the table in the farmhouse. A dozen hand grenades lay on the table. Each leader had carefully chosen twenty men from their own militia, most of whom had served in Iraq or Afghanistan. The three leaders had been told only that Galvin had a plan that would overthrow the government and give the three of them incredibly powerful positions that would eventually net them far more wealth than any of them could imagine. The three men weren't privy as yet to the entire plan, and they had serious doubts that it would work, but the lure of untold riches and power was enough to whet their appetites and get them to comply with Galvin's requests. They had been instructed to choose ten men each who were combat hardened, and another ten who were reliable drivers. This they had done, but they still hadn't heard the whole plan, and what they were hearing now placed severe doubt in the three men's minds.

"Too risky," Luke Tyler said. "Won't work."

Galvin knew his plan might be a hard sell, but he believed he'd be able to convince the three leaders once they heard more.

Galvin spoke with passion. "We have the firepower and manpower to do it. It's risky, but so was Bunker Hill. Men died for freedom for all white men. It's what militias like yours and mine have been waiting for."

Bob Stern wasn't convinced. "You think with one fell swoop we can knock out the entire government?"

Galvin slowly nodded. "An attack during the State of the Union address. The president, vice president, and line of succession will be wiped out, except for the designated survivor, also known as the doomsday survivor."

Galvin noticed that the men appeared confused, so he continued, "The doomsday provision was enacted in case of a nuclear attack. One unnamed cabinet member is kept far from DC during the speech. He or she will become president, but the country will be in chaos."

Smitty Brown said, "You'll never kill them all—no way."

Galvin's face brightened. "Ah, that's where my plan B comes into play," he answered confidently. "They'll all be ushered to a bomb shelter, where my trap will be sprung."

Galvin stood up and walked over to a map pinned to a wall depicting downtown Washington, DC, the center of which was the Capitol building. Galvin slammed his fist on the building, on which were the letters *MVIEVTZHRMYFMPVI*. The men paid close attention.

Brown asked what was on all their minds. "Those letters—what do they mean?"

Galvin turned around and viewed the letters. "It's a code whose meaning you'll be privy to when the time comes."

Stern didn't like what he was hearing. "And exactly when is that time? The State of the Union address is tomorrow. My men, like yours, might need some time to train. And if you've got some secret plan or something, I think you need to level with us, or I'm out of here."

Galvin stared at their faces and explained, "First, your men will only have to follow the instructions I'll be handing out to you tomorrow morning. Certainly, the drivers know how to drive, and the men firing the weapons have already been trained to do so. All they have to do is follow the exact instructions you'll be giving them. Also, I have inside information as to who the designated survivor will be, and suffice it to say that this person is a sympathizer. I've been assured that the new commander in chief will have to declare martial law, which suspends habeas corpus. Our enemies will then be arrested and held without ever being charged with a crime. The military and militias will take over local government. Every county in the nation will be under the rule of the men who have the guns. Our nation can then get rid of the vermin that are polluting our land."

Galvin walked back and leaned with his hands on the table. The hand grenades gently rolled toward him. Forcefully, he concluded, "Gentlemen, it's the most noble thing any human being will ever do in this lifetime. Oklahoma City was nothing compared to this. This is our chance! This is revenge for Waco!"

The combination of his argument and the force of his personality had the men spellbound, but they weren't fully won over. They needed to hear more of his plan before they would commit their men to it.

Tyler announced, "My ten good ol' boys are familiar with this kind of firepower. Most of 'em served for Uncle Sam, some in Iraq, but all they know is to be ready for something big as soon as we give the go-ahead."

Galvin nodded approval. "I've compiled a list of your good men and mine. Makes close to eighty true-blue believers we can trust, but we can't let 'em know the plan until the last possible moment."

"When can we see the equipment?" Brown asked.

Galvin sat back in his seat. "This afternoon. And you won't be disappointed." He knew they were still unsure of his plan, but he also knew they would be impressed with the artillery and other firearms he'd managed to accumulate over the years. He also knew they would have to learn of his plan B, the chief plan, very soon, but the later they were informed, the safer his plan would be. He trusted these men, but he knew that, depending on circumstances, even the most trusted cohort could turn on him.

The men left the farmhouse, leaving Galvin and Webster alone.

Webster looked out the window. After the cars left, he asked Galvin, "What about Timothy Connor?"

Galvin sat down at the table and spun one of the grenades. "Ever play spin the grenade?"

Webster was annoyed. "I'm serious. Are you certain trying to find him is still worth it?"

"Not to worry. We'll get him soon enough."

"What makes you think so?"

"I got a connection in the local PD. We'll get him."

"If you ask me, I think we should forget about him. There was nothing in their apartments. Why take unnecessary risks?"

Galvin stopped the grenade from spinning. "I'm not asking you, am I? Just do your job. Let me worry about what's worth the risk and what isn't."

Webster eyed Galvin dubiously. He wondered if there was more to his obsession with finding this Timothy Connor than Galvin was revealing. But without knowing exactly what information Frank Valone had stolen from them, it was difficult for Webster to come to any valid conclusion. For now, he would wait and see what transpired.

CHAPTER 24

Tɪᴍ ᴡᴀs ᴏɴ the telephone in their room at the Skylight Motel speaking with Detective Sykes. Allie sat on the bed watching him.

Tim announced, "Got what they were looking for. It must contain dynamite stuff if they're so intent on getting it, but I'm not sure what it might be."

"Dynamite stuff, huh? Great choice of words."

Tim laughed. "I get it."

In a serious tone, Sykes said, "You've got to turn it over to us. The FBI's been looking for these jerks for over thirty years."

Recent events made Tim reticent to put his trust in anyone. "It's our ace in the hole. If I give it up, I lose my only bargaining chip. They know we can identify the two assholes that killed Sam. Also, the material I've got contains photos with names, a plan to overthrow the government, and a list of potential targets including the Capitol building."

"Wow." Sykes was impressed. "Tell me where you are, and I'll come get you. You need protection."

"Yeah, like they protected my mother."

"Know something?"

Tim swallowed hard. "She was murdered by...by one of them a long time ago."

"Listen to me. With your information, we can catch the sons of bitches. Without it, you might be on the run forever. Is that what you want for your girlfriend?"

Tim glanced at Allie. There were dark circles under her eyes. Maybe Sykes was right. Who knew how long they'd have to run? And with the police and the FBI protecting them and trying to find Sam's murderers, maybe he and Allie would be okay. His mind was made up. He glanced at his watch—10:35. "I'll be there in about thirty minutes."

Allie watched as Tim hung up, and she began to grab her coat.

Tim thought for a second. "You're safer here. If these guys are watching police headquarters or spot my car on the way there, I'd rather be alone."

Allie was tired, and if the police and Tim thought this was the best way finally to be done with this ordeal, then so be it. "Okay, but we should probably try to buy a cheap cell as soon as possible."

"Maybe I can get one on the way back." He walked out.

After hanging up with Tim, Sykes dialed out. "Barnes, it's Sykes. Looks like the case might be cracked open by your local PD. Connor is delivering the info the perps were after on a silver platter." It was difficult for him not to sound too smug. He knew the FBI loved taking the credit for solving a crime, even when most of the legwork was performed by the local police department.

A half hour later, Webster and Red pulled up at the Skylight Motel. They got out of the car and walked into the motel office. Webster carried a dozen roses and was wearing a florist's logo on his shirt. Webster had paid the owner of the shop a hundred dollars for the shirt. Neither Webster nor Red relished the thought of traveling together, but Suggs was with Galvin keeping an eye on the police station, waiting for Tim to arrive.

At the same time, Tim's car was only a few blocks from the police station. The metal box and all its contents were on the seat next to him. He surveyed the surroundings, but he detected nothing unusual.

Red waited in the lobby of the Skylight Motel while Webster, holding the flowers, talked with the male clerk at the front desk.

"Got a delivery from Timothy Connor for his girlfriend."

The clerk checked the computer for the room number. "Room 124. Outside. Turn right."

Webster lifted the flowers in the clerk's direction and said, "Thanks a bunch."

The clerk chuckled at the pun.

Tim's car was now two blocks from the police station. He glanced in the rearview mirror and spotted a car directly behind his with two men in the front seat. He instantly recognized Suggs, one of the killers from his apartment, but he had no way of recognizing Galvin. Suggs was sitting in the passenger seat, pointing a gun at him.

Tim floored the accelerator, and the other car followed close behind. Tim thought about stopping in front of the police station and jumping out, but he wasn't certain they wouldn't shoot him on the spot, grab the metal box, and drive off.

Tim's car picked up speed. He made a left at the corner and a skidding right at the next. He wasn't losing them. A garbage truck up ahead signaled to turn right. Tim gunned the engine and made a wide turn. His tires squealed as he barely missed the truck, swerved around it, and sped off down the block.

The garbage truck completed the turn onto the narrow street. Cars were parked on both sides of the street, and the garbage truck stopped to pick up garbage.

Galvin's car screeched to a stop. Galvin and Suggs were stuck behind the truck.

The truck's driver got out and walked to the rear doors of the truck.

Galvin leaned on the horn, which startled the driver. "Move that piece of shit, jerk!" he shouted harshly through his open window.

The driver gave Galvin the finger as he began to pick up one of the many garbage bags piled high on the sidewalk.

Galvin jumped out of the car and got directly in the man's face. "I said move it!"

The driver threw the bag into the back of the truck, sneered at Galvin, and said with a heavy Hispanic accent, "Give a fucking minute."

Galvin contemptuously said, "You're not even a real American."

The indignant driver shoved Galvin with a vengeance.

Enraged, Galvin whipped out his knife and plunged it into the man's gut.

The driver felt the knife bite deeply into his stomach. He clutched Galvin's throat as Galvin continued to rip the knife across his abdomen. The man slumped to the street as his life drained away.

Galvin glared down at the man, wiped the bloody knife across the man's shirt, and said, "At least now you won't breed any more like you. *Auf wiedersehen.*" Galvin rushed back to the car and backed it out of the street. They'd lost Tim for now.

Webster knocked on the door to room 124 while Red stood off to the side, out of sight of the peephole. They heard Allie's voice.

"Who is it?"

"Delivery of flowers from Timothy Connor."

From inside the room, Allie looked through the peephole and saw a man in a florist's shirt holding a dozen roses. She wondered how Tim could have been so thoughtful with all that was on his mind. But recent events had taught her to be extra cautious. "Leave them outside. Thank you."

Webster kicked in the door and rushed in, followed by Red, who slammed the door, but it was broken and remained slightly ajar. Fletcher barked at the two men.

At the sound of the crashing door, Allie jumped back into the small room. Webster ran in, dropped the flowers, and grabbed Allie. She attempted to scream, but Webster clamped his hand over her mouth. Red had followed directly behind, and she immediately recognized him.

"You!" she tried to scream through Webster's hand.

The two men wrestled a struggling Allie to the floor and held her down. Red lifted her blouse and bra, and he began to fondle her bare breasts as Allie squirmed and tried to fight, but she was no match for the two men.

She managed a muffled call through the strong hand of Webster. "You piece of shit!"

Webster told her, "I'm gonna remove my hand. If you scream, my fist is gonna knock some teeth out."

"It's a feel or a beatin'," Red cheerfully announced, squeezing her nipples.

Allie was mortified at the violation, which would normally have made her cry out in pain. But her anger overcame both her hurt and her revulsion, and she answered defiantly, "I'll take the beating, you motherfucking asshole."

Red stopped squeezing and removed his hands. "With such big balls, how do you get your panties on?"

Webster took control. "Stop messing around and fix her bra and shirt, dickhead. We got work to do."

Red slipped her bra back over her breasts and pulled down her blouse.

The two men got up.

Red ordered, "Stand up and put your hands behind your back."

Allie begrudgingly stood and did as she was told, hoping that if she didn't fight back, they wouldn't harm her. She fearfully wondered what they had in store for her.

Webster tied her hands behind her back as Fletcher continued to bark at them.

Red took out his hunting knife, held it out in front of him, bent over, and lifted the knife as though ready to stab the dog.

Allie shrieked, "Run, Fletch! Go!"

Red leaped at the dog, but Fletcher squirmed away just in time, and Red crashed to the floor. Fletcher squeezed through the door, ran out, and hid under a parked car, trembling.

They gagged Allie. Red took a bottle of ether from his pocket, poured some of it onto a rag, and held it over her face. Her eyes fluttered and closed, and she was allowed to slither to the floor. Red slipped his hand under her blouse again.

Webster was out of patience. He smacked Red on the back his head with an open hand. "You're a sick puppy. Help me, moron!"

Once again, Red took this slight as an egregious offense. "Don't fuckin' ever hit me again!" He silently vowed to put Webster in his place one day.

Webster ignored Red's protestations as he unfolded a duffel bag, into which they stuffed Allie. He and Red then tore the room apart. Finding nothing, they carried the duffel bag out, threw it into the car's trunk, and took off.

Fletcher barked at them from under the parked car.

Tim was parked at a local tavern. He used their pay phone to call Allie's motel number. It rang and rang with no answer. He hung up and tried again with the same result. *Could she be in the shower?* He doubted it, and although he knew she couldn't be in any danger at that motel, he was unsettled at the fact that she hadn't answered his call. He put the car in gear, and it lurched forward.

Still in his car, Galvin used his cell to call Webster. "We lost him. What happened at the motel?"

Webster replied, "We got his girlfriend. We tore the place apart, but nothing was there."

"I didn't expect there to be. Connor was delivering it to the cops, but he's a scared jackrabbit right now and will probably hold on to it once he finds out we got his girl. In fact, he's probably going back to the motel right now to check on her, so that's where we're heading. If we're lucky, we'll beat him there. What's the room number?"

"124."

Galvin ended the call.

CHAPTER 25

As TIM WAS speeding toward the motel, he wondered, *How did they know I would be at the police station and at exactly that time?* Something was wrong; he felt it in his gut. Would they also know about the motel? A cold sweat began to permeate his clothes. Allie was there alone. Tim frantically searched for a pay phone until he found one inside a BP gas station. He grabbed the phone book and dialed the number for the Skylight Motel.

The manager picked up while watching a game show on TV.

Tim shouted, "It's Tim Connor in room 124. Please tell Allie that she might be in danger, and to call a cab and get out of there. Tell her to call Sykes at the police station."

The manager turned down the volume on the TV and said, "Hold on a second. You're going way too fast. In fact, she was probably pleased with the dozen roses you sent."

"What? I sent no roses." He felt his heart pounding in his chest. "Please check out my room. I'll stay on the phone. If she's there, tell her to pick up your phone in your office. Please...this is an emergency."

The manager sighed, not knowing whether Tim was telling the truth or full of shit. This was an inconvenience that would make him miss some of his program. "Okay, hold on." He sounded put off as he put the phone on hold.

The manager strode to room 124. He saw the broken door, peeked into the room, opened the door all the way, saw no Allie and the room taken apart. He rushed back to the office and picked up the phone. "She's not there, and the room was trashed. Who's paying for the damage?"

Tim ignored the question. "Call the cops. Tell them Allie Sommers has been kidnapped."

"I'm calling, but only because the room is destroyed."

"I'll pay for the goddamned room. Tell them she's been kidnapped."

"Okay. I'm calling right now." He hung up and dialed 911.

Tim hung up. He wanted to call Sykes, but he had no change left. He turned and saw the attendant outside standing by a car. Tim rushed out and shouted, "Hey, I need change for a dollar."

The attendant replied, "Just a minute."

Every minute he had to wait was an eternity to Tim.

At police headquarters, Sykes sat with Barnes, who had arrived ten minutes earlier. Both men fidgeted in their chairs as they waited for Tim to arrive. Barnes impatiently glanced at his watch. It was 11:30 a.m.

Another few minutes passed in silence. Barnes looked at his watch again. "Now it's been almost an hour. Real crackerjack operation here."

Sykes was obviously pissed off, but said nothing.

Bored, Barnes glanced down at Sykes's ring and pointed at it. "Marine Corps?"

Sykes was happy the ice was broken. "I served in Vietnam in '72."

"No shit. I was there in '72. Army. You see any action?"

"I was lucky," Sykes said. "Almost none, and came back sane."

Barnes chuckled. "And still carrying weapons."

Sykes asked, "You ever shoot anyone on the job?"

"Never even had to draw my weapon. As you know, the FBI usually gets involved after a crime has been committed. Rarely do we have shootouts like on TV."

"Yeah, same for detectives. But when I was a patrolman in downtown Baltimore, I drew my gun plenty of times, but only once did I actually get involved in a shooting."

"No kidding. What happened?" Barnes was genuinely interested.

"We got word that someone was robbing a closed liquor store late one night. My partner and I were the closest responders, and our black-and-white arrived just as two guys were attempting to leave the premises. We stood behind our vehicle and ordered them to get down on the ground and drop their weapons, although it was so dark we weren't certain they had any weapons on them. They froze in place for a split second, and then they both drew guns and opened fire with semiautomatics. They sprayed the vehicle. Glass was flying everywhere. We attempted to return fire as best we could, but they continued to fire away while running down the block. Nobody got hit, and the perps got away."

"Were they ever caught?"

"With the small amount of money they stole, they were probably druggies. My guess is that they probably got caught later on for some other infraction. They almost always do."

"You guys were outgunned."

"Tell me about it."

Barnes shook his head. "Too many guns out there."

"It's their Second Amendment right." His voice was matter-of-fact.

"You know, I'm sort of a history buff," Barnes responded. "I've looked into that amendment, and it was written in order to maintain a standing militia that could be called upon to defend the United States from foreign invasion or from a tyrannical dictatorship. It was passed when all we had were muskets that could fire only one bullet, and then it would take a good minute to reload. The amendment was never meant to have the average citizen walking the streets with assault weapons that can fire ten rounds a second."

"Yeah, where does it stop?" Sykes agreed. "Should anyone be able to walk the streets with hand grenades or bazookas?"

They nodded their heads in agreement. For the moment, the atmosphere had changed for the better.

Barnes added, "Even just one bullet can change the course of history, and that one bullet may have resulted in you and me serving in Vietnam."

"One bullet?" Sykes was confused.

"Well, maybe two."

"How so?"

"JFK might not have committed over half a million troops to Vietnam like Johnson did. There are recordings of Kennedy, who was also somewhat of a history buff, saying that no country could defeat the Vietnamese people. He pondered pulling our advisors out of there. That's the first bullet. The second bullet hit his brother, Robert Kennedy, who ran in 1968 on a platform of pulling us out of that shit hole as soon as he got elected. Sirhan Sirhan's bullet ended that."

"Yeah," Sykes said. "Nixon kept us there for four more years, and maybe thirty thousand more dead soldiers."

They became solemnly silent for a moment, each man remembering many friends and fellow soldiers who had needlessly died or had come home crippled.

The phone rang. Sykes swiftly answered, "Detective Sykes."

Using the pay phone at that BP station, a frantic Tim shouted, "They got her!"

"Who got who?" Sykes asked.

Barnes said, "Put him on speakerphone."

Sykes did so.

They both heard Tim shout, "They spotted me outside your station, but I managed to lose them. But how'd they get Allie at the motel? And how'd they know I'd be at your station?"

Sykes glanced at a frowning Barnes. "Did you use the room's phone?"

Tim was confused at the question for a moment. Then he realized what Sykes was asking. "You mean the call was traced without you knowing it?"

Sykes looked at Barnes, who smirked. Sykes said, "Been done before, but look, we still need your information."

"But if some cop is on their payroll...in fact, maybe it's you!" He was more incensed than he could remember being before, especially now that it looked as if Allie's kidnapping had been aided by someone inside Sykes's police station.

"You gotta trust me." It was a tepid response.

"I trust myself, asshole." Tim ended the call.

Barnes turned toward Sykes. "Somebody's dirty here, and he thinks it might be you. If it is…" Barnes pointed accusingly at Sykes. Their brief truce had ended.

Tim had never felt more isolated in his life. Allie had been kidnapped, and he didn't have a clue how to find her. The kidnappers had trashed the room, but both he and the evidence hadn't been there. He thought they might want to strike a deal with him—Allie for the material—but with no cell phone and no motel room to return to, how would they contact him? He felt as though he were in a dark abyss with no way out.

Tim immediately left for an AT&T store he'd passed earlier on the way to the police station, and although he didn't fully trust Sykes, he intended to give Sykes the cell number. At least the police would be able to contact him if something important happened, especially if the kidnappers contacted them with their demands.

He found the store and purchased a cheap, throw-away phone with a twenty-five-dollar SIM card. He then called Sykes and told him to contact him immediately if he heard from Allie's kidnappers.

Sykes promised to do so, knowing that the demands of the kidnappers would determine whether he honored that promise.

Ten minutes later, Galvin and Suggs pulled up to the Skylight Motel. Two patrol cars were already in front of room 124.

Galvin turned to Suggs. "They know she's gone. I doubt Connor will be coming back. Let's get back to the farmhouse and see what the girl can tell us." He pulled out of the parking lot.

Galvin was confident that any and all information she might have would be easily obtained. He knew a variety of ways of making someone spill their guts, but he hoped he wouldn't need to use his talents. He'd never tortured a young American woman before, but if he had to, he planned to show no mercy.

CHAPTER 26

AT NOON, GALVIN, RED, Webster, and Suggs were sitting in the main room of the farmhouse intently watching a video on the television.

The screen showed the Branch Davidian compound burning in Waco. The narrator described the event: "The roaring inferno took the lives of almost eighty men, women, and children of the Branch Davidian cult, including its leader, David Koresh."

Galvin had tears in his eyes as he watched. His breathing became shortened with the thought that in that conflagration were his wife and two daughters. He clenched his teeth as his face quivered.

The documentary then switched to showing the aftermath of the bombing of the Federal Building in Oklahoma City. The narrator said, "The explosion took one hundred and sixty-eight lives, including thirty children who were attending the day-care center."

A spontaneous cheer erupted, and the men applauded with enthusiasm. The paradox regarding innocent children had escaped them.

Galvin smiled broadly at the grisly sight of crushed babies.

The program changed to a forest where they saw the Unabomber's shack and then the Unabomber, Ted Kaczynski, in orange prison garb and handcuffs.

Galvin stood and shut off the TV. "Unabomber. No organization, but his intentions were good. There are thousands of Ted Kaczynskis out there waiting for the right moment to mobilize, to join forces with an organized front."

He looked at Red. "Red, bring the girl in."

Red left the room and quickly returned with a frightened Allie. Her hands were still tied behind her back. Red shoved her onto a chair at a small table. While sitting tied to a chair in the next room, she'd heard the name of Vance Galvin being used, and she knew that in this room was Tim's biological father. She now stared at the face of the only man who could be old enough to be Tim's father, and she hoped he wasn't the monster Dan Connor had written about in his letter to Tim. She was taken aback at the resemblance between Tim and Galvin.

Galvin sat down at the table, opposite her. The men wondered what Galvin had in store for the attractive young woman.

Red stood behind Galvin, and he shot her a sinister smile as he stretched both arms toward her and squeezed the fingers of his hands as though squeezing her breasts.

Allie's fearful demeanor changed as she spoke to Red, almost as if in a trance, using her best acting voice, "Fool! You think that life is nothing but not being stone dead."

Red's smirk vanished as he shot back, "Pretty tough for someone who looks like a liberrian."

Allie winced. "Bet you were never in a *liberry*." *You dumb shit,* she thought to herself.

"Was so, smart-ass." He was insulted. He'd been there once or twice.

Galvin had heard enough and calmly said, "Red, don't embarrass yourself."

Pleading his case, he said, "Major, she's wrong! I been to—"

"Shut the fuck up!" Galvin shouted.

Red glared at Allie with hatred, but backed off.

Allie turned to Galvin. "Major? I thought you were kicked out of officer candidate school."

"By some black ape. Did Frank tell you this?" He truly believed that if it hadn't been for that black colonel, he might eventually have achieved an even higher rank than major.

She knew she shouldn't mention Mick, and she therefore hesitated before answering. "Police have an FBI report on you."

Galvin accepted her answer and folded his arms across his chest. "You're being held by an army of patriots, and now I am a major." He gestured toward the other men. "These men are my lieutenants. Maybe one day you'll be calling me Mr. President."

Allie stared at him in disbelief. She knew she was facing a megalomaniac, and she feared she might not be able to reason with him.

Galvin continued, "We're going to call your boyfriend. I'm certain he wants his honey back and will deal with us. What's his cell number? You'll tell him you're okay and that we mean business. He'll understand."

Allie looked at Suggs. "He crushed it at Tim's apartment."

Galvin grunted. "I know you haven't got yours. Does Tim have it?"

Referring again to Suggs, she said, "Your guy over here destroyed mine too."

Suggs sheepishly said, "I thought it was a good idea at the time... you know, so they couldn't be called or traced by their phones."

Galvin understood, but with Tim on the run without a cell phone, Galvin believed he now had to resort to harsh measures. "I'm certain Mr. Connor won't be returning to that motel any time soon. I guess we go to plan B."

Galvin eyeballed her from head to waist. "Pretty one, aren't you? Wonder how pretty you'll be if your boyfriend has to put several pieces of you back together?"

Allie glanced around the room at the men and then back at Galvin. She nervously declared, "You know who Tim is, don't you?" She suspected, but wasn't certain, that Galvin knew Tim was his son. She hoped this knowledge might soften his heart, especially where she was concerned, since she might one day become—abhorrent as the thought was to her—his daughter-in-law.

Galvin answered, not caring at this point if the others knew he was Tim's father. "A mere slip of the sperm. His mother never understood what it was I was trying to accomplish."

The three men were stunned by the revelation.

"So you killed your own wife?" She tried to tread the fine line between conversing with Galvin and condemning him, knowing he held her fate in his hands.

Galvin mused for a moment and said wistfully, "After she tried to run off with that turncoat Valone, who took my two-year-old son. There were times I actually loved the little guy. Named him after my father." His demeanor seemed to change as he waxed nostalgic.

Allie took her cue, looked him squarely in the eye, and said, "Tim's still your son."

Webster silently began to fume. *Is that the only reason for all this trouble?* He gritted his teeth and waited.

Galvin gazed into the distance as he answered, "Not anymore… not my son anymore." Then turning back to Allie, he said, "These men are my sons and my brothers. You, my dear, are my bait. I'll get word to him through our friendly police." His deep-set eyes black suddenly became catlike slits. "We'll see how Tim reacts when he gets you back, one finger at a time."

He pivoted and ordered, "Red, untie her."

Allie began to quake. "Dan Connor called you a monster. I pray to God that you are not!"

Red cut the rope, freeing her hands, and she rubbed her wrists as an effort to increase the circulation.

Galvin appeared angry but in control, and he said to Red, "Grab her hand."

Allie's eyes darted around the room. She had an idea what Galvin had in mind, and she knew it could not be good. Speaking to no one in particular, she pleaded, "Please, don't let him hurt me."

The men ignored her request. Red hoped to witness something that would feed his sadistic appetite.

Galvin asked, "What's Tim got on us?"

She instantly latched on to the chance to appease him and not be hurt. The pace of her speech quickened as she intended to tell all she knew. "We found a bunch of photos, some lists, and other things."

"What things?"

"There was a letter addressed to Tim, telling him that you were his father and that you killed his mother." She was holding nothing back. "Also, one paper told of a plan, way back, to attack the Capitol."

Galvin still hadn't heard her mention the one major item that could foil the plot. "What else did you find, and who was in the photos?"

Knowing the photos were some forty years old with names she didn't recognize, she had paid little attention to them. "They were decades old, and we didn't know who they were of."

"Do you recall any of the names?"

At this point she was ready to tell him anything she knew. "Just someone named Mick." She stared at Galvin with the hope of seeing him satisfied.

Galvin already knew about Mick from Sam, but it was evidence concerning Brett J. Mannings that concerned him. "And no other names?"

She recalled Tim showing her a photo of someone who looked familiar to Tim, but she'd paid it little mind since she hadn't recognized the man in the picture. "I've told you all we found."

He sat back in his chair and rubbed his chin. "You and Tim might not know how that information can hurt us, but I guarantee the authorities will know. I still need for Tim to give me all he has before he hands it over to the cops or the FBI, and I believe I know how to do it."

Allie haltingly asked, "How can you do that if you can't reach him?"

Galvin leaned across the table. "You know what collateral damage is?"

She silently prayed he wasn't going with this where she thought he was.

With a pleased expression, he answered, "Well, you're it."

Allie's face revealed the terror building inside. Her voice quavered, but she called on her acting experience to put as much power into her words as she could. "They told me you were fools and that

I was not to listen to your fine words or trust to your charity. I know that your counsel is of the devil and that mine is of God."

Red asked Galvin, "Bible stuff?"

Uncertain, Galvin stared at her. He then spoke with scorn. "I can always tell a good actor or liar, and you're neither." He turned toward Red and commanded, "Hold out her hand. We'll start with something small."

He removed the hunting knife from the sheath attached to his calf.

Allie's eyes became two white orbs at the sight of the knife. She was now consumed by a swirling tempest of fear.

From behind her, Suggs grabbed hold of her right arm. She squirmed, but Red grabbed her left hand and forced it flat on the table. He held out her pinky finger.

Allie trembled. She shouted at Galvin, "I'm your bargaining chip!"

Galvin ignored her and placed the huge knife's serrated edge on her pinky.

She struggled with a vengeance but couldn't resist all three men. Her finger began to bleed as the knife started to slice into her flesh.

In stark terror, she screamed, "I play the piano!"

Galvin removed the knife. Her finger was bleeding but still intact. He said with little emotion, "My mother played the piano... especially when my father beat me. It drowned out my screams."

Galvin reached across the table and rubbed his hand seductively across Allie's damp cheek. He seemed to like her looks.

She recoiled from his touch. "You're old enough to be my father."

Red, still holding her finger in place, laughed and said, "But not too old to put his dick in your mouth when he tucks...I mean *fucks* you in at night. Did Daddy do that?"

The men laughed.

Allie's crimson expression changed from fear to resolve.

Red continued, "If we got daughters like you, we'd be fuckin' their brains out." He laughed like the baboon that he was, still holding her finger.

Allie declared, "My father was a saint."

Galvin cocked his head to the side. "You know, my father beat me plenty, but I never blamed him. Lost his job to niggers. Reverse discrimination laws passed by Jews in Washington. Did the saint abuse his little angel?"

Mustering all her bravado, Allie spoke with great conviction. "You perverts will see each other in hell!"

With a violent thrust, Galvin chopped off half of Allie's pinky finger.

Allie's plaintive howl pierced the room. She writhed in pain and horror at the gory sight of half her finger, with its sharply manicured nail, lying grotesquely on the table. She sobbed uncontrollably as blood poured from the stump.

Red laughed and said, "Shitty actress and a freak show piano player. What a combo!"

Many emotions flowed through Allie at once. She had prided herself on her looks her entire life, and now she would be forever disfigured. Were they going to chop off other fingers or parts of her? She trembled at the almost inconceivable thought. Her acting career, and certainly her piano playing, would be affected. In a matter of seconds her emotions ran the gamut from horror to fear to untamed anger—she imagined cutting off their genitals with a dull knife—and back to fear again. She prayed that Tim would soon deal for her release or that the police would somehow rescue her. She was crying in a way she hadn't since she was a little girl, but observing the jubilant expression on Red's face, she forced herself to control her sobs, trying not to give them the satisfaction of seeing her cry.

Webster left the room and quickly returned. He placed a bandage on the stump of her pinky. He felt a twinge of regret at having to mutilate such a young, good-looking woman, but he knew that she might be the first of many who would soon be considered collateral damage.

Red picked up the severed finger, wrapped it in toilet paper, and dropped it into a manila envelope, which they intended to deliver to the police.

Watching Red with her finger made Allie fall into an almost catatonic state. She was physically and emotionally exhausted. She felt as though she were having an out-of-body experience and would suddenly wake up to find herself snuggled safely in bed with Tim and Fletcher beside her, and her finger intact.

Red guided Allie to a bedroom, where he shoved her onto the bed, grabbed her bandaged left hand, and handcuffed it to the headboard.

Standing next to the bed, Red made an obscene gesture with his tongue and index fingers as though licking her genitalia.

Allie didn't vocalize the utter contempt she felt for this degenerate, but the expression on her face said it all. She envisioned herself sinking her talons into that sick prick's eyeballs.

Red blew a kiss in her direction and walked out.

When he was gone, Allie gave in to depression. If Tim or the police couldn't find her, what would happen to her? Would Galvin and his men simply let her go? Or would they do far worse things to her before killing her? Horrible fates worse than death crossed her mind, and she cried softly.

CHAPTER 27

TIM SAT ALONE AT a desk in the dingy Baltimore motel room that he had just checked into. He didn't know what he was searching for, but he hoped it could give him something that might lead to Allie. He feverishly thumbed through the material from the metal box and viewed the photos. Several photos showed a farmhouse, and others a cabin.

The fact that they had kidnapped Allie was gnawing at his soul. He believed he would do anything to save her, even at the cost of his own life. Visions of destroying the people involved, especially the two who had killed Sam, permeated his soul to its core. He now spent every waking minute trying to find a way to rescue Allie. Would they want ransom? Or were they only interested in the contents of the box?

Was it possible they still occupied these secluded places depicted in the photos? It was a long shot, but Tim had nothing else to go on.

He picked up the phone and dialed. Someone answered, and Tim said, "Mick Yeager's room, please."

Galvin was working on the finishing touches to the assault, assigning men he believed would be capable drivers, and others who were experienced with the types of weapons he had stored, when his cell phone rang. It was his mole at the police department telling him that Mick was at the Morton Hospital.

Galvin ended the call and immediately called Webster. "Meet me here as soon as possible. We're gonna find my old friend Mick, see what he can tell us."

Galvin didn't know what to expect from Mick, but he felt it was worth the effort, especially since Tim's friend Sam had told him Tim had gone to see him. The last time Galvin had seen Mick had been in a prison hospital room decades ago, and Mick had been barely more than a vegetable. But what if Mick had recovered enough to recall things, especially about BJ? Galvin had to know for certain.

Galvin suddenly felt the urge to slaughter Mick slowly as he remembered a night just before Mick's incarceration. It was a night he'd relived over and over. He vowed to make Mick pay. A quick death would be too good for Mick. He relished the thought of torturing Mick.

After a half-hour drive to the Morton Hospital, Tim sat on the edge of Mick's bed with the photos spread out on the bedspread. Tim pointed at them. "Only you can locate these places." He glanced at Mick, searching for some sign of recognition.

Mick examined them and asked, "How ya know they're still standing, or that they still own these places?"

"I don't, but it's worth a try. They might be using the same hideouts they had years ago, and we've got pictures of these guys."

Tim picked up the photo showing BJ, scrutinized it closely, and said, "Why would this guy look familiar to me?" He handed Mick the photo.

Mick stared at it for a few seconds. "Funny...thought I once saw him on the boob tube, but the name wasn't BJ." He handed the photo back to Tim.

"On TV?" Tim squinted at the photo. "Damn, that's a very young Brett J. Mannings!"

"Big deal. Now take me to a concert."

"You haven't even earned a stinking CD. This guy is a bigoted congressman. Is this the same BJ you mentioned in those stories?"

Mick viewed the photo. "Same guy. So?"

"If he was in your gang, he was obviously part of some horrible criminal stuff. He's a long shot, but he actually has his sights on winning the next presidential nomination as a Republican, though I don't think they'd choose him. And if he was part of your group, he's got no chance at all."

"Hopefully not."

"Would you vote for a bigoted terrorist? He might even go to prison."

"You know what I'd do to him?"

"What?"

"I'd make him listen to Barbra Streisand music for the rest of his fuckin' sorry-ass life." Mick chuckled.

Tim was now losing patience. Time was of the essence. "No time for stupid jokes. If he's still with these guys, he may have a lot to gain."

"Or lose. So whaddaya want?" Mick lit a cigarette with a shaky hand.

"You know their hiding places, their habits. Maybe one of these places was their headquarters or a place they lived for a while."

Mick exhaled smoke and thought for a moment. "There was one main farmhouse that they used, but it was so long ago. I don't remember exactly where it was. I do recall that it was somewhere down Route 65. That's it."

"But if we drive down that highway, maybe seeing some landmark or building or something might jog your memory."

"Why not let the fuzz handle it?" Mick curled up in his chair.

"There's a goddamn informer on the inside. Believe it or not, you're the only one I think I can trust." Tim's eyes pleaded for Mick to help.

Mick became twitchy. "Maybe I'll crack up again."

Tim pointed at the walls, and shouted, "Whaddaya got to lose?"

Almost in tears, Mick glanced at those walls and shrugged. "What if Galvin's still part of this? Can you waste him, your own—"

Tim shot back, "Allie's the only family I got." The thought that Vance Galvin might be part of the group that was behind all this had crossed his mind, but he'd always suppressed it. It was too painful to think that the person behind it might be his own flesh and blood.

Tim grabbed a piece of paper and ripped it in half. He showed Mick how the two ragged halves fit perfectly together. "Different, but they fit together. Get it?"

"You both seem a little rough around the edges there." Mick grabbed another cigarette, lit it, and nervously blew smoke rings.

Tim held the two torn pieces together. Then he raised the left piece and then the right. "The left one's me. In the whole world, the only piece that will fit it is this one." He held up his right hand. "That's Allie."

Mick took a deep drag. "If it's Galvin, he'll probably waste her no matter what." He blew smoke toward the ceiling.

"Only you can save her," Tim said. Thoughts of her kidnappers doing unimaginable things to Allie flashed through his mind. Tim had little faith that the authorities would be able to find her. They'd searched for decades and had been able to locate Mick only because he was crazy. *And here I am, counting on this mental patient to be able to find Allie.* He believed that although it was only a remote chance, Mick was his only choice.

Webster's car pulled up to the Morton Hospital. Galvin said, "Wait here. I need to do this myself."

"No problem."

Galvin quickly entered the building, arrived at the front desk, and asked the middle-aged female receptionist to see Walter Yeager.

The receptionist's phone rang, and she said to Galvin, "Just a moment."

Mick stared at Tim's pleading face, pondering his request. His mind was boggled by too many conflicting thoughts all at once. He hated Galvin and would have loved to put a cap in his ass, but he knew Galvin was crafty and would probably kill or capture him and Tim instead. Thoughts of being tortured by Galvin or his men did not sit well with Mick. He knew what these men were capable of. Yet here was Tim, begging him to help find Allie. Mick liked her. *But what if I can't find where they are?* Mick didn't want to be blamed for not remembering a place from so long ago. Then he thought about Tim's mother, Sara. He hadn't been able to save Tim's mother, but maybe now Sara was speaking to him from the netherworld, asking him to save Tim's girlfriend. It was the thought of poor Sara that made up his mind. "I *could* go for some Wetson's. Ten-cent fries and fifteen-cent burgers."

Tim's spirits rose. "McDonald's put them out of business years ago. You'll have to settle for a Happy Meal."

Mick mimicked Dr. Martin Luther King Jr. "Free at last! Free at last! Thank God Almighty, I'm free at last! And remember, you're taking me to a Stones' concert."

"If we find Allie, I'll buy you tickets for the rest of your life."

Mick got up, reached for his jacket, and said, "First I gotta pee."

"Okay. I'll go sign you out. Meet me at the front desk."

Tim walked out and strode down the hall to the front desk, where he stood in line behind an older gentleman who sported a full head of salt-and-pepper hair.

The receptionist hung up the phone and asked Galvin to show her some photo ID.

Galvin extracted his Texas driver's license and gave it to her.

She noticed the expiration date. "This expired about fifteen years ago."

Galvin had been able to obtain a Texas license just prior to joining the Branch Davidians using an old address, knowing that even if the FBI somehow got wind of his license, the old address would lead nowhere. But since the debacle at Waco, he'd avoided renewing it for fear that newer computer technology might trigger an immediate response by the authorities.

Galvin attempted to be as polite and charming as possible. "As you can see, that's my photo, with a touch more gray."

"How'd you get here?" she casually asked.

"I have a driver waiting outside." It was the truth.

Still standing behind Galvin, Tim fidgeted and glanced down the hall, looking for Mick. He hoped this man would hurry up and get the hell out of his way.

The receptionist printed his name on her computer, printed out a sticky guest badge for him to wear, and said, "I need to call Dr. Sung first."

"Sure."

She picked up the phone, dialed a number, waited a few seconds, and said, "Dr. Sung, I have a gentleman named Vance Galvin here to see Walter Yeager."

Tim's whole body was electrified. Standing in front of him was his biological father! Crazy thoughts careened through his head. Should he tap him on the shoulder and say, "Hi, Dad," or should he bash him over his head with a chair? But Tim prudently decided to go find Mick since he knew Galvin most likely had a weapon on him, and possibly several men stationed nearby. He glanced down the hall and saw Mick walking toward them. Tim turned and hustled as quickly as possible to Mick while Galvin was still waiting for the receptionist to get the okay from the doctor.

The receptionist told Galvin he'd have to see Dr. Sung first, and she pointed down the hall in the opposite direction from Mick's room. "Room 114."

Tim grabbed hold of Mick and spun him around, facing away from the front desk. Tim looked back to see Galvin walking away from them, toward Dr. Sung's office. Tim recalled speaking with Sung for a few minutes the first time he visited Mick, and he figured that Galvin would be with Sung for a similar amount of time. He spun Mick around again and ushered him toward the front desk.

Mick said, "What's going on? You're making me dizzy."

Tim anxiously responded, "I'll tell you in the car. Let's sign you out."

Tim spoke to the receptionist. "I'm signing Mick out."

She answered, looking at Mick, "There's another gentleman who wants to see you. He's speaking with Dr. Sung right now."

"Who w-wants to see me?" Mick stammered.

She glanced at her computer, and said, "A Mr. Vance Galvin."

Mick began to breathe heavily. "I don't want to see him. Sign me out right now."

"You're sure?"

Mick turned and walked swiftly toward the exit.

Tim said, "He's sure," and then followed Mick out the door without actually signing Mick out.

The receptionist called after them, but they were already long gone.

Tim quickly guided Mick to his car.

Both men's thoughts were going a mile a minute. Tim wondered if Galvin had come here to kill Mick. Mick wondered how Galvin had found him. But Mick also thought how he'd love to kill Galvin if given the chance.

Fortunately for Tim and Mick, Webster had never met either one, and he paid little attention to the two men getting into a white car. Webster couldn't help but take note of Mick's mode of dress, and he thought, *There's another nutcase, probably being taken out by a friend or relative.*

Meanwhile, Galvin left Sung's office with Sung at his side. When they reached the receptionist, she stopped them and said, "Dr. Sung, I'm sorry, but Walter just left in a big hurry with Mr. Connor. He wasn't even signed out properly. In fact, the man who Walter left with was standing right here behind Mr. Galvin five minutes ago."

Galvin, thunderstruck, gave up any attempt to be charming. "Fuck! Where'd they go?" he shouted at her.

She was taken aback and answered, "They didn't say."

Galvin turned and ran toward Webster's car. He jumped in and frantically asked Webster, "Did you see two men just leave?"

"Yeah, an older guy dressed funny and some younger guy. Why?"

"Shit! That was Tim and Mick. Did you see their car, and could you tell which way they went?"

Webster hadn't paid much attention to them, except for the fact that Mick was dressed like a hippie. "I remember they got into a white car…that's all, and I didn't see where they went."

Galvin took several deep breaths, calming himself. "Okay, it's probably not gonna matter. We gotta get back to our meeting."

CHAPTER 28

AN HOUR LATER, in a large warehouse located in a sparsely populated area of northern Virginia, Galvin showed off his matériel to Brown, Stern, and Tyler.

The cavernous warehouse was filled with bazookas, mortars, hundreds of assault weapons, pistols, and many hand grenades.

Galvin proudly walked the center aisle of the warehouse, trailed by the three men, as he described his ordnance, pointing out each type as he went along. "Over here I have five Israeli-made Mizo mortars, along with eight Soviet-made RM-38 fifty-millimeter light infantry mortars, and ten US-made M-19 mortars."

The three men nodded their approval as Galvin continued to show off his weapons.

"On the right, I have over twenty AK-47s that can fire ten bullets a second. On the left, I have mostly American-made bazookas. As you probably know, these rocket-propelled weapons were used primarily as antitank weapons, but are also quite effective against buildings."

"How many bazookas do you have?" Tyler asked.

"Seventeen."

"Nice," Tyler said.

Brown pointed at two trucks parked at the rear of the warehouse. "What are the trucks for?"

Galvin's face brightened. "Ah, those contain my *pièces de résistance*." He jauntily strode up to the rear of the trucks, turned around to face the three men, and said, "Gentlemen, feast your eyes." He slid open the door of the nearest truck. Inside, bolted to the floor, was a 75 mm Pack Howitzer cannon, also known as an M116. The men were amazed. Galvin remarked, "This Howitzer can fire three to six rounds per minute. In only a few minutes, my guess is that the men firing this could shoot at least a dozen rounds before making their escape."

"Yeah, and exactly how do they manage to escape?" Stern asked. The other men nodded—they had been wondering the same thing.

Galvin answered, "I've thought of that. We enter our firing zone with these two trucks and our other trucks and pickups, but we'll have several other vehicles strategically parked just hours before the assault. Forty of our men will drive while forty-five others will do the firing from the rear of the vehicles. Our men will quickly ditch the trucks they've fired from and run one or two blocks to these parked cars, in which they will make their escape. By the way, I've checked the weather reports, and they predict snow for late tomorrow afternoon and evening. I believe that God is helping us by shielding the men and trucks in a shroud of angel-white snow."

The three men muttered approval, but they were still waiting to hear Galvin's plan B. The three men had previously agreed that if any one of the three believed plan B was doomed to failure once they heard it, all three would gracefully decline to commit their men to the assault.

Galvin walked behind the second truck. He opened the doors and waved his hand as though introducing a young starlet to the audience. "Gentlemen, feast your eyes once again."

Bolted to the floor of the truck was an M16 rocket launcher containing twenty-four tubes capable of launching twenty-four rocket-propelled explosives in just seconds.

The men were highly impressed.

"How'd you get all this stuff?" asked Stern. "Fantastic."

Galvin waxed pensive. "Every job, passed over for promotion. They kept choosing some loser minority. Affirmative Action. Took my own affirmative action and began stockpiling weapons for the past twenty years. Some were stolen, some bought. You'd be amazed what the government throws out, sells, or seems to misplace and what you can buy on the black market from foreign countries."

Brown asked, "Where'd you get the money? This stuff don't come cheap."

Galvin paused in deep thought. "My loving wife, Lucinda, was a whole lot smarter than me when it came to our beautiful children." His face contorted for a moment. "Let's leave it at that, okay?"

The men knew it wasn't a suggestion.

Lucinda had known their involvement with the Branch Davidians was dangerous. After giving birth to her second daughter, she had seen TV advertisements for term life-insurance policies, which were quite inexpensive considering Lucinda and Vance's relative youth. Even though Vance had originally objected to throwing away good money, as he put it, she had convinced him that, for the sake of the girls and for her own peace of mind, they should each take out two million dollars of term life insurance. The girls would never have to worry about anything should something happen to one or both of them. Galvin knew he couldn't put his true name on the documents. Lucinda hadn't changed her name legally from Graham as yet, and so he applied for the policies using falsified documents for himself as Vincent Graham. The thought that he would be the sole beneficiary of two million dollars had never crossed Galvin's mind.

They continued to walk back toward the front of the warehouse. The three became increasingly impressed. Tyler asked, "How'd you manage to get a Howitzer? Kind of big to lug in the trunk of your car."

The men chuckled at the ridiculous image.

Galvin said, "The illegal buying and selling of arms is big business. Planes fly out of places like Belgium, Ukraine, and South Africa and deliver arms to places like Africa and Afghanistan. I was able to make contact with a Ukrainian arms dealer who had contacts in the Sudan, where the loose government makes keeping track of weapons almost impossible. With the right amount of money, I was able to have much of this weaponry shipped by barge up the Nile River, where it was loaded onto containers and shipped from Cairo to New York Harbor. Very few containers are ever inspected, and even fewer before 9/11. Most of the rocket-propelled grenades, mortars, and the Howitzer cannon were obtained that way. The feds believe we're an unorganized group of crazies who can only strike by driving a truck filled with explosives up to a building. They have no idea the firepower we possess, and the best is not even here."

Stern's eyes opened wide. "Nuclear?"

Galvin smiled devilishly. "Don't I wish. But just as lethal. Nerve gas planted in the president's bunker."

"No way," Brown said, shaking his head. "No way you can get in there."

Galvin appeared confident as he explained, "Let me worry about that. All you need to know is that it's all set. That's all I'm at liberty to tell you right now. When it's all over, you'll know everything."

The three men accepted Galvin's response. From what they had seen in the warehouse, they knew Galvin was a man of remarkable talents and tenacity. If he had been able to gather this equipment over such a long period of time, who could doubt his commitment or ability to carry out his plan?

Brown asked, "How certain are you that the nerve gas will do the job?"

Galvin understood their questioning of his plan, and he was actually glad, because it demonstrated that he was dealing with men of enough intelligence to ask these kinds of questions. It gave him confidence that these men would be able to accomplish their assignments. "Been doing a lot of research on nerve gas. If it's released in a sealed room, death will occur within one minute. As soon as they inhale it or have it on their skin, they'll get runny noses, tightness of the chest, and then difficulty breathing. They'll get nauseous and start drooling. And get this"—Galvin smiled sardonically—"they're gonna lose control of themselves by vomiting, shitting their pants, and pissing all over themselves."

The men laughed.

"Then they'll fall on the floor, twitching and jerking." Galvin made twitching and jerking motions with his arms and body.

The men laughed again. Galvin continued, "They soon go into a coma, have convulsions, suffocate, and die. This is so much better than a bullet to the head. I wish I could be there to see them suffer," he said with a sneer.

Galvin casually picked up a bazooka that was propped up against the wall behind him. He placed it on his shoulder and looked through the sight as he spoke. "Over eighty men, strategically placed, rapidly firing shells, will unleash enough force to bring down the dome, and maybe the entire building."

The men stared wide-eyed at Galvin as he put down the bazooka.

"Each vehicle should be able to fire at least ten rounds before escaping. Gentlemen, that's over four hundred bombs. If the line of succession survives, which they probably will, the president and all the major players will quickly be ushered to a shelter, where our trap will be sprung."

Tyler said, "A lot of our boys'll surely bite the bullet. Even Webster."

With obvious pride, Galvin answered, "They will have given their lives for the cause of mankind, and like Hitler's, their names will be enshrined forever." Then he wistfully added, "If only Hitler had been born in America."

Brown pointed at Galvin. "Maybe he's been reincarnated."

Galvin proudly accepted this as the supreme compliment.

Brown asked, "What about Connor?"

"He'll deal with us...guaranteed. There's no way he's going to ignore our demands once he gets her finger. Besides, I'm still monitoring events from the inside." He hoped his mole in the police department would continue to feed him timely and accurate information.

CHAPTER 29

AT 2:00 P.M., TIM was driving on Highway 65 in Virginia with Mick next to him in the front seat. The near miss with his father was making Tim's head spin. Would his father have greeted Tim with open arms had he found him there with Mick? Or was Galvin the monster Dan had made him out to be? Mick's stories seemed to confirm that he was.

Tim was still having trouble coming to terms with the scenario of how Galvin had lost him to Dan—Frank Valone—but at that moment, thoughts of Galvin would have to take a back seat to his real mission, which was finding Allie. The only thing Tim regretted was not seeing what his biological father looked like since he'd paid little attention to the man standing in front of him and only had seen the back of his head.

Mick was also thinking about the close call with Galvin, and he kept his mind off his former leader by looking through the CDs in Tim's glove compartment. He was not paying much attention to the surrounding countryside.

Tim impatiently shouted, "Look for some landmark or something."

Mick turned toward Tim and spoke uneasily. "What if I don't boomerang by dark? And remember, you needed to sign me out. Against the rules."

Tim was concentrating on his driving, and said, "Let 'em sue me, but keep your eyes on the road. Something's bound to remind you of where this farmhouse was." Tim knew time was of the essence.

The longer her captivity, the more likely something terrible would happen to her. He could only hope Mick would recall the location, and by some chance Allie would be there. He tried not to think of the next steps since he knew there could be tons of trouble waiting for them. But he knew he had no choice in the matter. His primal fears were overcome by the adrenaline rushing through his veins, and all he could think about was Allie's safe return.

Tim had given Sykes his new cell number, and he prayed he'd be called with some positive news regarding Allie, or at least the news that the kidnappers had contacted the police or FBI with their demands, which Tim intended to meet immediately.

Mick became twitchy and lit a cigarette. He wasn't used to being under pressure. Sitting in his room for so many years had become monotonous, but at least he worried about nothing. It was often a zombie-like existence, but it was free of pressure. If Allie was there and Mick couldn't find her, would he be blamed if something terrible happened to her? He'd endured so much guilt for all these years concerning Sara that he didn't know if he'd be able to survive taking responsibility for Allie. Watching the wafting cigarette smoke drift away settled his nerves a bit.

Tim saw him take a drag and said, "Light me up one."

Mick lit another cigarette and handed it to Tim, who inhaled greedily.

Mick noticed and asked, "Nervous?"

With a wry smile, Tim said, "No. I'm not expecting to live long enough to get cancer from these coffin nails."

Mick smiled and then made a discovery among the CDs. "You're not so square after all. You got *The Best of the Rolling Stones.*"

Mick inserted the CD, and "19th Nervous Breakdown" began playing. Mick started singing along with the tune. He began to laugh almost maniacally at the words, "It's just your nineteenth nervous breakdown."

Tim shouted angrily, "Concentrate on where we are! You said the farmhouse was around here. You better remember some landmark, or you'll walk the fuck home."

Mick stopped laughing and watched the landscape roll by. It was a blur of nondescript buildings and dull gray foliage.

At police headquarters, a female secretary walked into Sykes's office carrying a manila envelope. It was addressed, "To the detective in charge of Tim Connor investigation." The secretary knew that it was Sykes's case, and she handed the unopened envelope to him. There was no return address listed.

Sykes asked, "Where'd this come from?"

She answered, "It was apparently hand-delivered, dropped just inside the outer doors of the building. An officer picked it up and gave it to me. I came right here."

"Did he see who dropped it?"

"I asked him, and he said it was just lying there."

"See if you can get someone to examine the building's surveillance tapes. Maybe they'll reveal something."

"I'll get right on it." She turned and left his office.

Sykes tore open the envelope, finding a note and something wrapped in tissue paper. He read the note, which said, "Tell Connor to play ball with us or he'll be receiving more of the same. Tell him to be at the following pay phone at exactly 3:00 p.m. for our call. The phone is inside the Sunoco station at the corner of First Avenue and Duncan."

Sykes put the note down and picked up the tissue paper. He hoped against hope that there wasn't something terrible wrapped inside. He gingerly unwrapped the tissue paper, revealing Allie's nail-polished pinky. Disgusted, he dropped it on the desk. "Fucking bastards," he said out loud. He picked up his phone, called Landers, and asked him to come immediately to his office. After hanging up with him, he dialed Barnes's number and told him the same thing. Barnes said he'd be over in ten or fifteen minutes.

Twenty minutes later, Barnes, Sykes, and Landers stood in front of Sykes's desk, all with serious expressions. Sykes spoke to Barnes. "We received a woman's finger with a note telling us to tell Connor to make a deal, or more parts will follow."

Barnes's shoulders slumped, and he merely replied, "Shit."

"Landers and I think we shouldn't tell Connor. We need what they want. Besides, Connor doesn't trust us. We also believe they're not going to let her go, no matter what. She probably knows way too much."

"You realize," Barnes said, "that we're placing this Allie in even greater jeopardy if we don't try to cut a deal."

Landers spoke to Barnes. "Listen, we're trying to save a lot more than one life here. If we lose one to save many, it's the right move. Why don't you guys go home and let us handle this."

"Yeah, great fuckin' detective work so far," Barnes snorted. "The one guy we need thinks you guys are a disease."

Landers retorted, "We fucked up? You big FBI boys have been after these jerks for over thirty years."

"At least we're not helping them."

The accusation that someone in their department was helping Allie's captors was met with stony silence.

Barnes broke the ice. "Any ideas on this rat?"

"Could be anyone," Sykes answered.

Barnes looked at Sykes. "Trouble is, Connor believes that includes you. Who'd you tell besides me that Connor was coming here?"

"Just Landers."

Barnes glanced at Landers. "So some phantom traces the call from the motel and tips off the bad guys?"

Sykes and Landers eyed each other suspiciously.

After an uncomfortable pause, Sykes said, "We got a call from Tim Connor telling us that he bought a new phone, and he gave us the number."

Barnes asked, "And you've had that number how long?" It sounded like an accusation.

Landers answered, "Several hours."

Now Barnes was miffed. "You should have given it to me immediately. We're the lead agency now." Barnes smugly folded his arms in front of his chest.

Landers pointed at Barnes. "I don't need a goddamned lecture from someone who probably didn't have to answer all the questions on the FBI exam."

Barnes knew what Landers was alluding to, and he sarcastically answered, "I'm sure smart guys like you answered all the questions. Real smart guys questioned the answers."

The remark perplexed Landers. "Questioned the…you insulting my intelligence?"

"You don't even know what I'm talking about, do you? Kind of makes your question a rhetorical one."

Frustrated and angry, Landers fingered his gun.

Barnes looked down at Landers's hand and then at his face. "You're shitting me."

Sykes yelled, "Landers!"

Landers wore a sinister smile as he rubbed his holstered gun. "Got an itch. Sometimes you gotta scratch."

They would have needed a chain saw to cut the tension. Finally, Landers said, "I need a smoke." He left the room in a huff.

Barnes asked, "How did you receive the finger?"

"It was dropped off in the outer vestibule of our building. We're examining the surveillance tapes, but I doubt they'll reveal anything of value. My guess is whoever delivered it was smart enough to wear some sort of disguise."

"So all we can do is wait and see what transpires," Barnes reflected.

"Maybe we'll get lucky and something will turn up," Sykes said.

"Let's hope it's not another body part."

Sykes nodded and gave Barnes Tim's new cell phone number. "Oh, yeah," Sykes said. "We're also calling the Morton Hospital right now to see if we can speak with this Walter Yeager and see what he knows. We might even want to pay him a visit."

His intercom buzzed, and Sykes picked up. "Yeah?"

He listened for a moment and then turned to Barnes. "They got the receptionist at the Morton Hospital on the line." Then he said into the phone, "I'd like to speak with Walter Yeager, please." He listened for a minute and said, "Thank you." He hung up. He told Barnes, "He left a while ago with Tim Connor."

"I wonder what Connor wants from this Yeager guy?" Barnes said.

"At this point, he's probably grasping at straws."

At the farmhouse, Allie sat on the bed with her back against the headboard. Her bandaged hand was still handcuffed to the bedpost. She was alone and miserable. She knew escape from these men was impossible, but her hatred for them engendered thoughts within her that she never would have thought possible. She had always thought seeking revenge could eat a person alive. Perhaps Jesus was correct, and a person should learn to turn the other cheek. Well, she thought, maybe that was good enough for Jesus. After all, he was the son of God. She was the daughter of nobodies, and almost every thought in her mind was devoted to how she would take revenge. If it happened, it wouldn't be swift for them. They would die horribly, slowly, and painfully. She believed revenge would certainly be sweet for her.

Her thoughts were interrupted as Galvin walked into the bedroom. Galvin had called the telephone number at the Sunoco station for fifteen minutes beginning at 3:00 p.m., but only a station attendant had answered. "Your boyfriend didn't answer our phone call. If he doesn't deal with us soon, you'll be useless. Thought you'd like to know."

Through misty eyes, Allie asked, "How can you not call yourself a monster when you're willing to murder hundreds or even thousands of innocent people?"

Galvin pondered her question for a moment. "I've actually asked myself that same question. I'll answer it this way. When I was a kid, I watched an ant trying to find its way out of my bedroom. Maybe it was trying to get back to its colony; I don't know. I watched it for several minutes and actually felt sorry as it continued to struggle and fail, traveling this way and that. I finally stepped on it and flushed it down the toilet."

With sarcasm as thick as molasses, Allie remarked, "My, how interesting."

Galvin ignored her. "Years later, there was an infestation of ants in my mother's kitchen…maybe thousands of ants. We sprayed and stepped on them until not a single one was left alive. And you know what?"

"I'm all ears."

"I didn't feel sorry for even one of them. They were in my house, attempting to infest my world. So you see, killing one person who I might come to know might be a tad troubling, but killing thousands who threaten my home or family…that's no problem at all."

Allie's eyes opened wide in disbelief as she shouted, "People are not ants!"

Galvin placidly responded, "But far more threatening. Don't you see?"

Allie couldn't muster an answer. She knew that only a monster could equate innocent men, women, and children with insects.

Galvin was satisfied with his explanation. He started to walk toward the bedroom doorway and then turned around. "Oh, and before I dispose of you, I might give you to Red. He has this burning desire to play gynecologist." He shot her a sinister smile.

Galvin walked out, leaving Allie forlorn. Thoughts of revenge became feelings of despair once again as she envisioned Red's filthy hands and dirty fingernails probing her body.

CHAPTER 30

TIM'S CAR CONTINUED ON the highway. Every minute or so, Tim glanced at Mick and said, "Anything?"

But Mick only shook his head.

Tim was fearful that he might be wasting precious time by pinning his hopes on Mick. If Mick couldn't recall the location of the farmhouse, all could be lost. Horrible thoughts pierced his mind concerning Allie's treatment by her captors. Tim attempted to erase those thoughts by concentrating on his driving.

The Rolling Stones CD switched to the song "Wild Horses." Mick suddenly sat up straight. "Ya know, there was this motel I crashed at for a while…horses nearby…maybe a dozen klicks from the farmhouse."

Tim enthusiastically said, "Remember the name, and we can get the phone number to locate it."

Tim reached into his pocket and removed the cell phone.

Mick thought for a moment. "The name reminded me of some kind of a bird."

"What bird? A dove, an eagle, a robin? Think!"

Mick slouched down in the seat. "I am thinking. But the brain cells just ain't what they used to be."

Irate, Tim reached over and grabbed Mick by his collar. "Too much goddamned acid in the sixties?"

Mick was almost in tears. "Too much nirvana in the seventies, eighties, and nineties."

Tim roughly released his grip.

The cell phone chirped, startling them. Tim answered.

Barnes was on the other end. "Don't hang up. I'm Special Agent Calvin Barnes with the FBI. We need your help if we're gonna find your girlfriend."

"Did you speak with Detective Sykes?"

"Yeah, and that's why you gotta trust me. Someone at police headquarters is playing a nasty game. Your girl's gonna get hurt real bad if we don't find her soon."

"I don't know who to trust. Give me your number. If I'm in over my head, I'll call, but I only want FBI…no cops. Agreed?"

Barnes glanced over at Sykes, but he didn't hesitate to answer. "Agreed, but you can't take these guys by yourself."

Tim looked at Mick and said, "I'm not alone. I got the power of the Rolling Stones with me."

Never having met Tim, Barnes had little understanding of the kind of person Tim was, and he hoped Tim's cavalier quip about the Rolling Stones wasn't indicative of his ability to aid in the operation. But Barnes ignored the remark and proceeded to give Tim his cell number.

Tim grabbed a pen and piece of scrap paper from his glove compartment, wrote Barnes's number, and ended the call.

Tim scowled at Mick. "I'm gonna name every damn bird I can think of till you remember or go nuts again. Sparrow, pigeon, parrot…"

CHAPTER 31

Stan Urbanski's car pulled onto a deserted road. He drove until he came upon a lone metal mailbox with a badly faded number on it. The mailbox was rusted and in such disrepair it seemed not to have been used in quite some time. He checked the paper that Herrmann had given him; it was the same number. A dirt road wide enough for only one vehicle to pass began at the mailbox and disappeared into the forest. He knew there was only a fifty-fifty possibility that Alan Webster was his biological son. If he was, would Stan break the news to him? How would Alan react? Would he be happy to see his long-lost father? Would he already be aware of the fact that Oscar Webster wasn't his biological father? Or maybe Oscar really was his father. Would he be able to tell simply by looking at Alan? Or would they have to go through some kind of paternity test? He'd been told that Alan wasn't the kind of man to mess with. Would Alan become irate and try to hurt him? Or would he rush into his arms after having searched for decades for his true father? Stan had never had a son. Maybe this would be the beginning of something wonderful.

He was unsure whether this would lead to anything at all, but he turned up the narrow, bumpy road past the mailbox and headed for what he hoped would be his answer.

After he had driven slowly for about three hundred yards, a car pulled out from the thicket at the side of the road and blocked his path.

Stan's car skidded to a halt. Stan was surprised to see another vehicle in such a strange and isolated location. But maybe one of these men was Alan Webster. If so, he believed he would know it at first sight.

Red and Suggs jumped out of their car with guns drawn and pointed at Stan.

Startled, Stan opened his window, hoping that they meant him no harm. He scrutinized their faces and immediately knew that neither man could be Alan, as they both appeared to be no older than their late twenties. Stan began to explain who he was, but just then, a small bird flew into his window. Stan swatted helter-skelter at the bird with both hands as the terrified bird pounded his windows, trying to escape. Stan pressed the buttons that opened all the windows, and the bird was able to fly out. Stan breathed a sigh of relief and closed all the windows except the one on the driver's side.

Red and Suggs laughed at the sight, and they walked toward Stan's open window with their guns still aimed at him.

Stan composed himself, and he was surprised that the guns didn't scare him at all.

"What're you doin' here?" Suggs demanded.

Stan had no idea why the men would need to point guns at him. He asked, "What's with the guns?"

Red retorted, "Shut the fuck up and answer the question."

Stan smiled. "I can't do both."

Red looked confused. "What?" Through the open window, he pressed the gun against Stan's temple. "You some kinda smart-ass?"

Stan calmly answered, "I'm looking for a man named Alan Webster."

Suggs and Red glanced at each other with surprised and then bewildered expressions. Red pulled the gun away from Stan's head. They knew Webster was at the farmhouse, and they wondered how this chubby little guy in an expensive Lexus could possibly know that.

Stan noticed their reactions, and said, "So you know him."

Suggs stepped in closer. "What's he to you?"

"I got something he'll want."

Suggs stepped away from the car door and ordered, "Get out and lean against the car."

Stan obliged and was frisked by Red. Stan was clean.

Red said, "Turn around and tell us what you got, or maybe we put a bullet in your head." Red pressed the barrel of the gun against Stan's forehead.

Stan appeared cool as a cucumber, which the two men found unsettling.

Stan responded, "Then I'll be dead, and he'll be pissed off at the two of you, so go ahead and shoot." He closed his eyes. Maybe this would end his pain.

Red removed the gun from Stan's forehead. He looked at Suggs and said, "Guy's afraid of a bird but not a gun?"

Stan opened his eyes.

Red looked back at Stan. "Get in your car. We'll pull off the road and follow you up the road."

"Where am I going?"

"You'll see a farmhouse."

Stan got back into his car and watched as the other car pulled to the side. Stan then drove ahead of them, and the other car fell in behind.

The cars slowly navigated the narrow dirt road. Stan thought that in just a few moments he'd have his answers. He felt the anticipation building inside as he again wondered what Alan's reaction would be.

Inside the farmhouse, Galvin sat alone in the main room watching an attractive blonde news reporter on television. The reporter was interviewing Brett J. Mannings during a white power rally. A skinhead carried a sign that read, "Congressman Brett J. Mannings for President." Mannings was wearing a lapel pin that read, "America for True Americans." Even though the next scheduled election was almost two years away, Mannings wanted to get an early jump, especially if Galvin's plan never got off the ground. He trusted Galvin, but who knew if he would actually get all his ducks in a row? Maybe the FBI would step in and foil the plot. Or maybe the other leaders would have cold feet and back out. Mannings knew getting the nomination was a long shot, but stranger things had happened. Hadn't they once elected a black president? *Christ, that shows any damn thing is possible.*

The reporter asked, "What does your slogan mean to you?"

Mannings answered, "True Americans know its meaning."

The reporter said, "Some say it means keeping immigrants out. Others say it even means expelling certain people, especially undocumented Latinos. What about Miss Liberty asking, 'Give me your tired, your poor, your huddled masses yearning to breathe free'?"

Mannings waved his hand dismissively. "A fairy tale. Look at the quotas and restrictions for European immigrants as opposed to Asian or African. Face it. America is a racist nation…whites first, everyone else last."

"You get campaign contributions with fear tactics. Can money buy the nomination?"

Mannings contemplated the question and then answered with confidence, "Jesus had no money." He pointed toward the sky. "He just knew the right boss."

A scuffle broke out behind them. The TV camera turned away from Mannings and the reporter, toward the commotion, and the reporter began to describe the scene to her television audience. Several people attempted to rip the hate signs from the hands of the white power marchers. Fistfights broke out, and police officers charged into the melee, some wearing riot gear and carrying billy clubs. One white power marcher attempted to hit one of the officers with his sign, but he was taken down by a blow to his leg with a club. The crowd began to disperse in several directions.

Galvin's cell phone rang. He turned away from the TV and answered. He listened for a minute and hung up just as Webster walked in.

Galvin announced, "Connor made contact with the FBI, but my mole says they're not telling him about the finger or even that we tried to contact Connor. The mole might be able to contact Connor himself, but it's risky for him. Apparently they don't give a damn about the girl. They want Connor's information, but we have to make certain they don't get it. The good news is I doubt he'll give it to them knowing we want to trade it for the girl. It's his ransom money, so to speak, and in twenty-four hours, it won't matter anyway."

Webster appeared enraged. He paced the floor and then pointed at Galvin. "You're more interested in him than in what he's got! The girl would've talked if he had somethin' on us. He's probably got nothing, and risky is how the whole plan sounds to me."

Galvin, apparently unruffled, said, "Relax. You're military. Ever hear of diversion tactics? The real plan is plan B, but I can't tell you who's carrying it out or how, at least not yet. God willing, in twenty-four hours none of this will matter. And you have to believe me. Frank had damaging information on a certain person who's extremely important to our operation. Tim is now my son only biologically."

Galvin's little speech tempered Webster's concerns, but he was still dubious about the whole affair. "Okay, I'll be the good soldier, but if you fail and this sacrificial lamb gets out alive"—he pointed at himself with his thumb and then at Galvin with his index finger—"you'll be the first one I go for."

Galvin nodded, and then he looked back at Mannings on the TV and laughed sardonically.

Webster eyed Galvin with suspicion. He didn't like not knowing all the details of the plan, but for now he would wait and see.

They both heard cars pulling up the dirt road. The two men instinctively ran to a window and ducked down, peering out. They saw Stan get out of the first car, with Suggs and Red's car behind. Suggs and Red got out and walked up behind Stan. Both men carried their pistols down at their sides.

Stan took a few steps toward the farmhouse and shouted, "I'm looking for Alan Webster."

Galvin and Webster were momentarily stunned. Who could possibly know that Alan Webster was here?

Galvin turned to Webster. "You know this guy?"

Through the window, Webster stared at Stan's face. He slowly shook his head. "No way."

"You're sure you told no one about this place?"

"Of course not." Webster thought for a second, and he suddenly recalled telling his friend John Herrmann to call the cops if he didn't return, but he had told Herrmann to forget about the conversation. Could this guy have talked with Herrmann? Webster thought it wise to remain silent about it.

Stan walked toward the door. He knew Alan was in there, and if Alan was his son, he believed he'd be able to tell right away. Maybe he'd resemble his daughter, Kim.

Galvin shouted through the window, "Stop or you're a dead man."

Undaunted by the threat, Stan continued toward the door. He shouted back toward the window, "Are you Alan Webster?"

"Who wants to know and why?" Galvin asked.

"I got something for him."

Galvin pulled out his gun and turned to Webster. "We have to get rid of him."

Galvin opened the door and walked out.

Stan saw him and stopped thirty feet away. He studied Galvin's face and realized Galvin was too old to be Alan Webster. But something about this man seemed distantly familiar to him. He carefully scrutinized Galvin's face, and he tried to remember where he might have met him.

Curious, Webster walked out, also holding a gun, and stood next to Galvin.

Stan stared searchingly at Webster's face and asked, "What's with all the guns?"

Galvin smirked. "Protection. We're real isolated out here."

Although Stan could recognize no resemblance to himself in the newcomer's face, he said, "If you're Alan Webster, I need to give you this." He saw that this man was well over six feet tall and muscular.

Stan extended his arm while still staring at Webster's face. Stan was disappointed as he saw the resemblance between Alan and Oscar Webster. This was no son of his—he was certain of it—but at least he'd be able to give Alan a memento of his father.

Webster stepped forward and saw his father's name on the bracelet. He squinted at it and appeared dumbfounded.

Stan saw his expression. "I served with Oscar. He would've wanted you to have it."

Stan removed the bracelet and held it out toward Webster. Webster took the bracelet and solemnly slipped it on his own wrist.

Webster asked, "How'd you find me?"

"I found your tattooed friend, Herrmann."

Galvin turned to Webster. "Who's this Herrmann guy, and how would he know about this place?"

Chagrined, Webster answered, "When I first decided to come here, I didn't know what I was getting into. I told my friend that if I didn't contact him within twenty-four hours, he was to call the cops. I called him the next day and told him to forget about it. Seemed like a good idea before I met you. You know…just in case."

Galvin took several deep breaths. If this Herrmann guy had told this puny man where Webster was, would he tell anyone else?

But Webster beat him to the punch. He asked Stan, "Why would he tell you about this place?"

"I convinced him that I merely wanted to give his son…you… this bracelet."

"Who'd you tell you were coming here?" Webster asked.

"Absolutely no one."

"What's your name?"

"Stan Urbanski. Your father was a hero. As a kid, I lost my dad, a bomber pilot, in the Korean War, so we're sort of connected, maybe in more ways than one."

Webster nodded. "Except fucking Vietnam made me an orphan. Destroyed her too."

Galvin was surprised by the mention of Stan's name. He stepped right in front of Stan and said, "Stan Urbanski. Holy shit. You don't remember me, do you?"

A half smile crossed Stan's face. "When I first saw you, I knew I knew you from somewhere, but I can't recall where or when."

"Does the name Vance Galvin ring a bell?"

Stan's eyes opened wide. "From Hawaii!"

"Yeah, and you serving with Oscar is bullshit, isn't it?" Galvin knew he'd caught Stan in a lie, and he wondered about his motivation. Was Stan working with the police or the FBI?

Stan knew he had to tell the truth. "Look, everyone I asked about Oscar treated me better if I said I served with him. But I wore this bracelet until I learned that Oscar was pronounced KIA. On the internet, I read he had a son. I just felt I had to give the bracelet to him. I also read that Oscar married Beverly."

Webster was jarred at hearing his mother's name. "You knew my mother?"

"We met when I was on vacation in Hawaii, and a bunch of servicemen were there on leave for R & R."

From within the house, Allie shouted, "Help me! I've been kidnapped!"

Startled, Stan asked, "What's going on here?" He quickly breezed past Galvin and Webster and headed for the front door. Galvin pointed his gun at Stan, ready to shoot. Webster grabbed Galvin's arm to stall him, and he yelled at Stan, who was nearing the door, "Stop or we'll shoot!"

Stan ignored Webster's threat and continued toward the door. Stan muttered to himself, "Maybe *that's* why I'm here. Goodbye, my beautiful Kim. Goodbye, my little David."

Webster raised his gun and fired.

Stan grabbed his calf and went down at the doorway.

Webster explained the intentional miss to Galvin. "He knew my parents."

Galvin said, "I'm real touched. He should be dead." But Galvin let Stan live out of deference to Webster—at least for the time being.

Allie heard the shot and feared for the worst. Maybe her call for help had made them kill whoever was out there. What if it was Tim? *Dear God*, she thought. *Don't let it be Tim.*

Galvin told Red and Suggs to bring Stan into the house.

They picked up the moaning and bleeding Stan and dragged him into Allie's room, followed by Galvin and Webster.

Allie nervously asked, "What's going on here? And who's that?" She was relieved to see it wasn't Tim.

The men ignored her as Webster tied a rag around Stan's injured calf and leaned him against the wall opposite the foot of the bed.

All the men except Webster left the room. Stan was in pain but managed to ask Webster, "What's…going on?"

Webster said, "Tell me about my father."

Stan looked at Allie. "And who is she?"

Allie blurted, "They're planning to overthrow the government."

Stan said quietly to Webster, "Our fathers died defending it."

Galvin walked back in with a pair of handcuffs, handed them to Webster, and said, "Cuff him to that pipe and then come on out. We've got things to discuss."

Webster cuffed Stan's left wrist to a water pipe that ran along the floor and said, "I'll talk to you later." He left the room.

With her wrist still cuffed to the bedpost, Allie gently asked, "Are you okay?"

Stan nodded, put his head back against the wall, and thought how disappointed he was. He'd found Alan, knew he wasn't his son, and was now involved in something he never could have imagined.

"I'm Allie Sommers. Who are you, and why are you here?"

Stan groaned. "Stan Urbanski. I only wanted to give Alan Webster his father's bracelet. Seems I got a lot more than I bargained for. If I didn't know his father and mother, I'd probably be dead by now. But what's your story? And were you serious when you said these ragtag imbeciles were going to overthrow the US government?"

"It's not just them. I heard they've got hundreds of men."

Stan rubbed his injured leg. "Interesting. Galvin and Oscar actually spoke about the overthrow of the government way back near the end of the Vietnam War. I can't believe he's still at it. But why are you here?"

"My boyfriend's father was originally part of Galvin's group. He changed his name from Frank Valone—"

"Hey, I knew Frank back then too. Where's Frank now?"

"Killed by muggers."

"Sorry to hear that. I liked Frank. He seemed somewhat less than enthusiastic about overthrowing the government. Galvin was pretty persuasive, but I was a lawyer and thought they were just making idle conversation."

"You're a lawyer?"

"Not a very good one, unfortunately."

Allie glanced at the open door and said softly, "Listen, we've got to figure a way out of here, or we're both going to be killed. They'll probably only shoot you. Me they've got other plans for first." She hoped Stan might have help on the way or that he'd have some kind of plan.

Stan understood her plea. But at the moment, he saw no way out, and mostly he didn't care. He laid his head back, closed his eyes, and dreamed of a time when life had appeared wonderfully full of promise.

Allie saw that this lawyer, handcuffed and with a wounded leg, would probably be no help. Her momentary hope at having an ally turned once again to despondence.

CHAPTER 32

MICK WAS SLOUCHED IN his seat with his hands covering his head. They were still driving on Route 65, and Tim was still hoping Mick would remember where to go.

Mick squirmed as "Paint It Black" by the Rolling Stones played. Then he sat up straight as something from the song jogged his memory.

Tim was still naming every bird he could think of. "Cockatiel, pelican, sapsucker…fuck!" Tim was near tears in frustration. They would never find Allie at this rate.

"Wait!" Mick shouted. "Only it wasn't a bird. It was the Black Crane Motel. The name always reminded me of a bird, but they had this rusted old crane on the property that was too expensive to move. So they painted it black and hung a sign from it."

"Call information." Tim handed the cell phone to Mick.

Mick stared at it sheepishly. "Ain't never used one."

He handed it back to Tim. Tim dialed, waited, and said, "Yeah, the Black Crane Motel, Northern Virginia." A few moments later, he ended the call, banged the steering wheel, and exclaimed, "Shit! No listing."

"Someone around here's gotta remember that crane."

"That's if your mind isn't playing psychedelic tricks on you." Tim hoped Mick wasn't leading him on a wild-goose chase.

Mick slumped in his seat. He prayed he was correct. He didn't think he could withstand the effects of the guilt if he couldn't remember enough to find Allie. He had lived a long time with the guilt of what had happened to Sara. It had been one of the last straws that had put him over the edge all those years ago.

An hour later, as dusk neared, Galvin stood speaking in front of a dozen men in the main room of the farmhouse. "With God's grace, when we meet tomorrow night, America will be free from the mongrels that defile our white heritage."

The men were captivated by Galvin's charismatic presence. "Charles Darwin wrote a book about a hundred and fifty years ago in which he described how things change over time due to what he called the survival of the fittest. Gentlemen, we will soon demonstrate that we, the white Christian race, are the fittest, and it is we who will survive and change the world!"

The men were mesmerized by Galvin. His pep talk had emboldened them, and they believed anything was possible.

Galvin ended the meeting with a Nazi salute. The men saluted back and filed out, leaving only Galvin and Red.

Galvin told Red, "I'll be back as soon as I get things rolling at the warehouse."

Red smiled. "The bitch is in tender, lovin' hands."

Galvin walked out. Tim was not responding to his demands, so it didn't matter if Red took advantage of the girl. She would have to be killed soon anyway.

Red felt his penis begin to swell at the thought of fondling Allie's breasts again. He could hardly wait to see what the rest of her looked like with no clothes on, and the image of a naked Allie fully aroused him. He was certain she was a peach, one ready to be plucked. He envisioned his cock in her mouth and between those lovely breasts. He could hardly wait to be alone with her. He knew she'd put up a huge fight, but he had a plan that would make his conquest simple.

Tim's car pulled into a gas station. He got out and quickly approached the attendant, a man who appeared to be in his midseventies. The attendant eyed Mick's attire curiously. Mick flashed the peace sign at him.

Tim asked, "You ever hear of the Black Crane Motel?"

"Sure have. Stayed there a couple of times when I was younger. Know what I mean?" The attendant winked at Tim, looked back at Mick sitting in the car, and then asked, "You boys goin' to a costume party?"

Tim ignored the question. "I believe it might be closed. Where would that place be?"

The old attendant pointed down the road. "Five miles, turn right on 76 for ten more miles. Motel's gone, but that crane's still there. Lookin' to buy an old crane?"

"Not today."

Tim ran back to the car and drove off as Mick again flashed the peace sign at the attendant. The old man scratched his head as the car disappeared down the road.

Allie, still cuffed, was resting on the bed when Red, clearly drunk, appeared in the doorway.

Stan, still in pain and also still cuffed, watched from the floor a few feet away. Stan knew it was best to keep his mouth shut.

"What do *you* want?" Allie asked, putting as much venom in her voice as she could.

Red picked at a tooth with a toothpick. "Pretty tough, tied up and all. Thought you might like the company of a man." He spat a piece of food onto the floor.

Chin up, she said, "When you see one, send him in."

Red's face turned sour. "Real funny, bitch. Ya know, your loyal dog came right back, so I gutted him." Then he mockingly said, "Run, Toto, run!"

She didn't really believe him, but just the possibility of him having killed Fletcher made her wish she could gut Red.

He approached the bed.

Allie clenched her teeth and raged, "I'll scratch your eyes out, you bastard!"

"I can take what I want, tasty thing." He envisioned himself tearing all her clothes off.

"That's what you think, moron." She gritted her teeth and clenched her fists.

"Let's see. I get the ether, you sleep like a baby and wake up with a sore pussy and maybe a little salty taste in your mouth. Think about that." He grabbed his crotch and began to rub it.

Disgusted, Allie spoke in her stage voice, "All this is worse than the furnace in the Bible that was heated seven times."

Red was confused, but he continued rubbing his groin. "More Bible shit? Does my cock bring back juicy memories of Daddy?"

Stan had been watching and listening and decided he'd seen and heard enough. He scowled at Red. "Your memories of *your* father must be of him sticking his dick up your ass."

Red walked to Stan and, without saying a word, kicked him in the jaw. Stan slumped to the side, stunned. Red smiled, looked back at Allie, and winked at her. He then sauntered out.

Allie yanked on the handcuffs. Images of that cretin doing anything he wanted to her unconscious body almost made her vomit. She could taste the bile that was welling up in her throat, and she vowed to fight as hard as she could, feeling a sudden adrenaline rush. She braced herself for the bastard's return.

Red soon returned holding a rag in one hand and a bottle in the other. His face bore a sick smile; he was savoring the moment.

In singsong fashion, Red announced, "Time for the doctor's medicine."

He walked toward the bed and stood out of Allie's reach. Stan was beginning to stir again on the floor.

Allie tensed up and yanked hard on the handcuffs. "The others will be back any minute." She hoped that someone would return and put Red in his place.

Red burst out with a mocking laugh. "Where you been, girl? When they come back, they might wanna take their turns. You're gonna have a cock in every hole in your skinny body."

Allie trembled. She clenched her teeth and fists and fiercely yanked at the handcuffs as Red poured some ether onto the rag.

Allie braced herself for what she feared would be a fight for her life.

Tim and Mick pulled up to what remained of the Black Crane Motel—the huge black crane.

Mick thought and then said, "You go maybe a dozen klicks. Should be a dirt road on the right.

Tim put the car in gear and gunned the engine.

Tim was worried. He knew that Mick could easily be wrong. Maybe there would be no farmhouse, and even if it was there, Allie could be somewhere else. And if she was actually at this farmhouse, they would most likely be outmanned and outgunned. Still, Tim was on autopilot. Nothing and no one would change his present course.

CHAPTER 33

RED WAS HAVING fun tormenting Allie as he let the anticipation build. He waved the rag in front of her. "Ooowee. Gonna have me some prime meat for dinner. And am I hungry."

With her free hand, Allie pointed at him. "Come any closer and I'll kick the shit out of you, you degenerate," she shouted.

Stan rubbed his hand across his face and eyes in an effort to revive himself. He knew what Red intended to do, and it sickened him, but he felt powerless to help. He tried his best to think of some way to stop Red.

Still in a mocking voice, Red said, "Sticks and stones may break my boner, but ether will put you to sleep."

Red leaped on top of Allie, who kicked and scratched. He struggled to grab her free wrist and hold it down while trying to cover her face with the rag. She squirmed and fought hard against him, trying to buck him off. The fact that Red was drunk didn't help him. He struggled to apply the rag to her mouth and nose, but she was stronger than he'd thought, and she punched and clawed at him with her nails as an attempt to slash his face.

With his free hand, Stan removed both his shoes and threw them at Red, one at a time. The first one hit Red in the back, and he ignored it. The second one hit Red's head. Red turned toward Stan, and as he did, Allie punched Red in the jaw, knocking him off the bed.

A chagrined Red got up and began to kick Stan violently while screaming at him that he was lucky he didn't put a bullet in his head.

Stan attempted to block the kicks with his free hand and one good leg, but some of the blows got through. Stan tried to fight back, but with one arm handcuffed and one leg badly injured, he could do no more than try to fend off some of the blows. The thought raced through Stan's mind that if he had to die, this shouldn't be the way it happened.

Allie picked up one of Stan's shoes and threw it at Red, but it missed, and Red continued to kick Stan. Allie began to cry for Stan, and she shouted, "Leave him alone!" But Red continued his assault until Stan was unconscious.

Red was exhausted from his struggle with Allie and from kicking Stan. He turned and hollered at a defiant-looking Allie, "I'll get you later, and I won't be as nice to you as I was to that shithead." He pointed at Stan, and then he stormed out.

Allie's fight with Red bolstered her spirits at least temporarily. She knew this had been only a small skirmish. Her war was yet to come, and she began to steel herself in preparation for it.

After a few miles, Mick recalled that he would recognize the dirt road by a large rock at the side of the road near the mailbox.

Mick said, "Slow down."

Tim silently prayed that Mick knew where he was going, and that somehow they'd find Allie and rescue her. But as they approached, Tim began to think more rationally about the situation. He knew that if they were totally outnumbered, the prudent thing would be to call Agent Barnes.

Mick blurted out, "There it is. The road is just past that old mailbox."

"You're certain?"

"I recognize that big rock." He pointed at a six-foot-wide granite boulder that had been deposited there with other debris from a melting glacier of the last ice age.

"Okay." Tim took a deep breath. "Here goes nothing."

Tim cautiously turned the car up the dirt road past the mailbox.

Mick bit into his lip, having mixed emotions. He both wanted and didn't want to find Allie. Who knew what fate the end of that road might bring? What if he came face-to-face with Galvin again? He recalled what Galvin had done to poor Sara and why Galvin despised him so much. He shuddered just thinking about it.

Mick turned to Tim. "This is definitely the road to the farm-house." Unexpectedly, he said, "Let me out and then drive real slow."

Mick opened his door even before Tim began to stop the car. Tim immediately slammed on his brakes, but Mick rushed out before Tim could ask why. Mick quickly disappeared into the woods.

Tim was now worried more than ever. Where the hell had Mick gone, and why had he suddenly jumped out of the car? Had he cracked up again, or did he have some kind of plan? Was Mick afraid to face what might be waiting for them at the farmhouse?

With great apprehension, Tim continued to drive slowly up the narrow dirt road, his eyes darting from left to right at the thick foliage.

A minute later, a man jumped in front of the car and pointed a gun at Tim.

Tim was startled at the sight of the gun. But far worse was the fact that he'd been caught, and now his plan to save Allie was ruined. Maybe he'd even be tortured and killed, just like Sam. He felt the perspiration welling up under his armpits. He thought of putting the car in reverse and attempting to back down the long and winding narrow dirt road, but he quickly dropped the idea as Suggs ran to the driver's side window with his gun pointed directly at Tim's face.

Suggs shouted, "Get out and put your hands where I can see 'em."

Tim remembered the searing pain from the bullet that grazed his side. The dread he felt wasn't only for himself but also for Allie. He began to concoct some way to disarm this man as he opened the door and climbed out of the car.

As soon as Tim got out of the car, he recognized Suggs as one of the men who had killed Sam and tried to kidnap him and Allie. He stood facing Suggs and his gun, and he wondered what might happen next. Although the gun was still pointed at him, he now felt no trepidation, as his primal instincts and desire to rescue Allie overcame his fear. His hatred for one of the men who had killed Sam spurred him to plan on taking action.

Suggs's eyes opened wide as he recognized Tim. "Holy shit! It's you."

Tim stared at Suggs's gun. The gun should have frightened Tim, but all he could think about was taking revenge for Sam and, more importantly, rescuing Allie.

Suggs shouted, "Put your hands on top of your head and turn around."

But before Tim could do so, Mick emerged silently from the thick underbrush only a few feet behind Suggs.

Suggs took a step toward Tim, and seeing that Tim hadn't followed his command, he yelled, "I said, turn around and—"

Mick struck the back of Suggs's head with a large rock. Mick had held nothing back, using both hands to strike a powerful blow. Suggs went down, unconscious, with blood gushing from the back of his head.

Tim breathed a huge sigh of relief as Mick kicked Suggs's gun to the side and then began to take Suggs's belt off. Mick used the belt to tie Suggs's hands behind his back. He then dragged Suggs into the woods, out of sight. Mick grabbed hold of some long, thick vines, and he broke off some strands. He used the vines to tie Suggs's feet together.

Tim was impressed by Mick's quick actions and ingenuity.

Mick stood up and looked at Tim. "Always had a lookout."

"I'm glad you remembered. And that was one hell of a shot that scumbag took from you. Is he dead?" Tim hoped the son of a bitch was. He thought of Sam's body lying dead in a puddle of blood.

"Unfortunately, he still has a pulse. That's why I tied him up, but he'll be out for quite some time…I guarantee it."

Tim muttered to himself, "Too bad."

Mick picked up Suggs's gun and placed it under his jacket. The two got back into the car, and Tim began again to drive slowly up the dirt road. Both men cautiously surveyed the road ahead.

Tim asked, "How much trouble do you think we're in for?"

"No way to tell, but at least I got this gun, and I know how to use it." Mick knew that if the time came to kill someone, especially someone who deserved it, he wouldn't hesitate. His experience in Vietnam made sure of that. He'd shoot fast and shoot to kill.

Tim couldn't remember Mick sounding more confident. But Tim was anything but confident. "What if there's another lookout? And what if there are too many of them for us to go against?"

Mick thought for a moment. "They always had only one spot for any lookouts. And if there are a lot of them up ahead, we'll know by the number of cars and trucks parked outside. If we see too many, we can turn around and call the cops."

At that moment, Tim was regretting traveling up this narrow road. Maybe they should turn around and call the authorities right now. But the thought of wasting valuable time in finding Allie was enough to spur him on. And he wasn't certain if this place warranted a call to the police or FBI. Tim continued to slowly drive the narrow road with his eyes darting from side to side, carefully surveying the surroundings.

Mick told Tim to park the car about a hundred yards from the farmhouse, just around a bend in the road, but to turn the car around so it was facing their escape route. That way they wouldn't have to turn around or back up down the road later, in case they needed to make a quick escape. Tim parked the car along the tree line out of sight. He was impressed by Mick's abilities, and he thought that serving in the military must have had at least some good effects on Mick.

They exited the car and began to walk slowly up the road. After about fifty yards, they were able to see the farmhouse. Only one car was parked at the side of the house.

Mick softly said, "That's a real good sign."

Tim wasn't certain this meant there would be little resistance in the farmhouse. Maybe half a dozen men were using the one vehicle.

Seeing no one waiting outside, they stealthily crept to the rear of the house, crouched under a window, and peeked into the main room. They spotted Red walking into the room.

Tim reflexively tensed up and whispered, "That's the other guy who killed Sam." Tim's blood began to boil as he recalled Red pressing his gun between Allie's legs.

Mick quietly replied, "We don't know how many others might be inside. And we don't even know if Allie's there."

Tim knew Mick was right, but he also knew he had to continue his search. "Let's sneak around the house and look in all the windows. If you spot any trouble, I hope you remember how to use that gun."

Mick patted the gun and confidently replied, "I know how to use it."

Still crouching, they carefully made their way to the side of the farmhouse and peered into another window. Seeing no one, they went to still another window, where they saw Allie handcuffed to the bed. She was there, and she was alive!

Without thought, and to Mick's surprise, Tim ran around to the front door and burst through it. Red turned at the sound of the door crashing open, but his face was met by Tim's foot. Tim struck Red again and again with his fists and feet. Red attempted to reach for the gun in his belt behind his back, but Tim tripped him. Red landed on his stomach. Tim tore the gun from Red's belt and threw it across the room. Tim's rage was now beyond control. Sitting on Red's back, he grabbed Red's long hair and pounded his head onto the hard wooden floor until Red stopped moving. It was the second time Tim had pummeled Red, and Red lay unconscious on the floor.

Allie had heard Red's screams, and she knew something bad was happening to him, which she quickly prayed would be good news. She shouted from the next room, and Tim ran to her. His face fell—she looked wretched. But Allie's spirits soared upon seeing Tim. It was as if the weight of a cement block had been lifted from her chest.

"Thank God you're here!" Tears flowed down her cheeks. "But they'll be back soon." She hesitated and delicately added, "Including Vance Galvin." She watched for his reaction.

But Tim merely replied, "I know. We almost ran into him at Mick's hospital. He was obviously looking for Mick, but Mick's with me outside."

Tim was ecstatic at finding her, but he knew there was no time to celebrate. "Is anyone else here?"

Allie pointed at Stan. "Only the guy handcuffed on the floor."

Tim glanced at Stan and then at Allie. He stared at her handcuffs and quickly asked, "Where's the key?"

Allie appeared suddenly crestfallen. "Oh my God! One of the others has it." She envisioned herself trapped like a mouse in a snake's terrarium, ready to be swallowed whole.

"Shit!" Tim exclaimed. He tried yanking on the cuffs, but he quickly realized he wouldn't be able to break them or the headboard. He pivoted around the room, desperately searching for something to use. He heard Stan groaning on the floor, but his mind was focused on freeing Allie.

Mick appeared at the bedroom door carrying a rifle. "I tied up the son of a bitch in the other room. More guns around here than Parris Island." He looked at Tim and said, "Step aside."

As Mick placed the barrel of the rifle against the chain between the cuffs, Tim apprehensively asked, "Do you know what you're doing?"

Mick looked back at Tim and asked, "You got a better idea?"

Tim shook his head and stood back.

Now Allie nervously asked, "Are you sure you know what you're doing?"

"Gotta get you loose. Have no fear. Look away."

Allie turned her head to the side and closed her eyes.

Mick fired. The rifle's blast resounded through the room, causing Allie and Tim to flinch, but the chain snapped.

Allie was still crying as she leaped from the bed into Tim's arms. One half of the handcuffs would have to remain as a bracelet on her wrist, at least for the time being.

The blast made Stan begin to stir. They heard him moaning at the foot of the bed, and they noticed the blood-soaked rag wrapped around his calf.

Tim asked, "Who's that?"

She turned toward a pathetic-looking Stan. "He tried to help me, so they shot him, and then he tried to keep Red off me, so Red kicked the crap out of him."

Mick pointed at her taped finger, and then Tim noticed it.

"What happened?" he asked. He hadn't yet realized the permanent damage they had done to her finger.

Through tears, Allie tried to force a smile. "They said I only needed nine fingers to play the piano." She hoped her disfigurement wouldn't make her any less attractive to Tim.

"They cut off your finger?" Tim became incensed. He kicked a chair across the room. "Motherfuckers! Why'd they do that?" He envisioned himself slitting their throats. He felt as though he was going to hyperventilate.

Through misty eyes, she said, "They said they were giving it to the police with a note saying that more parts would follow unless you gave them the information they wanted. What did the police tell you?"

Tim breathed deeply and answered, "They told me nothing." Tim thought for a moment. "The bastards. They want the information for themselves and were willing to let them cut you up so I wouldn't give it to these guys here." Tim then apprehensively asked, "They do...anything else to you?"

"The asshole inside tried to," she said with a hint of pride in her voice.

"How'd ya stop him?" Mick asked.

Allie thought for a second and then proudly answered, "I became Saint Joan of Arc. Played her in college. Strong woman." Tears were still streaming down her cheeks.

Tim smiled sadly and then tenderly kissed her wrapped finger. They embraced warmly.

Mick said, "It ain't over yet. Grab as many guns as you can and get to the car. Be along in a jiff. I wanna leave a message for these bastards."

Mick walked over to Stan and shot off his handcuffs. Stan would also have to wear one cuff as a bracelet.

The proximity of the blast fully awakened Stan. He looked up groggily and asked, "Who are you?"

Tim answered, "It doesn't matter. We're here to help." He stared at Stan's bloody leg. "Can you stand up?"

"I think so, but might need a little help."

Tim helped Stan to his feet, and Stan leaned against the wall. Stan remarked, "We better get out of here soon. They're coming back."

Tim, Mick, and Allie gathered several pistols and rifles.

Tim ran to the parked car and drove it up to the farmhouse while Mick helped Stan limp out the door. They put Stan into the back seat and went back for the weapons and Allie.

Allie was carrying a rifle as she walked past Red. His hands and feet were tied with rope, and he was lying flat on his back. He had awakened, and his eyes were now wide open as blood seeped from his forehead. Red saw her walking by and spat in her direction.

Furious, Allie stopped in front of him, raised the butt of the rifle, and smashed it into Red's groin. Red shrieked and tried to cover his crotch with his tied hands. Mick saw her smash the rifle butt into his groin again. Red shrieked in agony as the rifle broke a couple of his fingers.

Allie screamed, "Fucking bastard!"

Mick dropped his weapons, grabbed her rifle, and stopped Allie as she was about to strike again. "Go. I'll take care of him," he sympathetically ordered.

Allie pulled her rifle back from Mick and stormed out the door, feeling a brief euphoric rush from having taken a modicum of revenge on the piece of shit.

Tim helped Allie into the front seat, and he got into the driver's seat. Stan was still slumped in the back seat, moaning.

Two seemingly interminable minutes passed. Tim and Allie strained to see where Mick was. Tim lit a cigarette. He smiled to himself. This time his hand was steady as a rock.

Tim blew smoke out the window and said, "Come on, come on. What the fuck's he doing back there?"

"Maybe he snapped," she answered. "Maybe he's waiting to kill them when they return, but there are dozens of them." She nervously twirled her fingers through her hair as she peered down the road, hoping they would get moving before the others arrived.

"Then he's Custer, and this is his last stand," Tim remarked.

From the back seat, Stan said, "And Sitting Bull is probably going to show up at any moment with his tribe. We're all going to die real soon."

"I'll give him another minute. Then I'm going back to see what the hell he's doing in there." He nervously tapped his fingers against the steering wheel.

Four cars loaded with Galvin and his men passed the black crane on their way to the farmhouse. Galvin and Webster were in the lead car with two other men in the backseat.

Webster had been wondering what to do with Stan and Allie. He believed Galvin didn't intend to hold them much longer, but he felt he had to ask. "What about the girl and Stan?"

Galvin had thought about them. "As soon as you get whatever information you want out of Stan, we've got to get rid of him. As far as the girl, if the cops or her boyfriend don't deal real soon, I'm gonna let Red, and anyone else who wants, do whatever they like with her. Then we bury her with Stan."

Webster agreed there was no other choice. He knew they had been drawn into this quite by accident, but he rationalized that these were only two of many who would die for their sacred cause.

Tim nervously scanned the area down the road. He knew Galvin and his men would have far more firepower than the few weapons they had taken.

Allie shifted uneasily in her seat. "Maybe Mick doesn't intend to return? Or maybe he's cracked up again?"

Tim said, "Something's wrong. I'm going back."

Allie said, "No! We have to get out or here." She grabbed his arm.

The rear door suddenly swung open, and Mick jumped into the backseat.

"Where the fuck you been?" said Tim.

"Had to wash up."

Tim shook his head and started the car. He headed as quickly as possible down the road, passing the spot where they had dragged the unconscious Suggs into the woods. He knew that the narrow dirt road would allow only one car to pass. If the others came that way, they would be trapped and would be forced to shoot it out with them. He prayed it wouldn't come to that as the car careened down the road.

Galvin's caravan was only half a mile from the dirt road as Tim's car arrived at the highway and turned toward the black crane.

Seconds later, Tim and Allie spotted several cars approaching from the opposite direction.

"That could be them," Allie fearfully said.

Tim shouted to everyone, "They know my car. Get down."

Allie and Mick slid down in their seats. Stan was already slumped over, out of sight. Tim grabbed the sun visor and swung it to cover the driver's side window. He hoped that they'd pay little attention to a car speeding by in the opposite direction.

Galvin's car was still leading the caravan of four. Galvin casually glanced at the passing vehicle with the lone driver. He did a double take as the car zoomed by, and then he shook his head, knowing it couldn't be anything. He spoke to the others in the car. "Must be getting antsy…so much at stake. I feel the weight of the entire Aryan nation on my shoulders."

Webster understood. "In one more day it'll all be lifted, and you'll be known as *der Führer*."

Tim breathed a sigh of relief. "It's them." Tim looked in the rearview mirror to see if they were turning around. Seeing the caravan continuing in the opposite direction, he asked, "Mick, what the hell did you do back there?"

"In 'Nam, I learned how to send messages."

"What kind of messages?"

"Messages the enemy tends to remember. Ones that say, 'You fucked with us. Now it's our turn to fuck with you.'"

Tim gave Allie a sideways glance and said, "Whatever you say, Mick. Whatever you say." At this point, the only thing that mattered was getting Allie back to safety. Revenge for her finger, and for putting her through so much, would have to wait.

CHAPTER 34

GALVIN'S CARAVAN OF FOUR cars turned up the dirt road. After a minute of driving slowly, they were surprised there was no sign of Suggs. Galvin remarked, "If Jim Suggs is drunk or asleep on the job, I'm gonna kick his ass from here to kingdom come."

Webster said, "Maybe he went back to the farmhouse to take a shit."

"Maybe. We'll soon see."

The caravan pulled up to the farmhouse. Fifteen men exited the cars and entered the house through the front door. Galvin had expected Red to be outside to greet them, and not seeing him, he strode into the bedroom. His eyes opened wide as he saw the broken handcuffs dangling from the bedpost and the pipe and no Allie or Stan in sight.

Galvin ran back to the main room and shouted, "They're gone! Anyone seen Red? And where's Suggs? He should've been at the road." Galvin became frantic as he wondered if the FBI had come and had arrested Suggs and Red. Maybe there was an ambush ready for them outside. Or maybe the cops or the feds were on their way to the farmhouse right now.

Several men scampered around the farmhouse. A few of them searched outside.

From the rear of the house, one of the men yelled, "Major, back here! Come quick!"

Galvin, Webster, and a few others ran to the back of the farm-house. Galvin stopped in his tracks, stared unblinking, and then slowly approached the object in question.

The men were stunned. One of them exclaimed, "What the fuck?"

Wedged on top of a broomstick stuck in the ground was the bloody severed head of Red. His open eyes stared blankly back at them.

The entire group stood in front of the pole and stared back, some mesmerized and some sickened by the ghoulishly fascinating sight.

Webster voiced all their thoughts. "Stan or the girl cut off his head?"

Galvin was deep in thought. Then a knowing smirk crossed his face. "No candy-ass lawyer or bitch did this. It's a message straight from hell."

They eyed Galvin curiously.

He didn't wait long to answer their unspoken question. "It says, 'Don't mess with me, motherfucker, or you're next.'"

"Connor did this?" Webster asked, incredulous.

Galvin shook his head. "I've seen this handiwork. Like Lazarus, I think my crazy friend Mick rose from the dead. We better burn the damn place to the ground. And find out where in hell Suggs is."

Webster took one last glance at Red's severed head before turn-ing away. Webster hadn't thought much of Red, but he knew he had been loyal to Galvin and the cause. He didn't believe Red deserved a gruesome beheading, and he wondered what kind of man or men they were now dealing with. The person or persons who could do this were apparently ones to be feared. Webster didn't know it, but Mick's message had a similar unnerving effect on all of them.

Two of the men drove a car down the road with their windows open, shouting for Suggs. Suggs had regained consciousness, and see-ing the car and hearing them calling his name, he shouted, "Over here. I'm over here."

They got Suggs back to the farmhouse, where he informed Galvin that he'd spotted Tim Connor driving a car alone, but that someone had hit him over the back of his head with something, possibly a rock.

This knowledge confirmed Galvin's suspicion that Mick was helping Connor since only Mick would have known that they always kept a lookout and where that lookout would be stationed. He knew that Mick had once been totally out to lunch, but maybe these many years had cured him enough to be of some aid to Tim Connor. He hated Mick for what he had done all those years ago almost as much as he had hated Frank. If Mick was here, Galvin vowed that Mick would regret this day in spades, especially for what he'd done to Red. Galvin knew Red was uneducated, but he'd taken Red under his wing and treated him almost as a son. Red was Galvin's most loyal man, and Red would have done anything to please him. Galvin became melancholy for the moment, thinking about his past losses, but he quickly recovered, knowing how much work lay before him and how important it was to the nation. Once he was in power, Galvin vowed to erect a statue in Red's honor.

The men torched the farmhouse after removing anything of value, and they drove away from the blazing structure, leaving Red's head stuck on the pole.

Tim's car turned onto a major highway. There were many cars and side streets, and they knew they were in the clear. Tim dialed the cell phone.

Barnes was urinating at a public restroom at FBI headquarters when his cell phone rang. He fumbled for the phone with his free hand. "Jesus fucking Christ. Can't even piss in peace." He managed to retrieve the phone and answered, "Hello."

"It's Tim Connor. I got Allie with me. You fuckers chose not to tell me about her finger, didn't you?" He made no attempt to hide his anger.

An embarrassed Barnes responded, "Look, I know how you feel, but understand that we're also trying to protect our government and maybe even the president himself. I'm sorry about her finger, but it somehow worked out, didn't it?"

"No thanks to you guys." He was angry, but he knew he needed their help.

Barnes happily changed the subject. "So what information do you have for us?"

"For one thing, I know where their headquarters is."

Barnes listened to the directions as he tried to zip his fly and hold the phone with his chin. "How many and how much firepower?"

"Dozens, and tons of firepower."

"Where are you now?"

"Don't worry about it. Just find these cocksuckers." Tim gave him the address and directions, and then he ended the call.

Barnes rushed out and raced down the hall. He had much to prepare.

Twenty minutes later, Tim, Allie, Mick, and Stan were still in the car eating fast-food burgers and drinks. It was after sundown, and they were parked in the Burger King parking lot with the car illuminated by the lot's overhead lights.

A young man, who looked like he must have just gotten his first driver's license, sat in the car next to theirs on Mick's side. The teenager and his two friends stared at Mick and laughed. Mick saw them, smiled back at them, and flashed the peace sign. The teenager gave Mick the finger.

Mick opened his window and yelled out, "Screw you, man."

Tim wheeled around in his seat and said, "Don't make a scene."

The boy got out of his car, stood next to Mick's window, and said, "What did you say?"

Instead of Mick, Tim got out of the car and faced the boy. He spoke very softly so that only the boy, and not his friends, could hear. "You got one chance to back off gracefully before I embarrass you in front of your friends."

Tim's tone and self-assured manner made the boy back down. The boy puffed his chest out, gestured in face-saving bravado, and then returned to his car, where he high-fived with his two friends.

Tim got back in the car.

Allie gave him a half smile. "Nice poker face."

Tim breathed a sigh of relief and bit into his burger. He swallowed and asked, "Where's Fletcher?"

Allie felt a lump in her throat. "That cretin Red said he killed him, but I'm not sure. I pray he's okay."

Her eyes welled up, and she changed the subject. "I'm sure the bastards will be gone by the time the FBI gets there."

"Did you hear any of their discussions?" Tim asked.

"They were going to use me as target practice for their dicks and then kill me. They didn't care what I heard." The surreal image of her finger lying on the table sped through her, and she momentarily felt like she was teetering on the edge of a forty-story rooftop, ready to fall to her death, grasping wildly at nothing but thin air.

Tim slowly shook his head and said softly, "Motherfuckers. Did you hear anything important?"

She gripped the edge of her seat as if catching her balance. Exhaling loudly, she said, "I don't know the details, but it involves hundreds and maybe thousands of crazies. Kept talking about taking back America for the white race. I heard one of them mention bringing down the government in one fell swoop. They all think God is on their side."

From the back seat, Stan said, "During the Civil War, Lincoln said something like, 'We shouldn't ask if God is on our side, but rather we should ask if our actions show that we are on God's side.'"

Allie remarked, "Great quote. I doubt God believes these low-lifes are on his side."

Tim finished his burger and grabbed Allie's half-eaten one.

Mick said, "Back then, we believed that with enough chaos, the government would either change or get voted out during the next election. The driving forces of that protest movement were radicals led by children of the elite who trashed their college degrees and hung posters of Che Guevara and Mao on their walls."

"And these militia guys?" Tim asked. He glanced at Mick's half-eaten sandwich. "Gonna eat that?"

Mick handed his wrapper to Tim.

Tim bit into the burger as Mick continued, "From what I been reading, these are more like janitors and Army veterans...publish half-literate newsletters under the logos of American revolutionary soldiers. The revolution of the sixties was run from the cities. This one's run from rural areas. We linked our fight against the war with fighting racism. Today, all they talk about is some bullshit white supremacy."

Allie and Tim were surprised by Mick's knowledge. Allie asked, "How do you know so much?"

Mick understood their skepticism, knowing his past history. "I became crazy from the war and stuff I saw after. I was a smart college graduate who went in believing in the war and came out knowing it was the devil's playground. Took me almost forty years to get back to some kind of sanity. I've had nothing but time on my hands for a very long time. You can read a lot of stuff when there's nothin' else to do."

"So what do you think they'll try to do?" Tim asked.

Mick shrugged. "They ain't waitin' around for the next election. They're planning on taking out persons of power. Maybe even the president."

As the teenager and his friends pulled out of the parking space, the boy gave them the finger again, which they ignored.

Allie brushed her hair from her face and asked, "Would that bring down the government? Four presidents have been assassinated before, and nothing terrible happened."

"Maybe," Mick surmised, "they intend to waste a whole lot more than the president. If they can coordinate the underground militia, maybe they can synchronize hundreds of assassinations."

"Doesn't seem possible," Tim said.

Stan had been listening to the conversation and added, "When they shot Lincoln, they also planned to kill the vice president and secretary of state." Stan groaned in pain from the wound in his leg but was able to continue. "They hanged a bunch of coconspirators of John Wilkes Booth, including one woman."

A thought bolted through Allie. "State. They mentioned the State of the Union address!"

"It's tomorrow night," Mick said. "Everyone'll be there…one fell swoop, remember? Maybe this will help." Mick pulled out a map from his pocket and unfolded it on the car seat. It was the map Galvin had pinned to his wall.

"Look at this." Mick pointed at the letters *MVIEVTZHRMYFMPVI.* "In Vietnam, Galvin always wrote in code for something important, and sometimes just for the fun of it, but I can't remember what the code was. But maybe it's nothin'."

Stan groaned again, and Tim said, "Let's get Stan to a hospital and go to my motel room…see if anything else in that box makes sense."

Allie turned around in her seat and looked at Stan. "I never thanked you, especially for having better aim with shoes than me. But why were you there?"

Stan became choked up and seemed to ramble. "The past is always safer than the future. My father bravely gave his life, and I almost wasted mine. I'm a grandpa. I gotta live!"

"Your wound's not really that bad," she said soothingly.

Stan looked at her and said, "Not what I meant."

The three others were caught up in the moment, and no one questioned his meaning.

They dropped Stan off at the nearest hospital. They left it up to Stan to explain his handcuff bracelet and the events that had transpired.

Although shot and wounded, Stan felt exhilarated. He had endured so much at that farmhouse, and yet he hadn't felt this good in a long time. He thought to himself, *Empowered—that's how I feel.* He felt he was now in charge. He could still kill himself at any time if he chose to do so. But he now longed to see Kim and little David so much that it hurt far more than his wounds.

CHAPTER 35

AT SEVEN THAT EVENING, ten FBI vehicles with their high beams on drove warily down the dirt road. The men saw black smoke rising in the distance, eerily lit by smoldering embers flickering like fireflies.

Barnes was expecting no resistance since he figured they would have vacated the premises once Tim rescued Allie, but still Barnes's caravan moved cautiously toward the smoke.

Barnes thought that maybe they intended to make a stand and fight it out like at Waco and Ruby Ridge, since Tim had informed him they had dozens of men and plenty of firepower. In 1992, Ruby Ridge in northern Idaho was the site of a deadly confrontation and siege between the Randy Weaver family and federal agents, including members of the FBI, that resulted in the death of Weaver's son and wife. Randy Weaver had refused an offer to become an informant in exchange for dismissal of charges of possession of illegal weapons. Public outcry over Ruby Ridge and the subsequent Waco siege helped to fuel the militia movement.

A police helicopter's engines could be heard droning overhead, and its pilot was to radio Barnes if he spotted trouble. Instead, Barnes heard the pilot saying, "I can only make out lots of smoke from a burned house situated in a clearing, but I can't see through the surrounding pine trees. Just be careful."

"We'll proceed with due caution," Barnes responded.

Two minutes later, they stopped in front of the smoldering remains of the razed farmhouse. Only the ruined stone fireplace and chimney remained.

Barnes and the other agents prudently exited their vehicles with guns drawn, and they began to search the area. Many of the men wore riot gear with plastic face guards and bulletproof vests.

The rising smoke blocked their view to the back of the farmhouse. Several agents made their way around the smoke toward the rear.

Seconds later, one agent shouted, "Look at this, back here."

Barnes and several agents rushed to the rear of the farmhouse. Twenty feet beyond the destroyed building was the stake with Red's head still stuck on top.

Barnes grimaced at the ghoulish sight and said almost to himself, "Sure as shit hope that's not a lawman."

The other agents gazed at the frightful visage. An agent asked no one in particular, "Who the hell would do this, and why?"

Barnes spoke up first. "It's a scare tactic meant to demoralize your enemy. I never saw this in Vietnam, but heard that this kind of thing was done by both the Viet Cong and Americans, warning each other that this could happen to you."

The agents stared at Red's head as if hypnotized until Barnes said, "See if you can find the body. It might be among the wreckage. And who knows, maybe some other bodies too. And search for anything that might remain that can tell us something about these creeps."

The agents began to search among the wreckage for bodies and clues of any kind.

Two dozen men led by Galvin stood in the middle of the warehouse, which was now a dimly lit munitions dump. Webster and the leaders of the other three militias—Brown, Stern, and Tyler—were there as well.

Galvin addressed the group. "We lose nothing as long as we keep Tim Connor on the run for another twenty-four hours. Of course, if we can catch Tiny Tim and his elves, we will."

Everyone laughed except Webster, who stood stone-faced. This business of finding Tim Connor had been about more than just locating Frank Valone's information, and it bothered him that Galvin had kept that knowledge to himself.

Galvin continued, "Got men watching the police, the FBI, and every other place they might show up. And when they do, we're taking no prisoners."

One man asked, "Ain't Tim Connor your son?"

Galvin contemplated his answer and said, "Genetically speaking, yes."

The men were awestruck by Galvin's apparent sacrifice. They saluted Galvin Nazi style while Webster smirked disdainfully.

The group shouted, "To Vance Galvin!"

Galvin showed no reaction. He had only known a cute little two-year-old named Timmy Galvin. This grown man named Tim Connor wasn't really his son. He'd been raised by Frank Valone, and Tim had believed that Frank—Dan Connor—was his father. He thought, *The men here don't realize how easy it would be for me to kill Frank's adopted son and send him to hell to meet with Frank.*

CHAPTER 36

TIM, ALLIE, AND Mick drove back to Tim's motel room. Allie was concerned about Stan, who had acted peculiarly during the drive. "I hope Stan will be okay. I think all those kicks to his head may have done something to him."

Tim said, "The hospital will take good care of him."

Allie turned around in her seat and spoke to Mick. "I wish you'd let me bust that bastard's balls. Why'd you stop me?"

Mick thought for a moment. "You don't need nothin' on your conscience. Believe me, I know about conscience."

Allie stared at Mick. Maybe he was right. But she hoped Red would get what was coming to him one day.

A while later, Allie and Mick sat on the bed looking at the contents of the metal box. Tim had left to bring back drinks and snacks.

Although exhausted, Allie was able to muster enough strength to question Mick and try to make him recall anything that could be of help.

She pointed at the photos and papers. "Come on, Mick. Something here has got to lead to something we can use."

Mick pouted. "If it'll make you happy, I'll look again."

Mick examined each photograph and document on the bed. He picked up one of Dan Connor's handwritten notes, and he was reading it when the door to the motel room swung open.

Tim rushed in with Fletcher in his arms.

Allie's jaw dropped, and she screamed, "Fletch!"

She leaped from the bed, ran to Tim, and grabbed Fletcher, smothering him with hugs and kisses. Fletcher licked her face excitedly with his tail wagging a mile a minute.

Allie said, "I thought you went for food."

"On my way a thought occurred to me. You said Fletcher ran out of the room. I figured that the only place Fletcher could be waiting for you was at the motel. I called there, and the manager had him."

She continued to hug an excited Fletcher.

Tim looked at Mick, who was examining a piece of paper.

Mick said, "It's not much, but Frank wrote about some corporation he helped form."

"Corporation? My father?"

"It wasn't IBM," Mick said flatly. "Just a dummy corporation called Bunker Hill that could buy things so nothin' could be traced to any individual. Maybe it still owns stuff."

"He's a genius," Allie said as she put Fletcher onto the floor. "Maybe it still owns property, you mean?"

"Worth a try," Mick answered.

Allie suggested, "We might be able to research this Bunker Hill."

Mick appeared not to hear her. He was sitting on his bed staring at the map and scratching his head, focusing on the block letters written on Galvin's map.

Tim said, "According to Sam"—he paused and took a deep breath as mentioning Sam's name raised a plethora of emotions—"sales of property have to be recorded for tax purposes, and it's public record."

Tim turned to Mick, who was staring at Galvin's map. "What are you looking at?"

"These letters gotta be somethin' simple. Galvin used them to confuse the Viet Cong in case we were caught." He scratched his head. "But I just can't seem to connect the dots." Mick turned to Allie. "So how can we get information on the properties?" Apparently he had been listening.

"The Internet," she answered.

"Don't you need a computer?" Mick probed.

"There are places that rent time," Allie answered.

They packed up a few of their belongings, but left Fletcher behind since they thought dogs might not be allowed in a computer store, and as they were leaving, Tim quietly mentioned to Mick, "She's a hotshot with computers."

Mick whispered back, "She's hot any way you look."

Tim glanced admiringly at Allie as she opened the door to the car.

Mick said, "Don't blow it, man."

Tim nodded. He knew he had to give Allie her space, even if it meant her leaving for Hollywood for a couple of months. If she decided to stay there, maybe he could open up a martial arts school out there. Maybe she'd even agree to marry him, he thought.

A short while later, the three entered a Kinko's and paid for time on a computer.

Allie sat down and began to research Bunker Hill properties using nine fingers, which caused her to struggle with the keys a bit. Her typing was further hampered by the handcuff bracelet with its piece of chain dangling. Her frustration was clear to Tim and Mick. They both felt for her but said nothing. They knew she'd have to work out her frustrations on her own.

While tapping the keys, she said, "I'm cross-referencing Bunker Hill with the tax rolls, asking for property purchased from 1968 to the present."

They viewed the changing screen. Her anger had now become resolve. She knew it was her mother's gift. *No one can tell you what you can and can't do.* It was that credo that prompted her to believe she could become a successful actor.

Fifteen minutes later, Allie touched the screen and remarked, "Look. Bunker Hill bought three places." She printed them out.

They left the store both excited and nervous about what they might find. But all of them agreed it was a long shot, since it had been so many years that these places were purchased. Maybe there were now condominiums or shopping centers where Bunker Hill's properties had once stood.

They stopped at the motel to pick up Fletcher and then drove into Virginia, seeking the three locations. Allie was acting as navigator, reading a road map while Tim drove. Mick shared the rear seat with Fletcher.

"Turn left there." She pointed.

Tim turned the car onto a deserted road just as snowflakes began to fall. In the distance, gathering dark clouds hinted at the severe change in the weather that was predicted for the next afternoon and evening.

Allie nervously asked, "What if we run into them?"

Mick patted the rifle that lay across his lap. "We've all got guns now. We shoot first and ask questions later." Mick didn't disclose the hatred he felt for Galvin or the reasons for it. Beautiful, sweet Sara's image kept crossing his mind.

Tim and Allie both nodded, but their apprehension was obvious.

Tim lit a cigarette and said, "Look, if we come close to finding anything, the prudent thing would be to call the FBI and let them handle it. As far as I'm concerned, we're on a reconnaissance mission—nothing else. I don't care how many guns we have, we're certain to be outnumbered and far outgunned."

"I agree," Allie said emphatically. "I'm not taking any chance of being caught again by those animals." She looked sadly at her wrapped finger.

Mick lit a cigarette. "I'm with you guys. If we find anything, we call the cops." Mick noticed Allie staring at her finger, and he felt sorry for her. "You know, I watch TV a lot and seen what doctors have been doing lately with wounded soldiers that come home from Iraq and Afghanistan. I'll bet you can get some kind of prosthetic that'll make your finger just as good as new and probably look real."

Allie's face lit up. "You think so?"

"I know so."

Tim nodded appreciatively toward Mick, and he hoped Mick's attempt at giving Allie back her future aspirations would work, and that she'd be able to play piano as well as she used to. He didn't want her to leave for California, but he also didn't want her injured finger to be the deciding factor. He wanted her to stay with him because she loved him enough not to want to jeopardize their relationship by leaving him for two months and possibly much longer. He believed if she was that good a pianist or actress, there must be plenty of opportunities in and around Baltimore and Washington.

After turning off the highway and traveling on several gravel roads, they came upon a dirt road that they believed led to one of Galvin's locations.

Tim remembered Suggs acting as the lookout at the farmhouse. "If somebody jumps out of the woods carrying a weapon, we fire first and get the hell out of here as quickly as possible. Agreed?"

Mick and Allie both agreed, although Allie wasn't certain how she would react if the time to shoot actually arrived. Her fingers were trained to tickle the ivories, not to pull a trigger.

Tim slowly drove the car up the road as the three of them glanced from side to side, watching for anything that might mean trouble.

One minute later they arrived at a huge snow-dusted field lit only by their car's headlights. The sole structure was the hunting cabin that Galvin's men used during their target practice.

They got out of the car, carrying their weapons, and walked toward the cabin, which they believed was probably deserted since there were no vehicles in sight. They cautiously walked up to the door. Tim turned on his flashlight.

They quietly and carefully opened the unlocked door to the cabin. It was empty except for an old wooden desk and one folding chair. Tim trained his flashlight on the wall, where the president's poster still hung with a bullet hole between the eyes. Other than that, the place was cleaned out.

"Look at this." Tim gestured toward the poster. "It's my guess they didn't vote for him, but that's just a wild guess."

Allie and Mick chortled.

They walked outside and into the field.

"This was no spot for picnics or parties," Tim said.

Allie scanned the open field, and declared, "Maybe lynching parties." She recalled how disturbed she had been at seeing old photos of African Americans hanging from tree limbs with their necks grotesquely cocked to the side.

Mick chimed in. "Training ground. Look at the tire tracks and all the spent shells." He picked one up and showed it to Tim and Allie. "And look at all the cans and broken bottles over there." In the distance they could see the shattered cans and bottles that had been used as targets.

Satisfied that this was a dead end, they got back in the car and left for their next destination.

They drove for a few miles and stopped the car, examining the map. After matching the address of the next property with the map, Mick said, "Forget number two. It's the farmhouse. On to door number three."

Twenty minutes later, they arrived at a deserted paved road surrounded by stands of evergreen trees. Once again, they approached slowly until they spotted a warehouse straight ahead. Tim stopped the car.

Mick offered, "A place like that could be booby-trapped."

Allie touched Tim's arm. "We could be walking into a nightmare. We should call the FBI and tell them about this place and about their plan."

Tim saw the angst on Allie's face and thought, *She's been through enough.* Also, a warehouse that size might be harboring any number of men, and the three of them could be walking into a virtual minefield. He turned the car around and picked up the cell phone to call Agent Barnes.

At ten that evening, a caravan of twenty vehicles rolled down the road and encircled the warehouse. A helicopter hovered overhead and shone its powerful floodlights at the front cargo doors.

Dozens of FBI agents, armed to the teeth, some in riot gear, drew their guns and aimed them at the warehouse.

When everyone was in place, Barnes spoke into a megaphone. "You in the warehouse. FBI. We have the building surrounded. Come out with your hands on your head in one minute, or we're coming in."

The minute passed with no response.

Barnes spoke into a walkie-talkie. "On my command…move in!"

An armored half-track rumbled toward the large double doors of the warehouse and smashed them open. The half-track's lights illuminated the interior of the warehouse.

Barnes waited apprehensively for a response, but he didn't have to wait long. The man in the half-track radioed, "Clear. Warehouse is clear."

Barnes and several agents entered the warehouse. It was totally vacant except for some empty wooden crates and cardboard boxes. Some of the crates and boxes bore labels identifying them as having contained all sorts of munitions.

They examined the floor and saw that it was covered in dust except for certain areas, and that there were tire tracks in the dust. Barnes bent down and rubbed the tire tracks with his finger. He noticed how clear of dust these areas were and said, "They were here with the goodies all right, and not very long ago. If all these dustless areas contained hardware, they might have a ton of stuff."

They returned to their vehicles. Barnes intended to make a full report to FBI headquarters immediately. He wasn't certain what the perpetrators intended to do with whatever had been stored there, but he was certain that it would be used for some kind of mayhem. It was his sworn duty to see that that never occurred.

CHAPTER 37

By 11:00 P.M., TIM, Allie, and Mick were back at the motel room. Tim was on the cell phone with Barnes. The call ended, and Tim announced, "Warehouse was empty, but they moved a lot of stuff out of there recently."

"Because of us?" Allie asked.

Mick said, "Because they might be planning to level the Capitol building. The animal has to be stopped. The things he did…those kids…your mother…"

Tim was jolted by the offhand remark. "My mother!" he shouted. Tim walked up to Mick, who tried to avoid Tim's glare. "You know what happened to her, don't you?"

Mick remained silent. His hand began to shake as he lit a cigarette.

"Don't you!" Tim hollered directly into Mick's face.

Mick shuddered and nodded his head. He began to bite his lip.

Still upset, Tim shouted, "And don't bite that fucking lip again!"

A tear began to roll down Mick's cheek as he said, "Tried not to think about it…sent me over the edge."

Calmer, Tim asked, "What happened? I have to know."

Mick composed himself, took a deep drag from the cigarette, and blew the smoke out of his nostrils. He had spent the last forty years trying to deny what had happened to Sara and why he felt so guilty. But these past few days had caused a change in him, especially now that he had been confronted with Tim Connor, the little Timmy

Galvin that Mick had helped to save. For better or worse, Mick felt he was finally ready to tell his tale.

Frank Valone, Vance Galvin, and BJ sat around the kitchen table in the farmhouse. Off to the side, Galvin's wife, Sara, was holding two-year-old Timmy, who was crying. Sara tried to soothe the toddler, but Timmy kept crying.

Annoyed, Galvin said to Sara, "Can't you shut the kid up?"

Frank shrugged. "Not bothering anyone."

"It's bothering me, and it's my kid, so butt out."

Galvin stood up and strode toward Sara, who fearfully backed away, holding Timmy tightly. She kept backing up until her back was against the wall.

Galvin placed his big hand over Timmy's face, covering his mouth and nose, muffling Timmy's cries. Sara timidly attempted to stop Galvin from hurting him. She feared Galvin and had regretted almost from the start of their relationship that she had ever met the charismatic, good-looking Marine. She knew Vance was attracted to her long blonde hair and Scandinavian good looks. But she soon found out that there were plenty of other women with equally good looks who attracted the attention of her husband. The one positive thing she had achieved from their relationship was Timmy. In her heart she knew that one day she would have to muster enough courage to take Timmy and leave.

Sara tried to pull Galvin's hand from Timmy's face. Galvin struck her hard across the face, sending her flying against a wall, where she slumped to the floor, sobbing and rubbing her bleeding mouth, still holding Timmy with her other arm. Timmy was unhurt but was screaming at the top of his lungs.

Frank jumped up and went to Sara. He knelt down and cradled her head in his arm tenderly.

Mick became agitated, feeling sorry for poor Sara.

"You all right?" Frank asked Sara.

Sara gazed at him in a way that Galvin didn't like.

Frank waited until Timmy had calmed down a bit, and then he walked over to Galvin. Frank yelled directly in Galvin's face, "Don't ever fucking hit her like that again."

"She's my wife, Frank. My wife! Don't you ever forget it," he shouted through clenched teeth.

Galvin was jealous and edgy. He was a time bomb ready to explode.

Later that night, Frank and Sara, hidden by darkness, met deep in the woods that surrounded the farmhouse.

Frank put his hand on Sara's shoulder. "You, me, and Timmy can get a new start. Mick too."

Sara handed him a metal box wrapped in plastic.

Frank stared at it and said, "What's this?"

"Evidence, including photos. It could be our insurance."

Frank cradled the box under his arm and said, "Okay."

She anxiously peered into the darkened forest and said, "Vance is going drinking with the boys. Soon as they leave, I'll grab Timmy and my stuff. I'll meet you at the diner with the pickup."

Frank solemnly said, "You got to be careful. You know what he's capable of doing."

"I'll be careful."

They embraced and kissed.

They both knew what they were risking, but Frank had seen enough of Galvin and his tactics. He knew Galvin didn't love Sara, and Frank felt that she and Timmy would be better off far away from him. Frank believed that Galvin's obsession with the government would eventually get them all killed. This was the only way out for him, Sara, and Timmy. They could move to the West Coast, maybe Oregon or Washington, where he knew there were hippie communes, and start a new life. It would be wonderful, he thought.

Sara, too, had had enough. She initially had been drawn to Galvin by his attractiveness and strength of personality. Raised in Scarsdale, New York, she was an excellent student who attended Vassar College in Poughkeepsie beginning in the fall of 1968. She'd been raised in a well-to-do, conservative household, and as she had only sisters, the Vietnam War was an abstraction to her until she was exposed to a storm of variant ideas and philosophies in college. She became submerged in a sea of dissent that fought the government's dogmatic stance on the war. Many hoped that with the election of a new president in November of 1968, the US could begin to pull out of that quagmire, but it wasn't meant to be. Nixon continued Johnson's insistence that somehow, in some way, the light of victory would soon be visible at the end of the long, dark tunnel.

Like so many college students in the late sixties and early seventies, Sara became radicalized, attending sit-ins and peace marches. She began to dress hippie style and listened to the music of many counterculture artists, such as Pete Seeger, Bob Dylan, and Joan Baez. Smoking marijuana became almost a daily routine as she and her friends dreamed of a better world to come while voraciously munching on potato chips and other such treats.

The summer of 1969 gave birth to the Woodstock nation. Sara and a few friends traveled the two hours by car to Bethel, New York, to be among the several hundred thousand who spent three days listening to the music of artists like Jimi Hendrix, The Who, the Grateful Dead, Janis Joplin, Jefferson Airplane, Richie Havens, and many others. For three days, nearly half a million people lived elbow to elbow in the most exposed, crowded, rain-drenched, uncomfortable conditions, and yet there wasn't so much as a fistfight. Sara marveled at how peaceful it had been, with so many people of every race and religion living in harmony. To Sara, it was less a music festival than a total experience, a phenomenon, and a happening. On opening day she heard a festival official announce, "There are a hell of a lot of us here. If we are going to make it, you had better remember that the guy next to you is your brother." Everyone remembered. Woodstock made it. She thought how wonderful it might be one day to live on a commune, in harmony not only with the others in the commune but with Mother Earth as well.

The final chapter to her conversion to radicalism was written when, in May of 1970, National Guard troops opened fire on unarmed college protestors at Kent State University, killing four and wounding many others. If the government could open fire on its own people who were protesting an ill-advised war, what might be next? Concentration camps for protestors?

She managed to earn a degree in sociology in June of 1972.

Later that summer while in Washington, DC, to protest against the war, she had a chance meeting with Vance Galvin at a local bar. She had been a slim-figured high-school cheerleader, and her blonde hair and pretty face attracted Galvin. He proposed to her only two months after meeting her, and in spite of protestations by her parents, she was married to the handsome, charismatic Galvin one week later by a justice of the peace.

But Galvin's sexual appetites seemed to know no bounds. It didn't take long for her to realize that he was cheating on her, especially while she was pregnant with Timmy. On several occasions, after an argument, she asked him why he had even married her. His answer was always the same: he wished he hadn't, and if it weren't for Timmy, he'd have been gone long ago. His remarks left her crestfallen. She dreaded becoming a young divorcee with an infant to care for. She hated to admit it to herself, but her parents had been correct in their appraisal of her husband.

Later at the diner, Frank and Mick sat at a table with empty coffee cups. Frank was worried. They both lit cigarettes.

"Should've been here by now," Frank said.

He slid out of his seat, but Mick grabbed his arm and said, "If Galvin sees you, he'll be suspicious. Let me go. He thinks I'm nuts. I'll make up some story about why I had to go back there."

Frank agreed, and Mick took off for the farmhouse.

Minutes later, Mick arrived and knocked on the door. The door swung open to reveal Galvin, obviously drunk, holding a gun, and apparently crazed.

"Ah, Mick. Just in time to see how justice will be done when we're in power."

Mick entered the room and gasped as he saw Sara lying on the floor, with blood oozing from the side of her head. Her long hair obscured much of her face. Timmy was crying and cowering in the corner.

Mick looked at Galvin and screamed, "What did you do?" Then to Sara he shouted, "Sara!"

Galvin trained the gun on Mick. "Wait till you see what's in store for that whore's son. She was gonna sneak off with Frank and desert us."

"No way. They—"

"Save your breath," he remarked as he waved the gun at Mick. "Sara confessed. Now I have to execute the deserters. Isn't that what's done in war?"

Mick smelled liquor on Galvin's breath. Mick frantically surveyed the room as Galvin, still holding the gun, approached Timmy. Mick trembled and looked at Sara. "She's alive, right?"

Speaking casually, Galvin answered, "If she is, she soon won't wanna be. Look. I took a trophy, like in the good old days."

Galvin held his arm out toward Mick. He opened his hand. In Galvin's bloody hand was one of Sara's ears.

Mick became dazed. "Sweet Jesus! Not Sara!"

Without thinking and with no regard for his own life, Mick lunged at Galvin. The gun fired but missed. Mick screamed, and with an amphetamine-like adrenaline rush, he threw Galvin against a wall. Galvin's head struck the wall, momentarily stunning him.

Mick turned, scooped up Timmy in his arms, leaped out the door, jumped into his car, and sped away.

Galvin got up screaming, ran out the door, and fired several shots at Mick's fleeing car. He then ran for his own car and gave chase, but Mick was able to escape.

Tim and Allie were glued to every word. Tim was highly distressed, knowing that the people Mick was describing were his father and mother and even his two-year-old self.

Mick was sweating profusely and was very unsettled, appearing almost to be in a trance.

After taking several deep breaths, he said in a subdued manner, "I loved sweet Sara, the prettiest, nicest girl around. She was attracted to that animal by his good looks and charm. I told Frank that someone ratted and she was dead, killed by Galvin. I couldn't tell him about her ear and felt guilty as hell not knowin' if I left her alive to be tortured some more. Couldn't take it. Cracked up at the cemetery, and Frank took me to some hospital." Mick looked off in the distance, staring at nothing, and shouted, "*Chat dau ho chung!*"

Soothingly, Allie said, "There was nothing you could've done."

Mick looked down at his hands through blurry eyes, avoiding Allie's gaze as he softly answered, "Could've stayed…beat the shit out of Galvin. Instead I ran."

Tim placed his hand lightly on Mick's shoulder and said with sincerity, "And maybe saved my life."

There was silence in the room.

Although he knew the odds were slim, Tim asked, "So it's possible my mother is still alive?"

Mick began to hyperventilate at the question. He'd felt guilty all these years for telling Frank she was dead without knowing for certain. *Could she be alive?* he thought. He had rationalized that perhaps she had left Galvin and made a new life for herself far away from him, and since Frank never had attempted to find her, maybe she had thought Frank was willing to let her go. Or maybe she had thought Frank was dead, and that was why he hadn't tried to find her. Or maybe she *was* dead. Mick slowly regained control of his breathing. "I guess it's possible," he said.

"What does *chat dau ho chung* mean?" Allie asked.

Mick blinked as though a bright light shone in his eyes. "How… how do you know those words?"

"You've said them a few times since we met."

Mick swallowed hard, took several deep breaths, and then screamed and fell onto the floor. He curled up in a fetal position and began to shake and sob.

Allie went to his aid, but Mick lashed out at ghosts of his past, and his hand struck Allie's shoulder. Mick was somewhere else.

Tim tried to grab Mick, but Allie pushed him gently back, and then she comforted Mick in her arms, tenderly stroking his face.

"It's okay. You're with friends," she soothingly said.

She continued to stroke Mick's face, and he settled down. Tim helped him to sit up and placed his back against the foot of the bed.

Mick took several deep breaths. He was sweating but composed.

"You okay?" Allie asked.

Mick stared off into space and spoke deliberately, vocalizing something he hadn't since Vietnam. "We had the firepower. They had the willpower. They tried to demoralize us by cutting ears and noses off our dead. They even stuck the heads of our dead on poles. We did the same. It's what I became good at. The words mean…"

Mick swallowed hard, and that crazed, faraway look came into his eye again. He shouted, "Cut off their heads! It's what I did to that piece of shit today at the farmhouse. I stuck his head on a pole."

"He was dead?" Allie asked, sounding surprised.

He turned to Allie and smiled crookedly. "Now he is."

Although shocked by the idea of Mick decapitating Red and sticking his head onto a pole, Allie and Tim now had a better understanding of Mick's madness.

Mick was clearly relieved by his confession. The years of having to bottle up the outrageous things he had seen and done in Vietnam had tied his soul into a knot, and now that soul was freer than it had been in a long, long time.

Allie stared off to the side with a smile. Jesus or no Jesus, revenge was sweet. She yawned. "I'm dead tired."

Tim agreed. "It's been a long day." He pointed at the bed Mick was leaning against and said, "Mick, that bed's yours."

Mick deadpanned, "How come you get to sleep with the pretty gal?"

Tim jabbed back, "I called it first."

Mick looked down at Fletcher and said, "I guess I get to sleep with you."

Fletcher cocked his head to the side.

For Tim and Allie, it had been the longest and most trying day of their lives.

CHAPTER 38

AT NOON THE NEXT day, while Tim, Allie, and Mick were resting and eating sandwiches for lunch in their motel room, John Simpson and several Secret Service agents boarded a gleaming Gulfstream jet, where they were greeted by the pilot.

"Welcome aboard, Mr. Secretary," the pilot cheerfully said.

Simpson smiled, settled into his seat, and exhaled. The plane would be taking him to his mother's home in Kansas, where he would be protected by many Secret Service agents in the event that some incredible disaster, such as a nuclear attack, hit Washington, DC. As the designated survivor, he would then be sworn in as the next president of the United States.

Simpson knew what would then have to be done. In order to ensure that the transfer of power proceeded smoothly, he would declare martial law and immediately restrict individual rights, including the right of habeas corpus, so that political enemies could be held indefinitely without trial. He might also have to pardon certain persons who, like the nation's founding fathers, would now be considered patriots instead of traitors. Whether someone was a traitor or a patriot was merely a matter of timing and perspective. Galvin and his compatriots would be given the highest honors and roles in the new government.

Simpson would see to it that America would reverse course back to its proper white Christian roots.

He ordered a double Jack Daniels, which he hoped would help keep his nerves from fraying. The moment of truth was only hours away. He prayed Mannings's confidence in Vance Galvin was justified.

At 4:00 p.m., Tim, Allie, and Mick were killing time by watching TV in their motel room when Tim's cell phone rang and he tentatively answered, "Who's this?"

Landers was on a pay phone several blocks from police headquarters. "It's Detective Landers. We've got information on your mother. She might still be alive."

Mick and Allie saw the astonished look on Tim's face as he scribbled an address on a piece of paper and hung up.

Tim's eyes drifted to the window as he said, "Landers wants to meet in a parking lot at eleven tonight. My mother might still be alive!"

Mick leaped to his feet, agitated. "Sara? Alive? God, I hope so." The idea of seeing Sara once again both thrilled and unnerved Mick. If she was alive, it might lift years of guilt off his shoulders, but facing her and knowing that he had left Galvin alone with her, perhaps to torture and torment her some more, made him dread seeing her. But far more importantly, he had taken Timmy and given him to Frank to raise. Had Sara tried to find Frank and Timmy? If so, it would have been difficult, as Frank had immediately fled and had changed his name to Dan Connor. And Mick had told Frank that Sara was dead, so Frank would never have tried searching for her. Mick thought, *If Sara is still alive, will she ever forgive me?*

"Was there a chance she was?" Tim asked, hoping for a miracle. "Could the ear have been a trophy from the war?"

Mick shook his head slowly. "It had fresh blood on it, but that doesn't mean she was dead."

Allie frowned. "Parking lot? Sounds fishy to me."

They pondered the thought for a moment, and then Mick spoke up. "Let's meet. Only this time we'll be carrying the weapons we took. Allie, ever shoot a gun?"

"Not really."

"Then I think Annie Oakley needs some target practice."

Galvin and the other militia leaders—Stern, Tyler, and Brown— were seated on folding chairs in the living room of an abandoned house deep in the hills of Northern Virginia. After destroying the farmhouse, they had been forced to find a secluded meeting place. Stern, who lived not too far from the abandoned house, knew that the family had moved out six years before and had left it in such bad condition that the bank couldn't unload it.

Galvin addressed the three leaders. As he spoke, his words came faster and faster, building to an emotional crescendo. "More than eighty trained men are ready to risk their lives for the cause of mankind. You men will have positions of power in our new government. A few minutes after twenty-one hundred hours, we will begin the overthrow of a tyrannical liberal government, save the Constitution, and make this the nation it was meant to be—a white Christian nation. White power!"

The men were clearly impressed with Galvin. They yelled back in unison, arms raised in a Nazi salute, "White power!"

CHAPTER 39

JUST BEFORE DUSK, Tim and Allie were shooting pistols at tin cans in a deserted field. Determined, Allie managed to hit a few. Fletcher hid under a bush, shaking with the sound of each gunshot.

Mick was a few yards away by the car, scrutinizing Galvin's map and pondering the code.

He looked up at Allie as she hit another can. "This chick's ready."

Allie accepted the compliment with pride. She'd always believed she had exceptional hand-eye coordination, perhaps as a result of being a proficient pianist. But instead of envisioning notes on pages of sheet music, she instead imagined Galvin and his men writhing in pain as her bullets struck them between their eyes and between their legs.

Tim glanced at his watch. "You guys hungry?"

Allie ignored him, and asked Mick with excitement, "Teach me to shoot a rifle."

Mick shook his head. "M-16's recoil will knock you backward." His eyes opened wide as he repeated, "Backward? Eureka! His code had somethin' to do with the word *backward*. It's there, right in front of me, but I can't seem to grasp it."

Allie said, "Maybe it'll come to you. Sometimes if you try too hard, you can't remember something."

Tim said, "I think that's enough practice. I'm starving. Let's find some decent place to eat.

Although some time had passed since the burning of the farmhouse, Galvin still couldn't get Red's image out of his mind. Red was often a dimwit, but he was loyal to his core and would have done anything Galvin asked of him. The fact that Mick was probably involved made Galvin's blood boil. Crazy Mick had stolen his son and given Timmy to Frank to raise as his own. The loss of Timmy hadn't hurt as much as the thought of that traitor Frank Valone attempting to steal his wife and child, leaving their group diminished and disorganized. *That fucking whore Sara deserved what she got.*

Webster walked in, approached Galvin's makeshift desk, and said, "We got him."

"Bring him in."

Webster left the room and immediately returned with Bobby Smalls. Bobby stood in front of the desk, drunk. Bobby had never met the major, and he was thrilled to be in his presence. The fact that he'd been summoned to see Galvin made Bobby believe Galvin had something good in store for him, Abby, and his unborn child.

Galvin calmly asked, "What were your instructions?"

Bobby unsteadily answered, "Get my vehicle 'spected."

"Very good. Do you remember why?"

Bobby scratched his head, wobbled a bit, and tried to think. After a few seconds he replied, "So...so no cop would stop me for somethin' stupid...like...like...no taillight."

"And what else were you told?"

"By twenty-one hundred hours, have my truck in DC. Park at...uh...the corner of Duncan and Second—no, Third! Yeah, I think Third. At twenty-one-oh-eight, Bill will open fire and keep firing using the prede...prede—"

"Predetermined."

"Yeah, predetermid coordits till he runs out of shells."

"Were you told not to drink?"

Bobby attempted to stand up straight. "Ain't been drinkin', sir."

Galvin and everyone else in the room knew he was lying. Galvin looked at Webster, who rolled his eyes. Galvin got up and put his arm around Bobby's shoulder. "Not following orders in time of war could be considered treason."

Bobby looked bewildered as he attempted to make sense of Galvin's statement.

Galvin walked Bobby outside with his arm still around him. He guided Bobby toward the back of the house.

Webster followed fifteen feet behind.

"You know what one rotten apple can do to the barrel?" Galvin asked in a fatherly tone.

"Uh…spoil it, right?" Bobby was pleased with his answer.

"And we can't have that, can we?"

"No sir, we—"

"*Auf Wiedersehen.*"

Galvin pulled out his pistol, placed the barrel behind Bobby's ear, and fired. Blood spurted out of his head like water from a hose as Bobby crumpled to the ground.

Webster strode up behind Galvin. He was shocked and angry.

Before Webster could get a word out, Galvin said, "This garbage could have ruined it for millions of true Americans. The importance of discipline cannot be underestimated. Take care of this mess."

Webster retorted, "The kid's got family!"

"Then they should have taken better care of him," he casually answered.

"Like you and your son?"

Galvin sneered at Webster, pointed a menacing finger at him, and then stormed off without uttering a word.

Webster silently fumed. He feared that Galvin, in his zeal to overthrow the government, was beginning to spin out of control. Webster hoped that after they accomplished their mission tonight, a more stable person would take on the leadership role in the new United States government.

At 7:30 p.m., Harold Smalls was wearing out the rug in his home. He glanced at his watch for the hundredth time. He picked up the phone and dialed.

"Carl, if he's been drinkin' again, I'm gonna shoot that no good son of mine right in the ass. I'm supposed to take off for my rendezvous point, and so's Bobby, but his wife ain't seen hide or hair of him. Make a couple of calls. Okay?"

Harold hung up and thought, *Where the hell is he?*

Tim, Allie, and Mick had just finished eating dinner at a Bob's Big Boy restaurant. They walked outside and got into Tim's car as Mick continued to grapple with Galvin's code. "I know it's simple. Just can't remember."

"It's probably nothing anyway," Tim said.

"Yeah, you're probably right."

At eight that evening, Harold Smalls was still pacing back and forth in front of the telephone that hung on his kitchen wall. He knew his son would have trouble keeping away from the booze. Bobby always drank more when the pressure was highest, and it worried Harold. What if he didn't show up? What if he was in a drunken stupor in some bar? Harold knew that Bobby was far from the smartest man in town, but Bobby had always been a good son, never getting into any serious trouble. Except for his excessive drinking, Bobby had been a good husband to Abby, and she was due any day now. Perhaps Bobby would grow up a bit and take on the responsibilities of being a father. Maybe Vance Galvin's plan would work, and maybe he and Bobby would soon have respectable jobs.

The phone rang, and Harold immediately grabbed it. "Hello?"

Seconds later, Harold's face became contorted. He dropped the phone, fell onto a kitchen chair, put his head between his knees, and began to moan. His only son had been executed by the very man that his son had pinned his hopes and dreams on: Major Vance Galvin. He would have to break the news to Abby. Bobby's soon-to-be-born child would have to grow up without his father. What had Bobby done to deserve execution? Harold thought long and hard as to what he should do. He was supposed to leave right now with his vehicle, meet with another man, and travel to their designated location.

CHAPTER 40

AT A FEW MINUTES past eight, Galvin, Tyler, Stern, and Brown were seated in front of a television at their makeshift headquarters in a hotel room near downtown Washington, DC. They were anxiously watching the buildup to the president's address on Fox News.

Galvin glanced out the window and noticed flurries of snow floating past the window. Galvin gleefully remarked, "I knew it! God is definitely with us. The low ceiling and swirling snow will make it harder for them to scramble any choppers to try to follow our men as they make their escapes."

Brown offered, "And harder for them to follow in their rear-wheel-drive police cars. Almost all our escape vehicles are four-wheelers."

The others nodded and watched the television, waiting nervously for the moment of truth to arrive.

At around 8:15, many trucks, vans, and pickup trucks left from different points and headed for various locations close to the Capitol building, each with an assortment of firepower. A few of the vehicles were located in Baltimore while most of the vehicles traveled from Virginia. The drivers had been instructed to plan their trips so they would arrive at their designated positions within one or two minutes of 9:07 p.m., when the president was expected to step up to the podium for his address. The timing was essential. Galvin knew that a parked van or truck could appear suspicious, so the plan was to stop the vehicles at their assigned locations and immediately begin opening fire. Even if the men began firing at precisely 9:07 with the president not at the podium, it wouldn't matter, as the president and the line of succession would be ushered to the safety of the bomb shelter. There, the trap would be sprung. The rest would be history.

There were thirty-nine vehicles in total, each carrying some type of ordnance that would be able to launch explosives at the Capitol at relatively short range. Each vehicle was manned by one driver and at least one other man in the rear of the truck or van who would do the firing.

Two hours earlier, they had parked their escape vehicles a bit farther from the Capitol building.

The men had been instructed to fire as rapidly as possible for up to two or three minutes, possibly firing as many as ten shells each. They would then drive to positions near their escape vehicles, ditch their trucks, duck between buildings and through alleys to their escape vehicles, and head out of the city to safety, making certain they weren't followed. If they were followed and couldn't make a run for it, they were to use their superior firepower to open fire on their pursuers and then make their escape.

As the president, who was still at the White House, made final preparations for his address, legislators and members of the press filed into the Capitol building.

Tim drove the three of them back to the motel room where they planned to watch on TV for any crazy events that might unfold during the president's address to the nation. Mick was in the rear seat, constantly mumbling the word *backward.*

Tim and Allie were getting tired of Mick's mumbling. Tim said, "If you don't shut up, I'm gonna have to slap you upside your head. You're giving me a headache."

Mick sat up straight. "Stop the car!"

Allie said, "Mick, he's just kidding about slapping you."

"I know that. Just stop the car."

Tim pulled the car over to a curb.

Mick got out of the car, carrying the map. He walked to the front of the car and placed the map on the hood. He looked at Tim and Allie, who had followed him, and excitedly said, "Backward and forward."

Tim and Allie merely stared at him, not understanding what he was getting at.

Mick took a pen from his pocket and, across the top of the map, wrote the letters of the alphabet in order from *A* to *Z*. Under those letters he wrote the alphabet again backward from *Z* to *A* so that it appeared as follows:

A B C D E F G H I J K L M N O P Q R S T U V W X Y Z
Z Y X W V U T S R Q P O N M L K J I H G F E D C B A

Mick pointed at the letters. "See, *A* is *Z, B* is *Y,* and so on. I knew it was somethin' simple."

Tim and Allie nodded in understanding as Mick began to match Galvin's letters with the reverse alphabet code, carefully converting the letters on the map to something intelligible. Two minutes later it was decoded.

Galvin's letters, MVIEVTZHRMYFMPVI, became *NERVEGA-SINBUNKER.*

"Mick was right," Allie declared.

Mick was puzzled. He looked up at the two of them. "Nerve gas in what bunker?"

Tim and Allie mulled over the question.

Allie said, "I'll bet if there's actually an attack on the Capitol building during tonight's address, the president and maybe a lot of bigwigs go into a bomb shelter of some kind."

Tim grunted. "You think a nobody like Galvin has a way to get nerve gas in there, with the Secret Service and all?"

"Maybe," Mick surmised, "somebody like BJ. A lot at stake, remember?"

Allie grabbed Tim's arm. "We have to warn them. But who—"

"FBI Agent Barnes. I got his cell number." Tim tried his cell, but the screen was dark. "Shit! Battery's shot, and the charger's back at the motel."

Mick shouted, "What do we do?"

"We're gonna have to find a pay phone," Tim quickly responded.

They got into Tim's car and drove, knowing that every minute lost might lead to a disastrous result, not only for the president, but for the entire nation.

The vehicles carrying the men and weapons began to approach their assigned locations. If they arrived early, they were to keep driving, killing time until they could meet the deadline. It was now 9:00 p.m., seven minutes till the Second American Revolution. Galvin had faith in these men. They had been handpicked for their zeal to bring down the present government. The men firing the weapons had been chosen because of their experiences in the military; most had seen action in Iraq or Afghanistan.

The Capitol building was now packed with the most powerful people in the world. The First Lady entered to applause, and she took her seat.

Seated in the audience was Congressman Brett J. Mannings. He nervously checked his watch: 9:04. As a member of Congress, he'd been able to determine where everyone would be taken during the attack. He'd learned that the line of succession—the president, the vice president, the cabinet, and the speaker of the house—would be taken to a room that was equipped to act essentially as a war room. In this way, if there was a nuclear attack on the city, the president would be surrounded by his advisors, such as the secretaries of defense, homeland security, and so forth. They knew that if indeed the Capitol building became ground zero for a nuclear blast, vaporizing the building and everyone in it, at least the designated survivor—in this case, John Simpson—would be alive to legally assume the reins of government, resulting in a relatively seamless transition, provided there was enough of America remaining to govern.

Mannings left his seat and headed toward the men's room. He approached the door, looked behind him, and then discreetly walked down a staircase toward the basement level. So far, he'd heard nothing out of the ordinary, but if all went as planned, he expected to hear explosions at any moment. He knew that within seconds of the start of the bombardment, the president and line of succession would be ushered past his location, where he intended to blend in with the crowd, knowing that in the chaos no one would pay him any mind.

At 9:05 at FBI headquarters, Detective Barnes hurriedly called a meeting with several other agents. He spoke with urgency. "The caller gave details only an insider could know. This Harold Smalls said the leader, Vance Galvin, killed his son, Bobby Smalls. The Secret Service has only minutes to get everyone to safety. We gotta try and knock these jerks out before they begin firing."

Barnes and the men rushed out. Barnes felt the hair standing up on the back of his neck. Never before had he been assigned to anything nearly as potentially threatening to the government as this.

In downtown Washington, DC, police cars from every precinct began to patrol the streets. Hundreds of FBI agents and Secret Service agents began to take up positions in the streets, both on foot and in cars.

Tim, Allie, and Mick were now closing in on the center of DC, looking out the windows for a pay phone. They knew that time was of the essence: their car's clock read 9:06.

Mick was serious as he asked, "Somebody steal all the pay phones?"

"Not many left since everyone in America but you has a cell phone," Allie answered.

Mick pursed his lips and said, "Heavy."

CHAPTER 41

GALVIN WAS IN his makeshift headquarters. On the television, he and the other leaders anxiously watched the cabinet enter and take their seats.

With a confident air, Galvin announced, "In one minute, the president will step up to the podium. The rest will be known as the Second American Revolution. We're past the point of no return, so I can now inform you that plan B involves a trusted congressman planting nerve gas in the bomb shelter where the president and the entire line of succession will be, except for the designated survivor, who is one of us. Praise the Lord!"

The men turned their attention back to the TV. Unexpectedly, the legislators began to quickly file out. A TV announcer appeared on the screen and declared, "An incredible turn of events is occurring behind me. The entire floor of Congress is being emptied for what we have been told is a safety precaution. We've no word as to why, but the address will indeed be delayed. Suffice it to say that this is unprecedented in our nation's history."

Galvin was shaken but quickly recovered enough to take control again and assuage the concerns of the other leaders. "Someone goddamn ratted, but I expected as much. It won't matter. Plans A and B are in progress. Our men should be opening fire as we speak."

On the television, the announcer suddenly flinched as several explosions could be heard in the background. "Jesus! I'm hearing what I think is an attack on this building!"

More explosions could be heard through his open microphone as he began to scramble toward an exit. The camera showed that some of the ceiling was raining down on the mostly evacuated hall. The Secret Service was busily ushering those who remained to safety.

One of the Washington, DC, patrol cars noticed a panel truck parked in an unusual location. The patrol car pulled up behind the truck and turned on its lights. Two officers got out of their car and approached the truck.

The driver of the truck had an AK-47 on his lap. Through his side-view mirrors, he saw the two officers approaching. The driver's job was to open the back doors of the panel truck and allow the three men inside to begin firing the loaded Howitzer at the dome of the Capitol building. He knew he would have to kill the two officers first and that he would have no trouble doing so, since his weapon could fire ten rounds in one second. The pistols the officers carried would be of little use against such firepower. Sweat poured down his brow as he fingered the gun, picturing the two writhing in pain as he riddled their bodies with bullets.

Suddenly, the officers heard what sounded to them like bombs exploding in the direction of the Capitol building. They forgot about the truck, ran back to their car, and sped off toward the blasts. They heard many more blasts as they drove, and they hoped the United States wasn't being invaded by some foreign government.

The driver quickly ran to the back of the truck and opened the doors. As soon as the doors were open, the three men inside began to fire the cannon at the dome of the Capitol building. The driver immediately jumped back into the front cab, ready to make his escape as soon as the howitzer fired its few shells. The sound of the cannon fire was deafening, but the men reloaded and were ready to fire again when a different patrol car turned the corner. The patrol car's driver saw what was happening and pulled behind the truck. Upon seeing the Howitzer, one of the officers remarked, "Holy shit, a fucking cannon!"

Through their open windows, the police began to open fire with their pistols. One bullet struck one of the men, and he fell back into the truck. The officers kept firing at the open doors while the other two men ducked behind the cannon.

Through his rearview mirror, the driver observed what was happening. He leaped out of the truck and opened fire with his AK-47 at the windshield of the patrol car. The bullets shattered the windshield and ripped apart the upper chests and heads of the two patrolmen. The side of one officer's face was completely blown away.

The two men inside the truck fired two more shells and then shouted for the driver to get the hell out of there. The driver drove toward their escape vehicle.

In thirty-eight other locations, the attackers were facing similar situations. They were almost all able to fire at least one shell; many fired as many as ten. The men with the rocket launcher were able to fire seventeen rockets at the building before attempting their escape.

Webster was at the rear of a pickup truck firing mortars at the building. He heard sirens and hollered to the driver to begin making their escape in thirty seconds.

Tim stopped the car at a phone booth outside a closed gas station, but the receiver was missing. They were close enough to the heart of the city to hear the blasts in the distance. Tim yelled, "It's started!" He jumped back into the car and sped away.

Allie shouted, "There's got to be one working pay phone somewhere."

BJ Mannings was now the closest person to the stairs that led to the bomb shelter. He'd heard the shots, and he knew the legislators would be there in just a few more seconds. He patted the plastic canister under his jacket. In only moments, he would blend into the rushing crowd and enter the president's bunker. He knew that in the confusion, he'd be able to plant the device and pull the switch that would give him four minutes to escape. He took a deep breath and waited for what he knew would be considered a heroic deed. His name would be enshrined in all future history books. He was ready for the second coming.

The president and line of succession, including all the cabinet members except Secretary of Agriculture John Simpson, the designated doomsday survivor, were quickly ushered by Secret Service toward the shelter.

Members of Congress were led into various lower-level rooms.

As the Secret Service hustled the president's group past Mannings, he simply blended in with the crowd and entered the bunker.

Police cars, FBI personnel, and Secret Service agents were swarming everywhere. Gun battles began to blaze on dozens of streets near the Capitol building. Many of Galvin's men were being shot at and picked off as they attempted to fire mortars and bazookas from their trucks and pickups.

The president and line of succession were frantically herded through the shelter doorway by fifteen armed Secret Service agents. Mannings kept his head down and joined the pack as they entered the large room, which was equipped with maps, phones, computers, televisions, and other assorted items.

Two Marines turned huge wheels to seal the door shut and then stood guard as Mannings prepared to slip the plastic device from under his coat in the confusion. The device was equipped with adhesive tape, which Mannings exposed by pulling off the protective cellophane while it was still under his jacket.

Hundreds of law-enforcement officials attempted to block the side streets with their vehicles. Some of the attackers tried to run through the barricades of parked police cars and emergency vehicles, but the militia men were outnumbered many times over. Several wild firefights broke out. Some of the men were killed, and some others threw down their weapons and gave themselves up. Some of the men managed to escape, shielded in part by the swirling snow.

Barnes and Bronowski were cruising the streets in their car. They spotted a pickup truck. Webster had just finished firing mortar shells from the back of it. The two FBI agents leaped out of their car with their guns drawn and fired at Webster. Bullets struck around him.

Webster grabbed his gun and fired at Barnes, but missed.

Webster's driver opened his door and leaped out of the truck, but before he could begin firing his automatic weapon, Barnes put two bullets into his chest. The driver flew backward and landed on his back as the weapon flew out of his hands.

Webster shouted, "Fucking nigger!"

Barnes charged with his gun as Webster continued to fire back at the dodging and ducking Barnes. Barnes hit Webster in his shoulder, but Webster kept firing until a bullet struck him in the chest. He dropped to his knees as his empty gun fell to the side.

Barnes and Bronowki stealthily approached. Webster was still alive but dazed and bleeding profusely from his chest wound. Barnes jumped onto the back of the pickup and kicked the gun out of Webster's reach.

Webster was still on his knees and wheezing shortened breaths. He tenderly rubbed his bracelet, stared through blurry eyes at his father's name, pitched forward, and fell dead on his face.

Barnes, breathing heavily, turned to Bronowski and said, "First time a white man ever called me nigger to my face."

"Even in Vietnam?" Bronowski asked.

Barnes sat down on the pickup's tailgate. "My family's been here over three hundred years, but as the old slogan goes, 'No Vietnamese ever called me nigger.'"

A few battles still raged behind them.

Barnes inhaled deeply. "Maybe we'll win this war."

Bronowski understood.

Tim, Allie, and Mick raced toward the sounds of the gun battles. Suddenly, their path was blocked by a barricade of police cars. They stopped the car, hoping to have one of the officers make the necessary phone call.

Tim got out of his car and hurried toward the police barricade, where he was immediately confronted by a police officer who shouted, "This area is off limits. Go back." The officer pointed in the direction of Tim's car.

Tim blurted, "The president's in danger."

The officer pointed toward the battles raging behind him. "No shit, Sherlock. Now leave."

Exasperated, Tim said, "More than this attack! You gotta put me through to FBI Agent Calvin Barnes. I know his number."

"Great, then call him yourself. Now get going." The officer's patience was wearing thin.

"My cell phone's dead," Tim said frantically.

A second officer walked up behind Tim's car, looked in, and then he drew his pistol as he shouted, "They got weapons inside!"

The first officer drew his weapon, pointed it at Tim, and yelled, "Down on the ground, now, and put your hands behind your head!"

Tim stood there. "Just call Agent Barnes. He'll explain. We gotta warn the president."

The officer crouched with the gun straight out in both hands and demanded, "Down, or I swear I'll shoot."

Tim dropped to the ground.

The second officer ordered Allie and Mick out of the car and then forced them onto the ground by Tim's car. Fletcher remained inside, barking at the officer.

The second officer demanded, "Hands behind your heads."

Allie and Mick complied.

The officer noticed Allie's left wrist. He shouted to the other officer, "This woman's got a handcuff on one of her wrists."

The first officer glared at Tim and hollered, "What the hell's going on here?"

From the ground, Tim shouted back, "She was kidnapped by the attackers. Just call Agent Barnes, and he'll explain everything."

The two officers ignored their pleas and proceeded to handcuff their hands behind their backs.

Mannings sat on a metal chair and discreetly watched for a safe moment to stick the device under his chair and pull a tiny wire.

Tim, Allie, and Mick stood beside Tim's car with their hands cuffed behind their backs.

Allie attempted to plead their case. "We're no threat. You can be heroes with one phone call. If we're lying, take us in. If we're not…"

The first officer looked at their faces and then took out a cell phone. "If this is bullshit…What's the number?"

Tim gave him the number, and the officer began to dial.

With everyone scurrying around the bomb shelter, Mannings was able to press the device to the bottom of his chair and pull the tiny wire. He started a four-minute timer on his digital wristwatch, which immediately began counting down to zero.

Mannings then strode to the door guarded by the two Marines and said, "I'm Congressman Brett Mannings, and I've mistakenly entered the wrong room."

The clean-cut Marine said, "Sir, once the doors are sealed, we have standing orders not to open them unless ordered by the commander in chief."

Mannings glanced around the bustling room. The president and several others were on phones and monitoring events on computers and TV screens. Mannings looked at his watch. Beads of sweat began to form on his brow. He knew that nerve gas would lead to a horribly painful death.

He stepped toward the president and said, "Mr. President, I must leave. I…need to check on my constituents."

The president turned away from his computer monitor. He understood Congressman Mannings's concern but replied, "Sorry, Brett. For the safety of all concerned, the protocol is for the door to remain sealed until the all-clear has been issued. Is something wrong? You seem…" Observing the perspiration collecting on Mannings's forehead, the president placed his hand on Mannings's shoulder and said, "You're safe here."

Mannings looked frantically around the room like a caged animal. He glanced at his watch. Two minutes left. Everyone around Mannings was staring at him. His mannerisms were clearly not normal.

The president asked, "Brett, what's wrong? Tell me."

Mannings looked again at his watch. 110 seconds, 109, 108…

Sweat was pouring from him, but then a sudden serenity came over him. He'd seen dozens of men die in Vietnam for absolutely nothing. Now he could join his fallen comrades for an incredibly lofty cause. He knew he probably didn't have many more years left, but he was momentarily saddened that he wouldn't be around to see the revolution and its aftermath. Maybe they would erect a statue in his honor or rename a boulevard for him. He stared straight at the president and began to sing "God Bless America" in a strong voice. Mannings had no idea the song had been written by a Jew named Irving Berlin.

Barnes was standing next to his car, surveying the scene, when his cell phone rang. He answered, "Special Agent Barnes."

Barnes listened for only a moment before jumping into his car. He shouted, "They're legit! Do nothing. I'm only a few blocks away."

Several cabinet members had joined Mannings in singing "God Bless America." Mannings again glanced at his watch. One minute left. Fifty-nine seconds. Fifty-eight. Mannings had now reached a point of tranquility. He was ready to meet his maker.

Barnes's car, with siren blaring and rotating red light shining, skidded to a halt near Tim's car. Barnes leaped out of his car and spotted the three of them with the two police officers.

Tim shouted toward Barnes, "Call someone. Nerve gas might be planted in the president's bunker by Congressman Brett J. Mannings."

Barnes ran up to him. "How do you know this?"

Tim hollered frantically, "No time to spare!"

Barnes dialed a number as quickly as possible.

"God Bless America" was just coming to a rousing finish when the red phone rang, stopping everyone dead. The president picked up, listened, shot a look at Congressman Mannings, and then shouted, "Nerve gas planted somewhere in this room!"

Everyone began a frenetic search, turning everything over and looking in every corner. A Secret Service agent looked under a chair, grabbed the plastic container, and shouted, "Got it!"

The president ordered, "Unseal the door!"

The two Marines frantically began to turn the wheels that would open the huge metal door.

The president turned to the vice president. "Is John Simpson safe?"

"The secretary is in Kansas, sir."

"He may well be the next president." It was little consolation, but at least he knew the republic would still have a leader. He eyed the door and silently urged it to open as quickly as possible.

The agent, still holding the plastic container, ran to the door as the Marines turned the wheel.

Mannings checked the time. Fifteen seconds left...fourteen... thirteen. As the door began to open, he realized that all might be lost. He would be arrested, and the president would still be alive. In a millisecond, he knew what he had to do.

The clean-cut Marine grabbed the device from the agent and said, "I'll take it, sir."

Mannings's bulk suddenly blocked the exit. The second Marine, acting on instinct, put three bullets into the congressman's chest. He fell dead amid the screams of others in the bunker.

The Marine ran out. The president saluted the Marine through the open doorway as the Marine ran down the hallway toward an exit.

As a precaution, the remaining Marine swung the heavy door closed again.

The brave Marine reached the exit and pushed it open just as the gas exploded in his face, killing him painfully, but the remaining gas dissipated harmlessly into the snowy night.

CHAPTER 42

IN HIS TEMPORARY HOTEL headquarters, Galvin and several leaders nervously waited for a phone call that would tell them their efforts were a success, and John Simpson was the next president. If all went well, Galvin expected to hear from BJ. If he didn't hear from him, it could mean one of several things: the plan had failed, or BJ had been killed either by the nerve gas or some other means, or BJ had somehow been discovered and arrested.

Galvin hoped his mole in the police department would be able to gather enough information to let Galvin know the results if BJ was unable to call for any reason.

They had heard the roar of the cannons and mortars and the gunplay that followed, and now it was silent. Galvin had known all along that he might be leading some of his men to slaughter, and the death toll was likely to be high, since someone had obviously informed on them—the evacuation of the Capitol before the firing began testified to that. If the attack had gone as planned, he thought most of his men would have been able to fire their missiles and escape before the authorities knew what hit them. But plan B had been the real plan all along, and he prayed it had gone off successfully. BJ was a fine and brave soldier in the battle for American justice. He hoped BJ had completed his mission and that America would soon be a beautiful place, a beacon of freedom once again.

After waiting for what seemed an interminable length of time, during which Galvin paced the floor like a caged tiger, his cell phone rang. He listened intently while the others watched, searching his face for some sign of success or failure. An expressionless Galvin listened for a few seconds and then hung up, appearing crestfallen. He turned to the agitated group of leaders. They knew from his face that it could not be good news.

Galvin drew a deep breath and said, "Gentlemen, we have failed. The nerve gas killed a Marine outside the building. All those inside were saved." Galvin had received no word about the status of BJ, but he knew it couldn't be good. Galvin had known BJ for more than forty years, and he was momentarily saddened by the thought that BJ might have chosen to go down fighting.

The men were silent, trying to digest Galvin's words and think about their next moves.

Stern asked, "What do we do now?"

Galvin quickly composed himself. He'd always known that failure was a possibility, and he had an idea of what he should say to his men. With as much dignity as he could muster, he said, "It has been an honor and a privilege to have served with you, but from this moment on, it's every man for himself. Perhaps our failed mission will not have been in vain. I believe that many true citizens will see this as the first battle of many to follow in our war against tyranny. I believe this will awaken the sleeping masses that will join our future efforts. God bless each and every one of you, and God bless the United States of America."

The men, including Galvin, rushed out of the room. They had cars parked nearby that would take them to their individual hideouts, where they would wait for word whether the surviving men would divulge their names and roles to the authorities. They expected that at least some would, so each leader had made plans to go underground if necessary. Some planned to flee the country, at least for a time. Galvin had other plans.

With their handcuffs removed, Tim, Allie, and Mick leaned against Tim's car while Barnes monitored events from his car radio. Allie held Fletcher tightly.

Barnes turned toward the three. "It's over. They're all safe, but it was a close call. I believe the president owes you, and so do the American people."

Tim was just beginning to realize the enormity of what had occurred, but he didn't feel like a hero. "Let's just say this was a joint effort." He looked at Allie and then at Mick.

"*Joint* effort. Anybody got one? Sure could use one," Mick joked.

Barnes laughed. "I'm a cop, but right now, if I had one, I'd share it with you."

They all smiled.

Allie asked, "Did they catch the bastard?"

"Which one? Take your pick," Barnes answered.

"Vance Galvin." There was venom in her voice.

"He was probably holed up somewhere directing the assault. I guess he thought he was some kind of general."

"Or at least a major," she said sarcastically.

"We'll get him sooner or later," Barnes said. "It shows how big this movement is. Not over by a long shot, but they'll never defeat real Americans."

Mick said, "They think they're the real Americans."

Barnes contemplated Mick's remark. "I hate to preach, but it's guys like you and me who helped defend this great democracy."

Mick nodded in full agreement. He very much understood.

Tim remembered Landers's call. "Hey, it's ten thirty, and we got a meeting tonight at eleven."

Barnes's brow furrowed. "Tonight? Can I ask with whom?"

"With Landers," Tim responded. "He said he's got information that my mother might still be alive."

"I hope you find her, but be careful out there. We know we probably didn't get them all, especially the ringleaders. Meet me at my office tomorrow morning, would you? I'll need to debrief the three of you and get statements about all that's happened."

They all agreed.

They shook hands with Barnes and left for their meeting with Landers. The three of them hoped Tim's mother was still alive. What a reunion that would be.

The basement of Sykes's police station contained a shooting range and a storage room filled with records concerning every imaginable crime. One particular minor crime was being investigated by Detective Sykes. As he thumbed through a pile of recent requests from detectives, a piece of paper caught his attention.

He perused it carefully and said out loud to himself, "Gotcha!"

CHAPTER 43

A FEW MINUTES before eleven, Tim's car pulled up to a deserted parking lot behind a group of industrial buildings. They cautiously surveyed the poorly lit area.

Sitting in the rear seat, Mick leaned forward and said, "Smells like an ambush."

Tim answered, "I agree."

They sat in silence for several minutes, monitoring every sight and sound, but there was no sign of trouble.

Tim asked, "Do you think it's possible my mother might be coming here?" He knew it was a long shot, but he hoped it might actually happen.

Allie answered, "Why in a place like this?"

Tim scratched his head. "Maybe she's as nervous as I am, not seeing her child in almost forty years. Maybe she got remarried and doesn't want her family to know about me or her past, at least not yet. So she picked a deserted spot to meet."

Tim knew he was grasping at straws, and so did Allie and Mick.

But Allie chose to play along. Maybe it could really come true. "I guess that's possible. You might even have a bunch of half brothers or half sisters."

Tim thought, *That would be wonderful—a whole new family to get to know and possibly even to love.*

"Still smells fishy to me," Mick said. "Didn't you say that this Landers guy was an asshole who didn't exactly like you? Why would he be the one to tell you about your mother, like he's trying to help you?"

Tim answered, "He's an asshole, but maybe he's trying to make it up to me."

Sitting in almost total darkness, they sat back and waited. Maybe they'd have all the answers soon enough.

A lone car with its high beams on turned into the huge parking lot about two hundred yards away. The three strained to see inside the car, but they couldn't see past the blinding headlights.

Allie asked, "Do you think that's Landers?"

Tim thought for a moment. "If it's him alone, why the hell would he have to meet us at such a deserted place? Do you think it's possible my mother might actually be in that car?" He knew his hopes were clouding his mind a bit, but he couldn't help himself.

Mick frowned. "You said there was a snitch on the inside, informing the bastards about you."

"Yeah, so?" Tim answered.

"It would be just like Galvin, the shithead, to do something devious. I suggest we get out of the car and get behind it, just in case."

They opened the doors and got out, pistols in hand. Mick also carried an M-16 rifle. They ducked behind the side of the car, out of sight of the approaching car. Allie held tightly onto Fletcher.

The car stopped a hundred feet from them. The car's headlights still shone in their eyes as they peeked through their car's side windows.

A lone figure got out of the car and closed the door.

Galvin called out, "I guess Detective Landers won't be coming after all."

Allie shuddered. "It's him. I recognize that voice."

"Who?" Tim asked.

"It's Galvin." Her eyes betrayed her fear.

Tim's body felt like an electric shock had just passed through it. The man behind that voice was his real father, and although he had no recollection of the man other than seeing the back of his head at the hospital, he knew he'd been raised by this man and the mother he didn't remember at least for the first two years of his life. He shuddered at the thought of facing him now, knowing what a monster he was. He had tortured his mother, killed his best friend Sam, and chopped off half of Allie's pinky. Who knew what else that cruel, sadistic freak might have done?

Still hidden behind the car, Mick hollered, "Galvin, you lowlife scumbag! What do you want?" Through the car's windows, Mick strained to see what was happening. He saw Galvin lifting something onto his shoulder.

Galvin shouted, "So after all these years, I'll come face-to-face with you again, Mick. And I suppose Tiny Tim and his Tinker Bell are with you?"

"You piece of shit! I should've killed you when I had the chance all those years ago."

"Well, you have it again. Why not come out and play? Friends, Romans, countrymen, lend me your *ears*."

Mick swallowed hard and began to shake. "He's mocking me."

Tim gritted his teeth. "He's actually making a joke out of cutting my mother's ear off. We gotta butcher the animal."

Mick tried to stand up, but Tim grabbed him and whispered, "It's what he wants. He's probably got some kind of night scope or something."

Mick obeyed and stayed put.

Still by his car, Galvin called out. "That rat-bastard phony father of yours fucked my wife, and Mick stole my son. If there's a hell, I hope Frank's looking up to see me kill you, Mick, and the son Frank poisoned against me."

Mick strained to see what Galvin was holding, and then he heard a clicking noise that jogged his memory. "He's got a bazooka! Keep low and keep the car between him and us." They turned to make their frantic escape.

Galvin saw their car in the crosshairs of the bazooka.

As the three scampered away, staying as low as possible and out of sight, they heard Galvin shout, "*Auf Wiedersehen.*" Galvin pulled the trigger.

The car exploded in a fireball as the shell hit it. Galvin stood and watched the pieces fall to earth. He walked toward the burning car.

Tim's mind was boggled by the thought that his own father had just tried to kill him. This knowledge frightened Tim, and as never before he realized that this man's wickedness knew no bounds.

Galvin walked around the car, but he was disappointed when he saw no bodies. He pivoted to see the three running toward the road. Galvin ran back to his car, loaded another shell, and gave chase. He ran as fast as he could, paused to take aim, and fired.

The shell exploded near them. It sounded like thunder, sent debris and shrapnel flying, and knocked Mick and Allie off their feet.

Mick's rifle fell to the ground, but Mick was able to hold on to his pistol.

Galvin dropped the bazooka and ran toward them with his automatic pistol drawn.

Tim helped Allie to her feet. She was still hugging Fletcher in her arms. Tim then attempted to help Mick, but Mick's leg was badly wounded, bleeding heavily from a piece of shrapnel.

Galvin was rapidly approaching.

Mick grabbed Tim's arm and said, "Save yourself and Allie. I'll hold the animal off." He clutched the gaping wound in his leg.

Tim saw that Mick couldn't run and said, "I'll hide her and come back."

Tim and Allie disappeared into darkness as Mick saw Galvin approaching at a run. Mick fired his pistol at Galvin but missed. Galvin fired several shots from his automatic. Mick's gun was no match for Galvin's, and one bullet slammed into his abdomen. Mick dropped his gun and clutched at his bleeding stomach.

Galvin ran up to Mick. He looked down at him, saw all the blood, and sneered. "In pain, you hippie freak? I hope so. Wait till you see what's in store for you. You gave me forty years of agony. You'll learn what no mercy really means."

Mick knew that he'd rather die than face what Galvin was capable of doing to him. He tried to stem the bleeding from his stomach with his hand. He was too weak and injured to do anything but wait and hope that Tim would kill Galvin.

Galvin scooped up Mick's gun, quickly patted Mick down to ensure he had no other weapon, and then ran after Tim and Allie, who were hidden behind a dumpster next to a building.

Tim looked at Allie and said as sincerely as possible, given the circumstances, "If we get out of this, I'm giving up gambling." They were panting heavily both from running and from fear. Yet Tim's fear was more for Allie than for himself. The thought of Galvin hurting her again steeled his nerves.

Allie asked with a broken smile, "Even on a sure thing?"

Tim said lovingly, "I'll make the exception." He touched her face and then rushed back toward Mick. Tim was partially hidden by darkness.

Galvin was in pursuit and managed to see Tim's shadowy outline in the distance. He aimed and fired his gun.

Tim heard the shot, crouched down, and jumped to the side.

Galvin then backtracked, making a circle to try to outflank Tim, but instead of finding Tim, he stumbled upon Allie, who was still hiding behind the dumpster and still clutching Fletcher. Her eyes betrayed her fear as she saw Galvin approach with his gun drawn and aimed at her. Heart racing, she began to raise her gun. Her hand trembled.

Galvin barked, "Drop the gun now or I'll kill the dog first and then you."

Allie knew she could do nothing but follow his orders. She prayed that Tim was close by and would shoot the degenerate bastard. She released her grip, and the gun fell to the ground. Fletcher barked frantically.

Galvin strode to Allie with his gun still pointed at her. He grabbed her and forced her to walk in front of him in what he thought was Tim's direction. He held the gun to her head.

In singsong fashion, he called out, "Come to Papa. I've got my future daughter-in-law and her Toto."

Tim spotted Galvin and Allie in the distance and shouted, "You killed my mother, didn't you?"

Galvin yelled back, "She was an obstacle and a traitor, so I buried her with the worms. Now drop your gun or I'll splatter her brains all over the place."

Galvin's answer jarred Tim. He had hoped against hope that Landers actually had information that his mother was alive and well. What a reunion that might have been. But that was not to be. Tim shouted, "So now you want to kill me?"

"I never wanted you. I told her to get an abortion, but no, she wanted a baby. Well, she got her baby and her lover boy Frank. Now maybe they're both in hell."

Tim retorted, "If there's a hell, I hope you burn in it for eternity. My mother and father are in heaven, you piece of shit. Now let her go."

Tim approached with his gun aimed toward Galvin, but Tim knew he couldn't shoot while Galvin was using Allie as a shield. Galvin's gun was still pointed at Allie's head, and she tightly clutched Fletcher in her arms.

Galvin seemed mildly impressed with Tim's show of bravado. "Guess Frank taught you something, but you're gambling with her life, Timmy *Galvin*. Now drop your gun."

Allie shouted, "Don't listen. He'll kill both of us."

With no fear for his own life, and a willingness to defend Allie at all cost, Tim said with a strange calmness, "They say the first stage of recovery for a gambling addict is to admit you have a problem."

Galvin shrugged, pressed the gun against Allie's temple, and said, "So what?"

Tim gritted his teeth and continued, "My name is Tim *Valone*, and I'm a habitual gambler, so…"

Tim walked toward Galvin with the gun pointed at Galvin's head. He stopped five feet away.

Father and son's eyes met.

Galvin was taken aback at how much Tim looked like him.

Tim said, "I'm gambling you'll drop *your* gun."

Galvin was still shaken by Tim's remarkable resemblance to him. "My God, you look like I did at your age. You used to call me Daddy. Would you shoot your own father?"

Tim seethed, "My father was Frank Valone. You killed my mother, and all my life I thought I did."

Fletcher's bark distracted Galvin. Allie bit down on his arm with all her strength. Galvin pushed her away, and Tim rushed at him, trying to grab Galvin's gun. They fell to the ground, each man trying to get at the other's gun.

Allie put Fletcher down, and with vengeful determination, she ripped the gun out of Galvin's hand. She threw the gun away and hoped Tim could now kill this freak of nature.

They struggled for a minute more, but Tim's martial arts abilities and youth were a clear advantage. Using his elbows and feet in addition to his fists and the butt of his gun, Tim was able to subdue Galvin, and he ended up lying with all his weight on Galvin's back. He placed Galvin in a stranglehold on the ground, and with his forearm around Galvin's neck, he began to squeeze as hard as he could.

Galvin managed to utter, while attempting to pull Tim's arm from his neck, "I'm your real father."

Tim continued to tighten his stranglehold. "Not anymore. This is for my mother, Sam, and Allie." Tim had never felt such primal hatred before. Every artery in his body throbbed with it. His grip tightened. Galvin's face turned bright red and then blue, but then Tim unexpectedly released his grip. He could not strangle his biological father, his own flesh and blood. Tim caustically remarked, "Some jailbird can be your boyfriend." He climbed off Galvin's back and pointed his gun at him.

Wheezing, Galvin caught his breath, and then he slowly stood up. He brushed himself off, and almost casually said, "I've been to prison. Won't happen again."

Their fight had brought the two of them close to where Allie had tossed Galvin's gun. Galvin cautiously crept toward it and then slowly bent down and reached for it with his eyes fixed on Tim.

Allie screamed at Tim, "Shoot him!"

Tim was frozen in place. He had never killed anyone before or even shot anyone, let alone his biological father. Tim saw his physical resemblance to this man, but Galvin was truly the monster Dan had described in his letter. He again tried to squeeze the trigger, but his finger refused to move.

Galvin kept his eyes glued to Tim's as he picked up his gun, stood back up, and pointed it at Tim. Neither man pulled the trigger. For the moment, it was a standoff—father versus son, Oedipus versus Laius.

Galvin's face showed mixed emotions as he spoke. "You...you're the only child...I have left." Thoughts of his two daughters burning in the Waco inferno flashed through his mind. Could he shoot his only remaining flesh and blood?

Tim ordered, "Drop the gun!" He was perspiring profusely.

Galvin now seemed remarkably cool. "I named you. My father's name was Timothy. Your grandfather."

"Put down the fucking gun!"

Pleading his case, Galvin said, "We share the same blood, so you were born with the power to lead. I can give you that chance."

Tim shook his head. "You're crazier than I thought."

Galvin sighed. "Then I guess it's *auf Wiedersehen.*"

Tim was confused. Was this Galvin's sign-off? Was he saying good-bye and ready to turn and run? Tim tried to squeeze the trigger, but his finger was frozen in place.

Allie screamed again, "Shoot the bastard!"

Tim saw Galvin's gun still pointed at him, but he couldn't pull the trigger.

A shot rang out.

Allie flinched and gasped at the sound.

Galvin wheeled around to see Mick in the distance still pointing the smoking rifle at him.

"*Auf Wiedersehen* to you, asshole," said Mick.

Galvin dropped his gun and clutched at his chest. He saw blood on his hands and managed to say, "I wasn't...gonna shoot."

Galvin took a step toward his only son and fell to his knees at Tim's feet. One arm reached out toward Tim, and then he slumped forward onto his bleeding chest. He was dead.

Tim stared at the body of the man who had conceived him and who possibly once had loved him, but he felt nothing but relief that this man—this monster who had hurt Allie and was willing to create so much more mayhem—would be unable to harm anyone else.

Tim and Allie hugged each other and then rushed over to Mick.

Tim bent down and cradled Mick in his arms. Mick was bleeding profusely from the wound in his abdomen, but he patted the M-16 proudly. "Like riding a bicycle."

"Great shot, Mick." Tim thought of trying to use Galvin's car to get Mick to a hospital.

Mick smiled sadly. "Saved your ass twice. Know why I like you so much?"

"No, Mick."

"Because you're just like your mother."

Tim nodded in appreciation.

Mick smiled and coughed harshly.

"Thank you, Mick, for everything."

"Never got me...to that Stones concert. But I got...satisfaction." Mick coughed again, gave Tim the peace sign, breathed heavily, and then stopped breathing.

Allie choked back a sob. "Is he dead?"

Tim grabbed hold of Mick's wrist and felt for a pulse. After several seconds, Tim sorrowfully said, "He's gone. Hopefully to a better place."

Tim dejectedly stood up, faced a tearful Allie, and then put his arms around her, holding her tightly.

Allie glanced back at Mick. He appeared strangely peaceful to her. She thought perhaps in his dying moments all the demons that had haunted him for so long had finally been exorcised from his tortured soul.

Allie let go of Tim, picked up Fletcher, and squeezed him tightly. "You're my little hero," she said, knowing it was Fletcher's bark that had drawn Galvin's attention away from Tim. She then turned back to Tim, gave him a kiss on the cheek, and hugged him with Fletcher snuggled safely between them.

Although Tim was relieved that it was all over and that Allie was now safe in his arms, he remained deeply saddened by what had happened. His mother, Sam, and now Mick had all been killed by

Galvin. Dan Connor, the father who had raised him as his own, was gone, but he had hidden terrible secrets for forty years, and he also had to hide the man he truly was, a man named Frank Valone whose moral compass always attempted to point in the right direction. Fate and an unjust, immoral war had been his nemeses. And no matter how much he tried to deny it, the man Mick had just killed was Tim's biological father—a man who had named Tim after his own father and who might have hugged and kissed him a lifetime ago. But the world was a far better place without him.

Tim smiled sadly to himself as he recalled the last thing Dan had said to him before falling asleep in his apartment. He knew Dan had been attempting to repeat the saying, "If you love something, let it go. If it comes back to you, it's yours forever. If it doesn't, then it was never meant to be." Tim stared at the love of his life as a gentle breeze swept her auburn hair across her beautiful face. Tim tenderly brushed her hair aside, and he knew that he would do exactly that— he would set her free.

CHAPTER 44

THE NEXT MORNING, DETECTIVE Sykes stood in front of Detective Landers's desk at police headquarters. Sykes decided to play cat and mouse with Landers.

Sykes looked smug as he said, "Found an interesting request in records. Seems you traced a call to a certain motel without authorization."

Landers hardly seemed concerned as he answered, "Thought we should know where Connor was so we could protect him."

Sykes had expected Landers to have an answer ready for him. He thought, *Let's see how he handles the next question.* "Connor called this morning and told me you were supposed to meet last night—that you had information about his mother."

Landers shrugged. "Turned out to be bogus, and I couldn't raise him on his cell to cancel."

Sykes's eyebrows turned downward as he asked what he believed would be the gotcha question. "Then how did Galvin show up?" He folded his arms across his chest and waited.

A crooked smile crossed Landers's face. "Maybe the mole tipped him off."

Sykes glared at Landers. He knew he was lying but had no proof. "Nice answers. But if I find you screwed us, I'll have your badge… and definitely your ass."

Landers answered with a poker face. "I've been researching this militia movement thing. It's far bigger than you realize and spreading every day through the Internet. They say it could even spread to law-enforcement agencies." Landers smiled like the Cheshire Cat.

Sykes begrudgingly nodded and gritted his teeth. "Watch your damn back. I'll be there every step of the way." He bristled and then turned to walk out.

Landers called out to him, "The real problem is there's an eight-hundred-pound gorilla waiting to pounce, and people like you don't even see it."

Sykes hesitated and then stormed out, slamming the door behind him. He silently vowed to get that bigoted son of a bitch one day.

Congressman John Simpson was seated opposite the president in the Oval Office of the White House. The president's large wooden desk was between them.

Simpson attempted to appear relaxed; he was anything but.

"John, you came within seconds of sitting in my chair. We haven't gotten all the parties concerned, but we'll get them. Count on it."

Simpson stared at the president. He was waiting for the other shoe to drop. A bead of perspiration formed on his brow.

The president continued, "The media will hound you about how it feels to have come so close, et cetera. Avoiding them will help this sordid affair die down and get the country moving forward. Will you do this for me?"

A small smile crossed Simpson's face. "Certainly, but with all due respect, Mr. President, there's much discontent out there that needs to be addressed."

The president stood, stone-faced.

Simpson felt the president was eyeing him with a touch of suspicion, but he thought maybe he was just feeling a touch of paranoia. Simpson took it as his cue to leave. He stood and turned to walk out.

The president stopped him by asking, "By the way…"

Blinking, Simpson slowly turned toward the president. Maybe this was the president's Detective Colombo moment, and he'd be arrested as a traitor.

"…how's your mother? I heard you were chosen because she was ill."

Simpson felt his heart beginning to beat again. "Recovering, sir. Thank you."

"Good. So is the nation."

Simpson forced a smile. He turned again to leave, and the smile quickly faded to a look of disdain. The plan had failed, but he had survived to fight another day.

Stan Urbanski's daughter, Kim, was attending to four-year-old David in her apartment in Philadelphia when her doorbell rang.

She opened the door, and Stan limped in holding a gift-wrapped box. The two embraced warmly. Stan placed David's birthday gift on a table.

Kim cocked her head to the side and asked, "Find what you were looking for?"

A broad smile crossed Stan's face. "Yeah, that today is also *my* birthday."

Confused, Kim placed her hands on her hips and replied, "No, it isn't."

Stan smiled contentedly as little David rushed into his arms.

At the Gardens of Faith Cemetery, Tim and Allie stood at Dan Connor's grave. They had just ordered a new headstone that would read in part, "Frank Valone, Vietnam hero and loving father."

Tim clasped his hands in front of him as he looked down at his father's grave and solemnly said, "You did it. You stopped them. Thanks for being my father."

And for the first time, Tim shed tears for his father, the man who had raised him as well as he knew how.

Allie noticed his tears, placed her arm around him, and tenderly asked, "More than for Bruce?"

Tim smiled sadly, took her hand, and walked proudly from the grave of Frank Valone. Turning back, he flashed his father the peace sign and said with deep sincerity, "So long…Dad."

Allie understood, nodded her head in satisfaction, and shed a tear herself.

As they continued to walk, they passed a trash can. Allie took the plane ticket from her pocket, ripped it in half, and threw it out.

Tim watched her and asked, "What about Hollywood?"

"You ever hear of local theater?" She grasped Tim's hand tightly as they walked away, content and comfortable in each other's company.

CPSIA information can be obtained
at www.ICGtesting.com
Printed in the USA
BVHW071231031118
532089BV00001B/168/P